"You could be in danger."

Ben didn't let it drop. "Stay with your friend tonight. We'll figure out where you should stay tomorrow night."

Sally fought to keep her traitorous knees from softening. "My sleeping arrangements don't fall within the purview of our partnership," she replied. "I'll decide for myself whether it's safe to go home."

He bit his lip as if fighting the urge to say something. She didn't care. She had a mind of her own, and her instincts told her to steer clear of Ben McNamara.

He came closer, towering protectively over her. "Wherever you stay, I need to know you're safe."

Something in his tone snagged her breath, and the heat in his eyes made her head reel. She was falling for him, hard and fast.

Her head told her this was no good, but the rest of her had all but given up fighting the attraction.

Dear Reader,

I must have written the first chapter of this book about forty times before settling on the final version. Between all of those iterations, the only similarity was the image of the heroine in a white trench coat that was longer than her skirt, leaving the hero to wonder whether she was wearing anything underneath. It seems like such a minor image from which to develop a heroine (and a book!), but from there, Sally Dawson unfolded in all of her fashionable and dramatic glory.

Sally knows who she is and she doesn't make apologies, and I greatly enjoyed bringing her to life. Of course, that life is turned upside down the minute she reunites with the gorgeous Ben McNamara. Ben is strong and kind, but he's also deeply flawed. The courage with which he sets about righting past wrongs is, in my eyes, what makes him heroic.

I'm very excited to share Ben and Sally's story with you! I hope you enjoy your time with them as much as I did.

All the best,

Natalie

THE BURDEN OF DESIRE

—

Natalie Charles

HARLEQUIN® ROMANTIC SUSPENSE

Recycling programs
for this product may
not exist in your area.

ISBN-13: 978-0-373-27864-0

THE BURDEN OF DESIRE

Copyright © 2014 by Natalie Charles

Printed in U.S.A.

www.Harlequin.com

Books by Natalie Charles

Harlequin Romantic Suspense

The Seven-Day Target #1750
The Burden of Desire #1794

NATALIE CHARLES

is a practicing attorney whose day job writing is more effective for treating insomnia than most sleeping pills. This may explain why her after-hours writing involves the incomparable combination of romance and suspense— the literary equivalent of chocolate and peanut butter. The happy sufferer of a lifelong addiction to mystery novels, Natalie has, sadly, yet to out-sleuth a detective. She lives in New England with a husband who makes her believe in Happily Ever After and two children who make her believe in miracles.

Natalie loves hearing from readers! You can contact her through her website, www.nataliecharles.net.

For Mom and Dad, with love and gratitude

Chapter 1

Sally Dawson sat in her car and waited for disaster. A meteor, perhaps, or a freak bolt of lightning that would knock out power to the city. Whatever happened, it would have to be significant enough to distract her boss from the morning meeting he'd called with her. In her experience, morning meetings with Jack Reynolds were never called to convey good news.

She smoothed a light gloss across her lips, puckered at her reflection in the rearview mirror and took a deep, calming breath. Her father had a term for what she was about to experience: a *Day,* with a capital *D,* to indicate the gravity. How tragic that she'd been too upset about this meeting to notice her surroundings until this moment. The sky was the radiant, cloudless blue that seemed unique to early autumn, and the air was clean. She heaved a sigh. The butterflies still flittered against her stomach, but she was already running late. Time to face the Day.

She tapped her hip against the door of the sporty blue BMW to shut it, balancing the tray of coffees in one hand and her briefcase in the other. A few members of the defense counsel bar were gathered along the steps to the courthouse, eyeing her and whispering to themselves. Sally was well aware of the rumors that preceded her. She was a spoiled trust-fund baby, petulant and dramatic. She could be brash and short-tempered. Headstrong. Stubborn. She worked for fun and didn't take it seriously.

Sally had heard it all before, and she'd stopped caring a long time ago. The gossip was as unfair as it was immutable. Besides, people could say what they wanted about her bank account or her temper. She was equally aware of her reputation for being an impeccably dressed fashion symbol, and there was some comfort in that. There was also some comfort in winning difficult cases and rising to the top of her department. In her experience, nothing shut up the naysayers like a show of competence.

"Good morning, gentlemen," she said with a knowing smile as she passed the gossipers. Her quirks had never bothered her. She liked who she was just fine.

The click of Sally's heels up the marble steps resounded like a battle march as she walked into the courthouse. She'd labored for too long over her wardrobe that morning, carefully considering each fabric for optimal effect, but some decisions could not be rushed. She'd finally settled on a gray Valentino dress with a plunging neckline, black Louboutin pumps and a Ferragamo handbag. Every perfect stitch of her clothing bolstered her confidence, the kind of confidence that comes with polish and excellent tailoring. She was unstoppable, a one-woman lawyering machine. These were her fatigues, and this was war.

Well, maybe not exactly war. A business meeting first thing in the morning didn't feel too far off from it, though. Jack Reynolds hadn't said much in his email, only that he'd seen her time sheets, and he was concerned about the long nights she'd been pulling while preparing for the Kruger murder trial. It's time that we discuss getting some help for you, he'd written. Someone who can sit second chair.

She would set Jack straight easily enough. She did *not* need a partner on the Kruger case. She'd managed to get along without one for this long, and jury selection was only days away. To bring on another attorney, catch him or her up to speed— Was Jack out to sabotage her performance? To throw a wrench in her perfectly oiled machine? No, she couldn't have that. Sally flew solo; she didn't need someone else cluttering up her cockpit, and the sooner her supervisor accepted this fact, the easier her life would be.

She frowned at her watch. It wouldn't help her cause that she was ten minutes late as a result of the wardrobe dilemma. She supposed she could blame the shoes, which forced her to calculate each and every step lest she tumble and break something. Black leather peep-toe pumps with an ankle strap weren't practical in Connecticut's autumn, but since when was fashion about pragmatism? She could concede the three-inch heels were high, but they were also beautiful.

Sally glanced down at her feet and changed her

mind. The shoes were divine. She would concede nothing. If she was lucky, Jack was running late, too.

She balanced the coffee tray and pressed her hip against the heavy metal door that led to the state's attorney's office. "Morning, Delia." She beamed as she swept up to Reception and planted a coffee on the desk. "This is for your troubles. I'll no doubt add to them today."

"Bless you." Delia swiped a finger across her temple to tuck a stray hair behind one ear. Sally had purchased hair dye for her once during a lunch break. Shade #47, glossy chestnut. "Jack's waiting for you in his office."

He wasn't late. Shoot. Sally beamed a smile that she didn't exactly feel. "Great, thanks!"

She continued down the hall, taking a breath when she saw that Jack's door was open. Sally always came prepared, and today was no different. She had a plan. She would pretend to listen to his concerns, but she'd already decided that to the extent Jack was feeling worried about her workload, she was feeling equally resistant to working with another attorney. This was why she'd spent last night preparing a compelling speech that would culminate when she peered out the window, turned her face to receive the best of the morning light and declared in a tone that conveyed both struggle with and acceptance of her circumstances, "The thing is, Jack, I just don't play well with others."

As a backup plan, she'd brought him a coffee. Another deep breath. This would work.

She rapped gently on the door, before entering and saying brightly, "Sorry I'm late. You wanted to see me?"

But that's as far as she got. Jack had a guest. So

much for blaming her shoes. So much for finding her best light in that lousy excuse for a window, and dramatizing memorized confessions. The skin on her arms prickled. She suddenly didn't care if Jack Reynolds chewed her out publicly and called her a lousy attorney on the record. She didn't care if her beautiful, expensive new shoes spontaneously combusted. All she cared about was the man talking to Jack. The man she'd once lived to hate.

Ben McNamara. The devil himself.

"Hey, Sally." Jack beamed as he gestured to the man. "I'm glad you're here. I wanted to introduce you two."

Ben gave her a cocky smile that showed the top row of his perfectly straight white teeth. "Hello, Sally."

He extended his hand, but she couldn't tear her gaze from his blue eyes. Those familiar cobalt-blue eyes behind those thin silver frames. Even now the anger bubbled in her gut. Just what did he think he was doing here? *Here,* on *her* territory. She made a point of looking at his hand before setting the coffee tray on Jack's desk and folding both her arms across her chest. Ben withdrew his hand and brought it down to his side. "Suit yourself," he said.

Jack looked back and forth between them. "You know each other already?"

"Oh, we've met." The tone of her voice was blistering. "Hello, Ben. It's been a long time." *And yet somehow not quite long enough.*

He was smiling at her as if they were old friends, which they were not. She'd like to pretend that they didn't know each other at all. They had no history worth revisiting, just a series of progressively bad

choices. Graduating from law school with someone
didn't make you friends. She hadn't so much as thought
of Ben in years now. And he had to show up now of
all days, just as she was preparing for trial. He had to
dampen her trial buzz. Damn him.

"We went to Columbia together," Ben explained to
Jack. "I remember Sally. She was second in our class."

Ben arched his eyebrow at her, and Sally's cheeks
burned with rage. She'd been second, and in some
false display of humility, Ben had neglected to mention that he'd been first. "Oh, Ben. No one cares about
law school rankings," she said through a tight smile.

"I couldn't agree more, Sal," he said easily, giving
her a little wink. "Nothing's more important than experience."

No doubt he believed his experience, whatever it
was, trumped hers. He was still smug and unbearable.
Good to know that some things really never changed.
Bastard.

He looked…all right, she supposed. Healthy. That
was good, that fate didn't smite him with some awful
disease, like leprosy or rabies. It wasn't as if she wished
rabies on him. Now, maybe she could've gotten behind
a good case of poison ivy—one that kept him up for a
night or two. That would only be karma. But rabies?
Too far. So it was good that he wasn't foaming at the
mouth and that he looked normal. Passably attractive.

She rubbed at her suddenly pounding temple.
Maybe "passably attractive" was an understatement.
He looked hot, as if he'd just wandered off a billboard
advertising that dark gray designer suit he was wearing. She could admire his bone structure, the sharp
angles on his jaw complimenting an aquiline nose. His

olive skin had darkened over an apparently leisurely summer, bringing attention to his deep blue eyes. He looked clean and showered and still raging with whatever pheromones he exuded that made women weak-kneed around him.

Other women, not her. His pheromones repelled her. Just the sight of him spiked her blood pressure and made her want to do rash things, like throw something hard through something glass to distract him long enough so that she could run away. And now he was watching her, waiting for some kind of response.

Just…damn him.

Sally Dawson, in the flesh, after all these years. Ben wouldn't expect her to be happy to see him. Still, he would have hoped that time would mitigate some of the animosity. He ran his gaze along Sally's slender frame. The years had been kind to her, at least. Her blond hair fell to her shoulders before curling loosely like question marks at the ends. She was glaring at him, all trench coat, bare legs and high heels. It entered his mind that she could very well be naked under that coat. His collar tightened.

She was still beautiful, but then Sally had never lacked the financial means to achieve beauty. He'd always had some trouble explaining her to other people. It was as if the high school drama queen had one day become bored with sunbathing and decided to use part of her ample trust fund to go to law school. He had to give her credit for sticking with the profession for this long.

"I didn't realize you two knew each other," said

Jack. He clapped Ben on the shoulder. "Then you'll be happy to know that Ben is joining our team."

Her eyes widened. "No." She looked at him as if he'd just kicked a puppy. "I thought you were working in Manhattan?"

"I left Pitney Stern years ago. Since then I've served as a Marine Corps judge advocate." His back straightened. Being counsel to the marines carried with it the pride of being in top physical condition. All marines were battle ready.

"He completed tours in Iraq and Afghanistan," Jack added.

"But now you're *here*. Why?"

Charming, the way her eyes narrowed to little slits as if she were deciding whether she should slip off one of those stilettos and stab him in the neck.

"Because we need him," Jack interjected. "We've been looking to hire someone for a while, and we're lucky to have him."

"Hmm." She sealed her mouth into a tight line. "I didn't mean to interrupt. Jack, when you're ready to have that meeting you emailed me about, I'll be in my office."

"This is the meeting, Sally," he replied.

That caught her attention. She blinked her wide brown eyes. "You called a meeting to introduce me to Ben?"

Jack arched an eyebrow. "Have a seat."

She eyed Ben suspiciously again and waited for him to sit before taking the chair beside him.

"You've been pulling fourteen-hour days. Working weekends," their boss continued. "You could've come to me sooner. You need some help."

"It wasn't a problem. It's *not* a problem," she corrected. "I'm preparing for a big trial. One that I'm perfectly capable of handling on my own." She sent a pointed glare in Ben's direction out of the corner of her eye. Cute.

"It's not an insult to you." Jack relocated a stack of files on his desk so he could lean forward to address her. "You know it's policy that we have two attorneys on large cases. You're so capable that I neglected to pay enough attention to the fact that you were going it alone for so long."

Her jaw tightened, and she gripped the seat of the chair. "So what's this mean?"

"I've asked Ben to help you out. Sit second chair. I figured you could get him acclimated to the office."

"Show me the ropes. You know, where to find the pens, how to make the coffee." He gave her what he'd hoped was a disarming smile, but she returned it with a glare.

"I like to do things my way, Jack," she said slowly. "I don't…play well with others."

He shook his head. "It's not negotiable, I'm afraid. The Kruger case is too large, and there's too much media attention. I regret not giving you more resources sooner."

Ben cocked his head toward her. "I look forward to working with you, Sally. We'll make a great team."

She gritted her teeth and said to Jack, "Are we finished? I have a busy day."

"We're finished. Thanks for your time."

"Super." She rose from her seat. Then she lifted the tray of coffees, twisted one free and set it before Jack, and proceeded to the door without another word.

As the sound of her angry footsteps receded down the hall, Ben was surprised to hear Jack chuckle under his breath. "What's the joke?"

"Oh." He waved his hand and leaned back in his chair. "Sally. You already know her, so I don't have to tell you that she wears her heart on her sleeve." He popped the top of the coffee she'd left for him and looked inside before taking a sip of the steaming beverage.

So that's what that was: wearing her heart on her sleeve. Here Ben had thought she was acting bratty and rude. "Has she been working here for long?"

"Since the day she passed the bar." The older man leaned back in his chair and opened the blinds behind his desk to allow some sunlight into the dark quarters. "Sweet girl and a hell of a lawyer. But when she gets upset about something... I don't have to tell you," he repeated, and dropped back into his seat.

"No. You don't."

Ben was all too familiar with Sally's dramatic tendencies. In law school, she'd had near nervous breakdowns as a matter of routine before finals. She'd show up to the library in ratty jeans and an old sweatshirt, her hair unbrushed, looking as if she hadn't slept in days. She would draw concern from their classmates with her dramatics and endless questions, and then she'd go on to earn one of the highest grades in the class. She'd routinely squandered the time and energy of those around her. He'd found it tedious.

Jack's chair squeaked as he shifted forward again. "Anyway, don't worry about her. You two will be working together on the Kruger case whether she likes it or not. There's always a slew of work to be done during trial, and Sally doesn't need to be a hero."

"No, sir."

"Funny. She sure got upset about you." Jack's bushy eyebrows rose mischievously. "Is there some history I should know about?"

Ben started. There was a history, all right, but not one their boss needed to know. Definitely not. "Like I said, we went to Columbia together. Same first year classes." He coughed to politely signal a change in subject. "You mentioned that you had some other cases for me already."

"I've got a stack of them. We had a retirement last month and everyone's been helping out, but as far as I'm concerned they're yours." His new boss slid a piece of paper with several columns across the desk. "Here's a table of the case names and file numbers and the attorneys you should speak with about the status."

"Great."

"I'm expecting big things from you, Ben. First in your class at Columbia, followed by an impressive military record. We're lucky to have you here. Anything you need, you just let me know."

"I appreciate that, sir." He waved the list of cases and rose. "I'll get started on these right away."

Ben walked along the narrow hall, taking in the gray speckled carpet worn thin down the center, and the white walls marked with odd scuffs and smears of grime. He stopped in front of his office, which was located directly across from a cluster of gray cubicles, empty except for boxes of documents piled on and around the desks. The area hummed with the sounds of distant conversations and electrical appliances, but his was the only warm body in sight. *Welcome to the neighborhood,* he thought ruefully.

He stared into the hole of a room and wondered whether his office was a converted utility closet. That would explain the size. At least the window was large. He tugged at the strings of the dusty blinds, which rose with a squeal. The window may be large, but it looked out onto the back end of a bar. Working late nights meant he would likely have a front row seat to drunken brawls, which meant he'd be seeing familiar faces at bail hearings. That didn't seem like a perk.

He dropped his leather briefcase near his desk with a thud. The wooden top was marred by thin grooves, he noted with a frown. A large blotter and calendar would cover up those scratches and dents, and at some point he might even forget about them. He looked around again, absorbing the fact that the walls needed a fresh coat of paint and the office chairs looked as if they needed fumigation. It was a place to work, that was all. He needed this start.

He may have grown up nearby, but Ben couldn't say that he'd ever expected to land in a town like Bedford Hills. Returning to the area in which he'd started signified failure to him. Now that his mother's health was declining, though, he needed to be close to her. He pressed his fingers between two slats of the dusty blinds.

He could admit there was something appealing about the quiet of the area. Nightlife consisted of a few downtown restaurants and bars, most of which closed by midnight. The old town had remnants of its farming roots, and aside from some of the downtown core and scattered subdivisions, properties in Bedford

Hills were large and houses far apart. He could leave work and slip away into silence and solitude. He'd been raised a few towns away, but no one here knew him. He planned to keep it that way.

Except for Sally. She'd known him once, the old Ben, before he'd gotten his life together. He'd heard that she was working as a prosecutor, but he hadn't realized she was stationed here. That made sense. If he remembered correctly, her family lived in the area, too.

He glanced around again. The office was claustrophobic, the view dingy. The desk was probably older than he was. Back when he was working on Wall Street, he'd had only the best of everything, and now he didn't even have an administrative assistant. What had he been thinking, coming here? He'd never get used to this place.

He didn't plan to stay for long.

She released her breath when she entered the threshold to her office. Her sanctuary. Sally loved everything about the space, from the onyx vase she'd set on the table in the corner and filled with fresh flowers each Monday, to the framed watercolors depicting the seasons in Bedford Hills and painted by a local artist, to the lavender cashmere pashmina scarf that she draped on the back of her chair in case the ventilation went berserk, as it often did. Her space was warm and filled with the things she loved.

A shiver darted down her spine. She was feeling angry, and that wasn't healthy. Her palm floated unconsciously to her abdomen, resting protectively over the spot where the baby was growing. She'd read that morning that it was the size of a poppy seed. Just a little ball of cells, really, and she couldn't help but already feel the need to protect it from everything hurtful in the world. She'd been eating healthy and thinking positive thoughts, because positive thoughts bring positive results. At least that's what the *Life Coach* podcast taught. She'd been listening to the series during her commute for a few weeks now. Today's message had been about making peace with failure. *As if they'd known I would walk into work and see failure eyeing me smugly.*

"Sally."

She groaned and spun to see Ben standing in the doorway. All the beauty and positive thinking in the world couldn't stop her blood pressure from spiking at that moment. She didn't bother to force a smile. "Can I help you?"

She observed his gaze sweeping across her office, her space, her things. He was appraising her. She studied him, trying to get a sense of his ruling, but his face remained inscrutable and he didn't comment. "I just wanted to tell you that there are no hard feelings."

The statement turned painfully in her chest. This guy had some nerve. She removed her trench coat with methodical deliberation and draped it across one of the chairs at the little conference table she'd set up in the corner. "I'm not sure what you're referring to."

He wasn't rattled. Cool Ben had the gall to never appear rattled. "Don't play coy. It doesn't work with me. We're colleagues now. I'm suggesting that we try to be civil, even if we can't stand the sight of each other."

She gripped her herbal tea, white knuckled. At another time, she might have calmly removed the cover and hurled the beverage at his glaringly white shirt and dull blue tie. But not today, because today she was above that. "It seems like you're under the impression I spend time thinking about you. Would it make you feel better to know that even if I tried, I couldn't muster enough interest to hate the sight of you?"

"You're funny, you know that?"

He stepped into her office and walked toward her purposefully, his gaze locked on hers, the beginning of a smile curving his lips. She watched him, alarm sounding across her body, her muscles frozen. He reached her desk and pressed his large hands down, leaning forward until he intruded upon her space, caused her to lean away. "We both know you care. At least enough to hate me as much as you do."

He reached forward with one hand and pretended to pick a piece of lint off her Valentino dress. Then he faked considering it before pretending to flick it away. Sally's blood pounded in her ears. He was close enough that she could smell mint on his breath. Too close. She grabbed a stack of files from her desk and stomped toward the filing cabinet. "Don't play games with me. You know the feeling's mutual," she growled.

"That I hate you?" He righted himself with a slight shrug. "I wouldn't say that. I've always thought you were…interesting." He lifted one of her business cards from the holder on her desk, turning it between his fingers before tucking it into his pocket. "This murder trial you have, for example. Jack told me about it. A homicide without a body? That's risky."

"Is it? I would think it would be riskier to allow a man to get away with murdering his wife just because he'd found a way to conceal her body."

Ben arched one of his eyebrows rakishly. "Maybe. But do you get beyond a reasonable doubt?"

He leaned one shoulder against the wall and watched her. As he stood there, he folded his arms across his broad chest, silently reminding Sally that he'd never wanted for dates. Women in their law class had draped themselves across him, baking him cookies and inviting him to join their study groups. It was pitiful, and he'd lapped up the attention shamelessly. Ben used women. That's who he was. Once, before finals, she'd walked into a quiet study room in the library and caught him with a topless girl straddling his lap, his hand snaking up her skirt. He'd had the nerve to smile at Sally over the woman's bare shoulder as if to say, *You wish.*

Well, she didn't wish. She had self-respect. Ben had never been formally attached to anyone. He used women and dumped them. She may have thought she loved him long ago, but he'd been very clear that he wasn't interested in any kind of long-term, monogamous relationship. She'd been fooled, but that was a distant and ugly memory. Ten years distant.

She slammed the filing cabinet shut. He may be hot, but he wasn't *that* hot, really. At least, she'd never understood the appeal. He had mahogany hair, slightly tousled, that he wore at a conservative length. He was tall, but not taller than six feet. He was clean-shaven, probably still tattoo-free, and just…generic. His only striking feature was his pair of deep blue eyes shrouded by long black lashes and strong eyebrows. Sally could admit that his eyes were beautiful. Even his glasses could be kind of hot on a different guy. But everything else about Ben was ho-hum. A playboy who liked to have one-night stands? Yawn. She preferred a man with a real edge and some substance that went beyond whatever was in his pants. A man who could make her laugh and think before he rocked her world. And since her broken engagement, she preferred no man at all.

"If you'll excuse me, I have some work to do." She headed toward the door.

"As do I. And I believe we're heading to the same place. Remember, we're partners now." He stepped aside and waved her through. "After you."

She rolled her eyes at his pompous formality as she brushed past, accidentally sweeping her shoulder against his chest. "Narrow doorway," she mumbled.

Her attention was gripped by the sight of seven of her colleagues huddled in front of a television set up in a vacant cubicle in the center of the office. They watched her as she approached.

"Sally, you may want to see this," Greg said, nodding his head toward the screen.

She squinted to make out the sight of the gray marble steps of town hall. A lectern was erected in the middle of a swarm of buzzing reporters in subdued jackets. "A press conference? What's going on?"

"Your guy Marlow called it."

That would be Dennis Marlow, the defense attorney who represented Mitch Kruger in the murder trial. He was a ripe pain in the rear.

"He called a press conference? On the Kruger case? And he didn't even have the courtesy to tell me about it?" As soon as the words escaped, she reconsidered her simmering fury. Marlow had fallen far short of courteous during the pretrial phase, so what was one more professional breach?

She was aware of Ben creeping up to stand behind her. He had all the space in the world, and he had to stand right *there,* where she could sense him, practically feel the heat as it rose from his body. She couldn't resist glancing quickly over her shoulder. Yep, there he was, old jerk face, making a conscious decision to invade her personal space and suck up all her air. She'd been much too polite earlier. She'd have to change that.

Her attention returned to the television as Marlow entered the screen from the right and stood behind the lectern, in a red tie and a black blazer that looked brand-new. "That tie looks expensive," she murmured, mostly to herself. Marlow didn't wear expensive ties.

"Must be an important press conference," Ben replied close to her ear. "Fancy tie, lots of cameras."

She didn't have the opportunity to respond before Marlow began to speak.

"I'm Attorney Dennis Marlow, and I represent Mitchell Kruger. My client is accused of murdering his wife almost a year ago. Mr. Kruger has maintained his innocence from day one, and his story has never changed. Namely, that Mrs. Kruger walked out after a heated argument and never returned. We have maintained sincere efforts to locate Mrs. Kruger, but to no avail. Her body was never recovered, and the state's evidence against my client has always been circumstantial."

Sally bristled at this bit of theatrics. Most evidence in any case was circumstantial—it wasn't as if criminal acts were routinely captured on video. Marlow knew better, but lines like "circumstantial evidence" often played well to juries.

The attorney continued. "We have cooperated with the investigation without conceding Mr. Kruger's involvement in his wife's disappearance. He was not involved. He, too, was a victim."

Sally glanced across the crowd of colleagues and caught her friend Tessa's eye. Tessa made a gesture as if she was about to vomit. Sally shook her head. Mr. Kruger was a victim now? Marlow was really pushing it.

"I'm pleased to announce that now, on the eve of Mr. Kruger's trial, we are about to clear his good name once and for all." Marlow looked up from his notes and gestured to the right of the screen. "My client couldn't have killed his wife, because she's with us here today."

Sally's blood rushed to her feet, and a chill settled in its place as a figure crossed the screen to the lectern. She'd looked at hundreds of pictures of Mitch Kruger's wife over the course of this investigation and in preparation for trial, imagining the terror the poor woman must have felt in her last moments. Sally knew Mrs. Kruger. The shape of her face. The shade of her white-blond hair. Her slender build.

Through private interviews with her closest friends and family, Sally knew even more than that. She knew that Mrs. Kruger liked country music, line dancing and beer. That she didn't care for gardening, but kept small potted plants that she tended with love. That she loved her shar-pei, Pookie, and would never, ever have willingly left him with Mitch. Sally knew that Mrs. Kruger was dead.

But then the woman smiled shyly at the camera and said, "Hello. I'm Ronnie Kruger."

And stupid Ben had the nerve to whisper, "Sally, I think there's a problem with your case."

Chapter 2

Ronnie had never been one for card games. The dubious honor of household poker expert belonged to Mitch. "Everyone has a tell," he'd once informed her over a gin gimlet on the rocks. "A twitch, a smile. Something that lets you know they're hiding something."

She'd taken a sip of her icy drink. Three glasses in, and she no longer pinched her lips against the sourness. "I don't," she'd said, lowering the glass to the table and licking her lips. "I come from a large family, so I've learned how to be a good liar."

"Is that a fact?" One corner of his mouth had lifted in amusement.

"Absolutely. In a big family, someone's always looking over your shoulder. I learned a long time ago that if I ever wanted any privacy, I'd have to know how to keep secrets."

He'd clinked the ice cubes in his glass thoughtfully. "Maybe you can keep secrets, but you can't hide them completely."

"Oh?"

He'd set his drink down and placed his hand on the table. Then he'd rubbed the tip of his forefinger against the pad of his thumb. "That's it, you know. Your tell. I noticed it when you told me you liked the restaurant I chose last week."

"Huh." He was right. She'd hated that restaurant. She'd raised her glass and downed the remainder. "And what's yours?" This was back in the days when they'd flirted with each other, when she'd still found something exciting and arousing about him.

"Not me." He'd winked. "I've eliminated all of my tells. That's why I'm a hell of a poker player."

She'd found him sexy and dangerous in that moment, for all the wrong reasons. Here was a man who could read her body's secrets while he remained almost a complete mystery to her. It was naive on her part to believe he'd never turn it against her. Liars lie, and erasing his own tell simply meant he was an especially practiced liar.

Unlike her. Ever since that conversation, she'd realized how right he was. She was a terrible liar. Her fingertips jumped and twitched when she felt nervous, as she did right now. A press conference? She hadn't expected that, and this lawyer that Mitch had somehow scrounged up gave her the creeps. He looked like a kid at his own birthday party, hopping around as if he was loaded up on cake and ice cream and drooling about the new bicycle in the driveway.

"This way," he said with a too-smooth smile as he

placed his hand on her elbow to pull her through the hordes of cameras and journalists.

Don't touch me. She yanked her arm out of his reach, but he didn't appear to take any offense at the gesture. The old Ronnie might have allowed him to continue to clutch her, for fear of hurting his feelings. The old Ronnie was demure to a fault. Self-sacrificing. She was the school nurse who listened patiently while kids talked about their fake ailments and shared disgusting information about their bodily functions and sexual habits. That Ronnie took it all in stride with a smile. That was the Ronnie who carried little breath mints in her pockets, those sweet red-and-white candies that she'd learned long ago were universally loved and accepted. *Sorry your menstrual cramps are so bad, honey. Would you like a mint?*

The new Ronnie didn't carry mints, and neither did she put up with crap like strange men acting overly familiar. *I don't care if you're his lawyer, his doctor or his priest. None of that makes us friends.*

Wormy. That was what the lawyer was. All smug and pleased as punch about her sudden appearance. "This is big," he confided as they pulled away from the crowd. He was a close talker, and for a second she wished she still carried those mints around. "Real big. You just blew a hole in this side of the prosecution's case."

Ronnie smiled tightly. "I'm only here because Mitch is innocent," she said in a forced saccharine voice. "I just feel terrible that this confusion has continued for so long."

They were heading down the sidewalk now, and Ronnie winced at the distance to the car. She'd worn

the wrong shoes, that was for sure. In fairness, she'd
had only a short time to get dressed after she'd arrived.
She'd barely been able to sleep on the plane, not knowing what she'd be in for once she landed. She'd gone
zombielike to the closet in her home and blinked at the
many clothes she'd forgotten about completely. Sweaters and sensible cardigans and so much beige. The old
Ronnie had liked beige. Maybe being in a bright land-
scape like Vegas for almost a year had changed her
taste. This Ronnie gravitated toward bright blues and
rosy-pinks. They reminded her of the desert sunset.

She'd selected a sensible white blouse, a cardigan
in a muted dusty-rose, and a string of pearls. She'd
paired the ensemble with a dull gray pencil skirt that
fell below her knees and black heels that pinched her
toes when she walked. The whole look was dull dull
dull. She used to be like this? This boring? No wonder Mitch—

Well. She wasn't going to think like that. All the
beige in the world didn't justify breaking marriage
vows. She wasn't going to make excuses for him.

She was done with old Ronnie. In her first week
in Vegas, she'd come across a fresh snakeskin that a
neighbor said had belonged to a rattlesnake. It was just
lying there on the side of the road, as if the serpent had
taken off its coat and then forgotten to collect it on its
way out of the sunshine. *It's a sign,* she'd thought. *This
is what I am now. New Ronnie, who's shed her old skin.*

She'd picked up the remnant, taken it into the motel
room she was renting, then spread it out on the bed.
She'd never been out West before, and had never seen
a snakeskin. The dull scales were brilliantly beautiful
under the light, and she'd tried to imagine the sheen

of the new ones. Each time the snake shed its old skin, she imagined, it would grow stronger, thicker and more deadly. Glossy and self-confident, it wouldn't fear anymore.

Hadn't Ronnie understood when she'd left Connecticut that night that she would never be the same? She'd started changing before she'd even climbed into the metallic cocoon of the airplane. But it wasn't until she'd found that snakeskin that she knew what she was changing into. In that moment when she'd noticed the discarded pelt from the deadly animal, she'd understood in her heart that she hadn't come out to Vegas to become a butterfly. She'd come out to become a poisonous snake.

"Ronnie." The lawyer beamed at her again. "I should've asked sooner if I could get you something. Breakfast, perhaps? A coffee?"

He'd placed his hand on the small of her back, and the contact made her cold. "I'm fine," she replied icily, and with a pointed glare at his arm. "And I'd prefer if you'd keep your hands to yourself."

Sally didn't have to turn to see who was barreling down the hall. Only one person had those footsteps. "Sally! Where is she?" Jack bellowed. He stopped when he saw her. "We need to talk."

Her stomach knotted. "Your office?"

"Yours. It's closer."

She swallowed the lump in her throat and tried not to sway from the reeling in her head. Ronnie Kruger was alive. Good for her, she supposed. Bad for the office, and really bad for Sally herself.

"I need to call Dennis Marlow," she said weakly,

stunned by what she'd just seen. "Mitch Kruger is still in jail." She placed her palm against her cheek and shook her head, which did nothing to order her thoughts. "I need to find out what's going on first."

Jack's face softened. "I'll stop by in a few."

She trudged to her office, well aware of the eyes of her colleagues following her. Now the calmness of her sanctuary offered little reassurance. She drew the blinds. Darkness was preferable—she needed to hide.

Marlow must have been waiting for her call, because he answered after the first ring. "Why, it's Sally Dawson," he cooed in an unctuous voice. "Lovely day, isn't it?"

"You've got some nerve, Dennis," Sally hissed into the receiver. "A press conference? A freaking *press* conference?"

"It's nice to finally hear from you."

"What's that supposed to mean?"

"You were my first call. I've been trying to reach you for hours. I left messages on your office phone."

Sally glanced at the device. Sure enough, it was blinking red to indicate she had a message. She sat in her chair, not wanting to admit that she'd been both late and distracted that morning. "I didn't get the messages. But there's no excuse whatsoever. You have a hundred ways to reach me." She took a breath, trying to steady her nerves. "So Mrs. Kruger…what? Wandered back into town this morning?"

"She called me last night and said she was flying in from Vegas. I only met her this morning, and verified her identity."

"And you couldn't give me a heads-up before sending out a press release?" Sally pressed her fingers against her shut eyelids. "Dammit, Dennis. You've turned this into a three-ring circus."

"Oh, come now," he said, clicking his tongue. "This was a circus long before this morning. This case has been held up by the state's attorney as an example of his staff's dedication. You're all so tough on crime and so clever that you don't even need a body to go to trial. The magic of forensic science and all that." He snorted. "I just shone the spotlight in a different direction. All of this works to my client's advantage, really. Maximum impact."

She rubbed at her forehead. God, was he right about maximum impact. The press was going to love this little gift.

"You need to file an emergency motion and withdraw all charges," Marlow continued flatly. "Have it heard immediately so Mitch can get out of jail. He's been held without bail for months. I hope it doesn't come out later that you've been withholding evidence that would have exonerated my client." His tone was pointed.

Withholding evidence. Marlow didn't need to come out and say explicitly what she knew he was thinking. The state had charged a man with murdering a wife who turned out to be very much alive. He'd be searching high and low for proof that the state had overlooked exonerating evidence to manipulate the investigation's outcome. A civil lawsuit could follow, and quickly. "I'd like to meet with Mrs. Kruger before I file anything. Once I verify her identity for myself, I'll file a motion to withdraw all charges immediately. That goes without saying."

"We're at city hall now. We can be at your office in

twenty minutes. Half an hour, tops." Marlow sighed loudly into the phone. "I probably don't need to tell you this, but this has been a long nightmare for my client. First his wife walks out on him, then the state brings charges against him for her murder. He lost his job. His son was set to testify against him. This proceeding has done immense harm to Mitch's reputation and familial relations."

Heat climbed into Sally's chest. "I'm not sure what you're implying, Dennis. The state may ultimately have been mistaken, but we aren't liable for any wrongdoing. We brought that case on sound forensic evidence."

He laughed drily. "Not so sound, was it? Not really, when the alleged victim is still alive."

Sally balled one fist and brought it to her lap, digging her fingernails into her palms. This was Marlow's little way of informing her that Mr. Kruger would be bringing one hell of a lawsuit. It didn't matter whether the suit was actually successful; the bad press would be damaging enough to the office. She bit her cheek until it hurt, to keep from saying anything she'd regret. "I'll see you in our conference room in twenty minutes."

"I'll be there with bells on."

She had no sooner slammed her phone down than Jack darkened her doorway. "Sally."

Her boss's hands were on his hips, and his face was red. Not angry red, just an alarmed shade of ripened tomato. That made two of them.

"You finish everything you need to do?"

She propped her elbows on her desk and rested her head in her hands. What a nightmare. "Yes, sir. For now. I'm meeting with Dennis in twenty. I need to meet the vic—*Mrs. Kruger*—for myself." How disorienting to hear those words out loud, when she'd spent nearly a year thinking of Ronnie Kruger as a concealed body, not a living woman.

"You want to tell me how it is that the murder victim in your case is holding a press conference?"

"Besides stating the obvious?" She looked up to meet his concerned eyes. "You can't be mad at me, Jack. I've prepared for that case exhaustively. I just…" She shook her head, not knowing what she thought anymore. "The evidence was good. Solid. It was Mrs. Kruger's blood on that rug. There was too much blood for her to have survived. It all added up." Sally rubbed her temples. It didn't make sense.

"It's my fault. The hours you've been pulling… I should've given you help a long time ago." He planted himself in her visitor's chair. His thick eyebrows pulled together, wrinkling the skin on his forehead, and he cursed. "We need to fix this. Quickly."

She thought of that press conference, how Marlow had chosen to drag Mrs. Kruger out into the spotlight to humiliate Sally, the office and the police. "He let his client sit in jail so that he could shock us all with the news." Her cheeks grew hot.

"We were about to bring a man to trial for a murder that never happened," Jack said, loosening his tie. "I don't think I need to lecture you on the seriousness of this."

Her heart fell to the floor. No, he didn't, but he may as well have with that last comment. The effect was equally humiliating. "No, sir. Believe me."

A quiet rage flickered in her gut. She'd worked her rear off to get to where she was—one of the lead attorneys in the homicide division. She'd worked late nights and weekends for the better part of a decade, sharpening her skills. This case was just like any other: she'd pored over the evidence carefully and taken her responsibilities seriously. Even if Jack didn't exactly see it, she was certain that the evidence had been manipulated and a trap set. Sally had spent most of her life being underestimated and taken lightly, and she'd worked hard to prove everyone wrong. No one was going to make a fool out of her.

She tried to keep her voice steady now, but it sounded shaky, as if her words were being dragged over gravel. "I'm going to review that file. I'm going to figure this out. Some crime was committed, and whether it was an attempt to commit insurance fraud or murder…" She looked at him. "I'll fix it. I promise."

"Sally." He leveled a gaze at her. "You're off the file. I'll review this myself."

Her heart galloped, and her breath quickened. Jack would review the files? And what if he found a mistake? She scratched at her leg. She hadn't made one, she was sure. But what if she *had*? She didn't want to be blindsided. "Jack, no one knows that case better than I do. You know me. You know I've always been forthright with you. Besides, this doesn't violate any ethical rules. I can examine the file as well as anyone."

"Sally, I want a review. You can't review your own file. That doesn't even make sense."

"I can review it."

They both turned at the sound of a voice. Ben stood in the doorway, his hands on his hips, and shrugged nonchalantly. "Jack already briefed me on it this morning, and I'm probably the least busy person in this office."

"Not for long," Jack said, unconvinced.

"Not for long. But for now." Ben crossed his arms. "I've prosecuted complicated cases. I had a few murder cases while on tour. I know my way around forensic evidence. Besides, Sally and I are partners on this case. You said so yourself, Jack."

He sat in quiet thought before shaking his head. "God knows I don't need to deal with investigating this mess, on top of everything else I'm doing." He eyed Ben and then looked at Sally. "What do you think? I'm inclined to let him do it."

She smiled tightly. "Then I don't think it matters what I think."

"Fine." Jack shrugged and rose. "Ben, it's now your file. I'm off to go try to explain this to the media sharks circling our office."

Sally glanced at Ben, who gave her a small wink and a nod. And this became, officially, the worst Day of her life.

Sally may have been spoiled, bratty and rude, but she had her back against a wall. What kind of man would he be if he let her squirm, pinned under the threat of her superior's review? *Win-win,* Ben thought with some self-congratulation. He'd relieved his boss of additional work, and he now held the upper hand over Sally.

Not that he'd use it. He was a gentleman, after all, and gentlemen didn't humiliate women. Having a little power over her might convince her to talk to him again, that's all. If she did, she might learn that he wasn't as vile as she thought he was. Not anymore.

He didn't want to admit that her cutting glares that

morning had bothered him. In the past, he'd made some choices he wasn't proud of. The womanizing. The drinking. He was finished with both. Maybe, if she agreed to speak with him again, she'd stop looking at him as if he'd stepped in something foul. Not that he cared what Sally Dawson thought of him. He didn't need the approval of a haughty trust-fund baby to sleep well at night. She'd always struck him as a little kooky, anyway. She did her own thing, traveled through life slightly off-kilter. He didn't care if she thought he was a decent person at the end of the day. She didn't matter at all. But he could repair the past by fixing his relationship with Sally. He hadn't always been decent to her.

He flung a self-satisfied smile at her. In response, she leveled a withering glare that would have peeled paint off a wall. Had he expected his charms to work that quickly? Sally sat back in her desk chair stiffly, her piercing glare informing him that he should drop dead.

"You probably think I should thank you." Her voice was a barely audible hiss. She rose, rounded her desk and stepped forward, closing in on him like a great cat evaluating its chosen prey. "I'm not going to."

"I wouldn't expect you to thank me," he replied calmly. "You probably want my head. But I heard Jack laying into you, and I think it's in your best interest that your superior not review that file."

"Oh?" Her eyes narrowed to menacing slits. "And why is that?"

He focused on those light brown eyes. He'd forgotten that they contained tones of gold—the exact shade of whiskey filtering late afternoon sunlight. Beautiful eyes.

He tore himself from their glare to close her office door behind him. "Look, Sally. A mistake was made. It's the only rational explanation, and whether it was made by you, the police or the crime lab, it happened. You brought a murder case for a victim who wasn't dead. That's a problem."

"It's not that simple—"

"No one said it was simple. But if I find the mistake first, I'll come to you. Maybe you can spin it and save your job, or at least your position in this office." He pulled up straighter and added, "I'm doing you a favor."

"A favor?" She gave an unlady-like snort and walked away from him, heading back to her desk. She didn't sit. Instead she leaned against it, her gray dress hugging her curves, and looking elegant and furious, preparing herself to give him a piece of her mind. "I'm not done with this case yet."

Ben stepped forward then. "I beg to differ. According to Jack, you're quite done."

"I didn't make a mistake. I know how risky it is to bring a murder to trial without a body. I was careful, and the evidence was good."

The neckline of her dress was plunging to dangerous depths. Ben brought his focus back to her angry brown eyes. "I don't care how good you think the evidence was. I've been instructed to review this file, and that means it's mine."

She tilted her head to the side and rolled her eyes. "You sound *so* military right now."

Before he could decide what she meant by that comment, she pushed herself off her desk and approached him once more. He was very aware of her lean, bare legs and the way her body teetered just slightly on those heels. Those shoes were ridiculous—amazing that she could even stand, let alone walk in them. Her legs, on the other hand, looked strong and smooth. She probably ran five miles a day. He fought the urge to reach out and touch them.

"Ben." Her voice had assumed a smooth, glassy tone, and her eyes were wide. "I'm going to level with you. I love my job, and I'm trying hard to save it."

The note of desperation in her voice tugged at him. Damn. She hated him, but he didn't hate *her*. He didn't want her to lose her job, and he certainly didn't want to be perceived as being responsible for something like that. "I'm just reviewing the file, not making any recommendations. I would never recommend that you lose your job." There, that should settle it.

But she continued to watch him, unblinking. He released a sigh. "You may as well come out and tell me what you want me to do. I've never known you to hold back."

She raised her chin. "I want to conduct the follow-up investigation with you. I need to know what went wrong, and if I can, I need to fix it. I need to save my job."

"You want to doctor the file? Cover your tracks?" He shook his head. "I can't agree to that. No way."

"No, that's not what I meant at all. Jack is locking me out of this case, shutting the whole thing down. But, Ben, the forensic evidence is strong. Mitch Kruger killed someone, I know it. I need a second bite at the apple. I need a chance to prove my case."

"I think you're going to have a hard time convincing anyone here to bring Mitch Kruger to trial again."

She chewed her bottom lip while she considered

this. "You're probably right. My credibility is shot." Her long lashes fluttered as she turned her gaze to him. "But yours isn't."

"Now wait—"

"I can help you review this file. I know everything about it, and you can provide the second set of eyes that Jack feels is needed. If I can convince you that Mitch Kruger committed murder, you can convince Jack that my judgment wasn't off. Not entirely."

"And you can keep your job." Ben crossed his arms. "But Jack won't like this. He wants an independent review."

"Fine, make it an independent review. Just let me tag along, treat me as a partner. A consultant. Tell Jack that it's too complicated and you think my input would be valuable." He caught the sweet scent of her hair as she leaned forward. "He'll listen to you. Besides, it wouldn't be strange for two colleagues to consult with each other. Not if we're already *partners*."

"Sally, I realize you don't want to lose control of the file—"

"You want to cut a deal?" She squared her shoulders. "Fine. Name your price."

"A deal?" He started. "What kind of deal are we making here?"

"You let me in on your review process and convince Jack to make me your partner. Give me a chance to save my job and make my case. I'll give you something in return. So what do you want? I'll do your dry cleaning, buy you coffee for a month…what?" She placed her hands on her hips.

He didn't care about dry cleaning or coffee. He allowed his gaze to venture lower, skimming the edges of her dress, the elegant curves of her body. There'd been a time in law school when he'd thought he could fall in love with Sally Dawson. Smart, quirky Sally, who was unlike anyone he'd ever met. Then he'd gone and ruined it. But now she needed him. Now he finally had an in. So what did he want?

"All right, Sally," he began coolly. "I'll talk to Jack, tell him I want your help. I'll let you tag along on my review interviews, and I'll promise to keep an open mind. If you can convince me that Mitch Kruger committed murder, I'll help you plead your case to Jack. But if I'm not convinced, or if I think an error in judgment was made…I can't promise results."

"Fine, I get that. And in return?"

He moved his hands to his waist. "Anything, right?"

She peered at him from narrowed eyes. "Keep it family friendly, Ben."

He lowered himself toward her, watching her eyes widen as he reduced the distance between them. "You sneer at me."

"I don't." But she blinked several times and leaned slightly away from him. *Busted.*

"You know you do. You've barely spoken to me since the first year of law school. You can hardly stand to look at me now, and we're going to be working across the hall from each other."

"Well, and so what?" She folded her arms across her chest like a belligerent child.

"So what? The 'so what' is that now you want something from me. You made my welcome as cold as possible this morning, and now you suddenly want us to work together."

"You're mad that I didn't smile at you enough?" She

rolled her eyes. "This is great. So what? You're going to get even, I suppose. Humiliate me? Make me wash your car in a bikini?"

That was an image worth dwelling on, but he had to stay focused. "Worse. I want a second chance." He pulled his back straighter. "I want you to have dinner with me."

It was as if someone had hit an erase button in her mind. She lost her words, her thoughts slid away into some great expanse of forgotten information, and all that came out of her mouth was, "Ha!"

Have dinner with Ben? Oh, that was rich. She'd put that one in her diary and read it the next time she needed a laugh.

His face was unmoving. "Is that all you have to say?"

"What else is there to say? How about, 'thank you, but I'd rather set my hair on fire.'"

"That seems like a dramatic response," he said mildly, then shrugged. "Suit yourself."

He turned and walked toward the door, leaving her standing there dumbly. "That's it? Suit yourself?"

He paused to issue a second nonchalant shrug. "That's the deal. If you're not willing to bargain, then we're done."

"And…what? What happens to your review of my files?"

"I'll proceed as Jack requested. I'll conduct some interviews, check under rocks for missing clues, exactly what you'd expect." He pulled at the knot on his tie. "I'll submit some kind of report to Jack, let him know how, exactly, a murder victim walked back into town. He'll take it from there."

Sally's stomach worked itself into a ball. "Without me? You mean you're going to cut me out? But I can tell you the subtleties of the case, who to talk to."

"I'll interview you, of course." Now he turned his gaze directly to her. "You'll be a part of my inquiry. But I'll do the rest independently, just as Jack requested. You were a brilliant law student, and I'm sure you're a good attorney, Sally. You shouldn't have anything to be worried about."

Her pulse quickened. He was going to complete a review of her file, and she'd have to sit back and wait for the result? Torture. She couldn't trust Ben with her job like that. What if he overlooked something obvious, and she was left formulating a defense? She had to maintain some control.

"I'll talk to Jack myself," she announced. "I'll explain the need to help you with your investigation."

"You can do whatever you want, but I think we both know that he's not likely to be receptive. But if *I* suggested it, on the other hand, told him that I thought it would be valuable to have your input at all stages of the review, given the time pressures..." His voice trailed off.

Sally opened her mouth to argue, but then snapped it shut again. Ben was right. If she asked Jack again to be involved in the follow-up investigation, she'd appear self-serving and even suspicious, as if she was trying to hide something. He'd already turned her down once. If Ben insisted that he needed her help, well, that just might work. Jack wanted an answer, and quickly. He would probably be open to anything Ben suggested as long as it might speed up his review. She frowned. "You're blackmailing me."

"Now wait a second." Ben spun to face her. "This *exchange* was your idea. You know my terms. If you don't want to do it, no problem. I can promise you I'll be a complete professional in my review."

"But your terms are…unseemly."

"Oh?" He raised an eyebrow. "I'm sorry you find the idea of having dinner with me so offensive."

She balled her fists. He knew how she felt about him. He knew this would be the one thing she couldn't take, but she wasn't going to give him the satisfaction of being right.

She could do this. Yes, it might be awkward to go out with him—the idea made her palms sweat—but she'd live. She could even fake a headache and leave early. No appetizers, no dessert. Really, what was the big deal? She'd suffer through an evening with him in exchange for having more control over a file she cared about. Dinner in exchange for information that she could use to save her job, repair her reputation and bring Mitch Kruger to justice.

"Fine," she said through clenched teeth. "I'll have dinner with you."

He didn't smile. She didn't expect him to. Her tight-jawed acquiescence wasn't a victory by any measure. Instead he nodded slowly and turned back to the door. "Then I'll speak with Jack about getting you involved with the investigation."

"Great. At least one of us will enjoy this." She flung her gaze to the far wall, directing her words to a large potted plant on the bookshelf.

Ben stood in place, and when he spoke, his tone had

softened. "Listen. I've done some things I'm not proud of. I was hoping that I could do this to make it… I'm not doing anything to hurt you."

"You want me to give you a second chance by coercion. That may work on other women, but it won't fly with me."

"Sally. Come on now. That was ten years ago—"

She wasn't listening as she bustled around her office. "I don't have time for soliloquies. I'm meeting Dennis Marlow and Ronnie Kruger downstairs." She picked up a few scattered pens on her desk and dropped them with a thud into the pen holder. Then she swept round her desk.

Ben stepped into her path. "Hold it."

He was in her way, his broad figure blocking her retreat. She had no choice but to stop. "What?"

"It's not just your file anymore. I'm going to that meeting, too, and I'll be going to any meeting that comes up. From now on, whether you like it or not, when it comes to the Kruger case, there's only 'us.' Got it?"

His hands were on his hips, his stance wide as he towered over her. Sally stared right through him without saying a word. Then she swept past him and out the door, as if he hadn't been there at all.

Chapter 3

Sally's angry head start didn't matter in the end. Ben caught up with her in three easy strides down the hall. Maybe the heels had been a mistake, after all.

"We'll take the stairs," he announced. "And on the way, you can explain your theory of this case to me. Give me your elevator pitch."

She rolled her eyes again. "Veronica Kruger disappeared almost a year ago. Vanished. Apparently she had a nasty fight with her husband, Mitch. Next thing we know, she's not showing up at work. The police investigate and their kid tells us he hasn't heard from his mom in a few days."

"Their son? How old?"

"Teenage son, sixteen at the time. His name is James. That's James, not Jim. He was set to testify that he came home late from a party on the night his mother disappeared, sneaked into the house and went straight to bed. The next morning his dad told him that she'd packed up and left after an argument. While he was at the party." Sally sighed. "James didn't believe it, and things between father and son have been tense. James was going to testify against his father. He thinks Mitch killed his mom. Thought. He's been living with a friend."

They reached the staircase and proceeded down it. Their voices echoed against the metal stairwell and cinder block walls. "But you weren't basing your entire case on James's testimony."

"Partly," she admitted. "But we're basing it in larger part on the forensic evidence. The police found an area rug in a Dumpster behind a store that Mitch passed each morning on his way to work, months after we first suspected murder. A store employee called it in because... God. You should see the pictures. It just *looks* like someone bled to death on it."

"And he threw it out? In plain sight?"

"A store employee saw it, and surveillance footage confirmed it. It was rolled up, but still messy. We think he may have hidden it in a storage unit and dumped it after the preliminary investigation cooled and the police gave him some breathing room. James identified it. He said the rug had been missing since the night his mom disappeared."

"It's like he wanted you to find it," Ben mused. "So that's your case? Missing woman and blood on an area rug?"

"The lab ran DNA tests. It's Mrs. Kruger's blood, and the amount on that rug proves a fatal injury. Police found blood spatter on the wall consistent with a gunshot wound. The blood had been cleaned up, but the evidence was not completely destroyed. Between all of that and James's testimony, we have ourselves a murder. I mean, we thought we had."

"Hmm."

Sally glanced over her shoulder at Ben. "What?"

"Just thinking," he replied.

"No." She opened the door to the landing, then froze in place. "We're partners now, remember? I told you my theory, so what are you thinking?"

He leaned into the door she held. She was surprised to see his forehead crease as he thought, evidence that he was taking this case, *her* case, very seriously. "I'm thinking about how a massive amount of Ronnie Kruger's blood could be on an area rug while she is still alive. Sounds like a lab error."

"Impossible. I've checked and triple-checked everything with the lab and the detectives on the case. I was about to go to trial, Ben. I *know* there wasn't a mistake."

"I'm not saying anyone's at fault," he said mildly. "I'm only suggesting that something was missed or maybe overlooked. In any case, the good news is we may have just found Ronnie Kruger's body." He gave Sally a wink as they exited through the door. She tried not to roll her eyes yet again.

Marlow was already in the conference room when they arrived. "Sorry I'm—we're—late," Sally said. Ben shut the door behind them.

"I don't believe we've met," the defense attorney said, rising from his seat and extending his hand to Ben. "I'm Dennis Marlow, and this is Veronica Kruger."

"Ronnie." The woman didn't exactly smile, but she wasn't unpleasant, either.

"Ben McNamara." He shook hands with Marlow and gave Ronnie a polite nod. "Ma'am."

Sally slid into a seat and studied Ronnie from across the table, trying to wrap her head around the idea of her. Ronnie Kruger had haunted her nightmares. Sally had imagined her screams and her fear. She'd hounded the police detectives about her, wanting them to extend searches for her body so the poor woman could receive a proper burial.

Sally had tried not to think about the grisly details of her death. Blood spatter patterns at the Kruger household had been blurred by aggressive cleaning, but illuminated by luminol, and they indicated Mrs. Kruger had been shot multiple times. A bullet recovered from the fireplace contained Ronnie's blood and confirmed the weapon had been a .357. Sally couldn't think about that final, awful end when the bullets had torn into her body. She knew some of her colleagues, like many homicide detectives, had to crack jokes to distance themselves from the daily horrors they witnessed. They called people "vics" and "perps" and used cold, impersonal language to describe the crimes. It was their only armor against evil.

Sally wasn't quite there yet, psychologically, although she supposed she might have fewer nightmares if she were. Instead, when she had a new case, she thought of clothes. This was what gave her insomnia: victims' clothing. When she looked at crime scene photos, she'd stare at the person's shoes and think about how alive he or she had been at the moment they'd dressed. At the darkest points of the case, when she questioned her abilities and her energy to continue, Sally had thought about Ronnie selecting her white blouse and beige khakis, not knowing those would be the clothes she would die in. Then Sally had fought on.

She blinked. But none of that was true anymore. Ronnie Kruger had dressed that morning, and she'd lived to see hundreds of more days, while Sally had worked to bring her nonexistent killer to justice. She tried to identify the source of the tension that balled the muscles around her neck. Was she actually angry that Ronnie Kruger was alive? Sally rubbed at her temple, where a headache had started to throb. No need to engage in psychotherapy right now. There were more pressing concerns.

Ben made his way around to her side of the table. Had he always been so broad-shouldered, or was that the marine in him? He carried himself as if he owned the room. She'd have to remind him that he didn't.

"I'm new to the office," he explained in an easy manner as he slid into the chair beside her. "Sally's showing me the ropes."

He gave her a smile. She gritted her teeth. "Mrs. Kruger," she said in a voice that sounded almost calm. "First of all, I'm glad to see you're doing well. It would be an understatement if I said that I was very concerned about you."

"And I feel terrible about that, believe me." The woman's hand flew to her heart, and her blue eyes widened. "Mitch and I had a terrible argument, and I'm ashamed to say I went a bit out of my mind." Her eyelids lowered and she shook her head contritely. "I left my son. My poor boy, James, was so worried. I had no idea."

Sally reached for the box of tissues beside her when she noticed that tears had started to well in Ronnie's eyes. "Please, help yourself. We're always well stocked with tissues around here." She slid the box across the table.

"Thank you." Ronnie took one out and proceeded to dab at both eyes and blow her nose. "The idea of Mitch being on trial for my murder? Well, I came home as soon as I found out."

Ben leaned forward across the table, his dark eyes staring intently at her. "That must have been some argument."

Ronnie sniffed, swiping the tissue beneath her upturned nose. "It was. I'm so embarrassed." She ran a finger below one eye. "I found out that Mitch was cheating on me. Had been for a long time. My world exploded." Her chin trembled.

"So Mitch was unfaithful?" Sally chewed on this fact for a moment. "He told us that you'd been arguing about something trivial. Specifically, that he'd left a mess in the kitchen that morning."

"Is that what he said?" For a flash of a second, she looked surprised. Then she quickly recovered. "I guess it may have started out that way. I'm not surprised that he didn't mention his infidelity. It's not the kind of thing he would advertise. It was a woman he worked with. Younger." Ronnie inhaled a ragged breath.

"Do you have the woman's name?" Sally reached behind her to open a small cabinet drawer. In her haste, she had forgotten to bring a pen and paper with her, but the cabinet was stocked with lined pads and ballpoint pens.

"I don't remember." Ronnie sniffled. "I've blocked out so many of those details. It's all like a bad dream now." Her chin twitched and her shoulders sagged as if she was about to crumple. "I was devastated. Our marriage, the life we built together, all of it was a lie. I blacked out."

"Amnesia," Marlow explained. "Mrs. Kruger doesn't remember anything after the argument." He placed a hand on her shoulder as she shuddered. "There now. No one's upset with you."

"I wouldn't say that just yet."

Sally's attention snapped to Ben. His mouth was pulled tightly as he studied Ronnie. "Ben, I don't think—"

"For the past year, law enforcement has been working hard to find you, Mrs. Kruger, and you're saying that you never had any idea?" He sat straighter in his chair. "And yet, after almost a year of amnesia, you regain your memory enough to come back home right before your husband is tried for your murder. I find that hard to believe."

He was in full litigator mode, his face blank, his muscular body imposing even as he sat at the table. Sally followed his gaze to Ronnie, who had balled her tissue in her fist. "I told you the truth. I woke up in Vegas without any idea who I was. No ID, nothing. I was treated at a clinic and released. I've been living in a motel and waiting tables."

"Mrs. Kruger has a number of people who can swear she's been in Vegas," Marlow interjected. "I called a few of them myself, and I'll email the list to the police."

"Copy us on that, please," Sally said. Marlow nodded and made a note.

Ben turned in his chair, still intent on watching Ronnie. Sally couldn't read his expression, but she was guessing that he didn't buy anything she'd just said. "Let's back up a minute. Now, you had an argument with Mr. Kruger. What was the nature of that argument?"

"It may have started out with something minor, but then I learned he was…that he'd been unfaithful." Ronnie's posture had shifted, and now she sat up straight in her seat. All her tears were inexplicably gone. "I remember that we argued, and I walked out. I don't remember anything after that."

"Did he hurt you?" Sally asked.

"No."

"So you remember that he didn't hurt you?" Ben observed.

Ronnie eyed him coldly. "Mitch has never raised a hand to me."

Sally nearly shivered from the icy glare Ronnie thrust at him. "Mrs. Kruger, I'm sure you've heard that we found an awful lot of blood—*your* blood—on an area rug that your husband discarded after your disappearance. Any idea how that blood got there?"

She blinked several times and looked around the room. "Now that I think about it, when I was in Vegas, I discovered this." She lifted a section of hair on the side of her head to reveal a thick, jagged scar. "I have no idea where it came from, but maybe I fell during our argument."

"Could explain the amnesia," Marlow interjected. "Bumps on the head, right?"

"You *think* you fell?" Sally's eyebrows shot up. The scar was ugly, but any injury that would have produced so much blood on the carpet would have been fatal. "Did you receive stitches?"

"I don't…" Ronnie turned to Marlow. "Am I in trouble?"

"Absolutely not. Ben, Sally, I'm not sure what the cop routine is all about. Maybe you should leave that to our fine men and women in blue." Marlow placed his hand on Ronnie's arm and leaned forward in his chair. "Mrs. Kruger has been through a terrible shock. She's told you she doesn't remember anything. Now, kindly do what you need to, to verify that she is alive, so we can reunite her with her husband, who is still rotting in jail. Any further questions as to what happened that night will have to come from a police officer."

Ben's face relaxed into an easy smile, and he turned to Sally. "Well, partner, you're the one who has to file that motion. Are you satisfied that Ronnie Kruger is alive?"

Sally studied her one more time. Ronnie Kruger had a small mole on the left side of her chin. All the missing persons reports had mentioned that mole, and Sally had seen it in each and every photo, and again right now when she looked at Ronnie. "Yes, I'm satisfied."

"Great." Marlow rose and indicated that his client's wife should do the same. "We'll stick around and wait for you to file that emergency motion. I expect we'll be pulled in front of the judge in no time."

"No doubt," Sally replied flatly.

She watched as Marlow held the door for Ronnie and then followed her out, closing it behind them. She exhaled. "I don't even know—"

"This stinks." Ben sat back in his chair. "She just told us a bunch of damn lies. What, are we supposed to believe she had post-traumatic stress disorder as a result of some argument with her husband?" His face darkened. "This is wrong."

"The cheating is all new," Sally said. "Mitch told us that they'd argued over dirty dishes."

The corner of Ben's mouth lifted in a wry smirk. "They didn't get their stories straight. Not surprising when it's been almost a year."

Sally felt something akin to relief creeping up her spine. Ben believed the Krugers were hiding something. Maybe she wasn't alone in this, after all.

She tamped down the feeling. Facts were facts, and facts alone would vindicate her and save her job. Besides, this was *Ben,* the man who'd betrayed her a hundred ways. She couldn't forget that.

"How did she get to Vegas?" he asked.

"Sorry?"

"She was in Vegas, right? How did she get there?"

He leaned closer, and Sally caught his scent. Soapy and clean, with a hint of vanilla. She felt hot under the intensity of his gaze. "Her car was found near a bus stop on the outskirts of town, about a mile and a half from the Kruger household. We assumed Mitch had dropped it off and walked home."

"But now we have to rethink that." Ben's forehead tensed. "She made it to Vegas, but she didn't take her car."

"She could have traveled by bus," Sally said. "Gotten off at the station and taken a series of buses to Vegas. The police asked around at the time of her disappearance, and flashed her picture. They never found anyone who recognized her, which we took as evidence that she'd never been on the bus, because she was dead." Sally tapped her fingertips against the tabletop as she thought. "But now that we know she wasn't dead, we can think about this differently. She didn't *have* to take a bus somewhere just because her car was at a bus stop."

Ben nodded as he picked up her trail of thought. "The police assumed that Mitch had dropped off the car at the bus stop after killing his wife. But now that we know Mitch didn't kill her, anything's possible. Especially if they were in it together."

"Yes. He could have dropped her off at the airport. The police never had a reason to check airline records." A nervous excitement sent Sally's heart pounding. "I have to call the police detectives. Maybe they can follow up on that."

Ben's jaw was set as he sat in quiet reflection. "Are we even sure she was really in Vegas? There could be layers of lies here."

That brought Sally back to reality with a thud. "Yes, she could be lying about Vegas. Heck, she may have even gotten a lift from a friend." Sally puffed up her cheeks with a breath and released it, fluttering her lips. "Even if they're lying, we don't know why, and until we do, we're living a public relations nightmare." She tucked a stray tendril behind her ear. "Regardless of our suspicions, now that I know Ronnie's alive, I need to formally drop the murder charges against her husband. Whatever happens after that…" Her voice trailed off. "All that work. It's like starting from square one, trying to figure out what happened that night."

"It's one step at a time, Sally. And remember, you're not working alone."

Ben looked as if he was fighting something, the way he stared uneasily at his hands. Then he glanced up.

He didn't need to look at her like that. All intense, as if he were actually listening to what she said. The hair on her arms rose as she remembered how he used to look at her back at the beginning of law school. Back when they'd been friends.

And then suddenly, briefly, so much more than friends.

She wondered what had happened to him, to have gone from an associate at an international law firm in Manhattan to a prosecutor in a small district in Connecticut. Sure, Sally loved the town, but she'd grown up in this area. Her family was here. Ben was from… actually, she didn't even remember.

She cleared her throat and rose. "I've got to get that motion out. We can talk later."

Ben nearly bounded up the stairs. After a dismal morning, he felt light with adrenaline. He couldn't get Ronnie Kruger out of his mind—her facial expressions, the way her tears had dried up the second he'd put her on the defensive. She hovered like a bad premonition at the edge of his mind. This time when he entered his office, he overlooked its small size. This job had just got interesting, and his heart was pounding.

What was Ronnie Kruger hiding? His mind hummed with possibilities. This could be a failed attempt at insurance fraud, or a publicity stunt. Maybe Ronnie had framed her husband for her own murder and then skipped town. This case could go a hundred different ways.

Ben helped himself to several boxes of files and settled at his desk. He paused before opening the lid to the first box. These were Sally's files, and whatever he found in here could put her job at risk. Ronnie Kruger may have pulled a hoax, but what if Sally had overlooked something obvious while compiling the case? He frowned. He was working a job, that's all. It wasn't his concern what Sally had or hadn't done. He couldn't blame himself if she lost her job.

He thought of her strutting angrily down the hall in those heels, and smiled to himself. How she managed to stand, let alone walk in those things escaped him. She was just as sexy as he remembered, with that exaggerated sway of her hips. Sally was larger than life, and it was impossible not to notice her. Everyone in their law class had known Sally. They'd all spent the first few weeks of school wondering why Columbia had accepted a ditzy prom queen, and the next few years regretting ever underestimating her. She'd walk into moot court, all smiles and designer clothing, and then proceed to wipe the floor with her opponent. He knew firsthand that underestimating Sally was dangerous business.

He studied the box again. He couldn't assume that she'd made a mistake. Sally might come off as a lightweight, but when it came to something she cared about, she was all business. The girl was dumb like a fox.

There was a knock on the door, and Ben looked up to see Jack enter. "How'd it go with Veronica Kruger? I went to ask Sally, but she's in court."

Ben shrugged. "Looks like she's alive, all right. Alive, and spinning some lies about what happened that night she went missing."

"What's her story?"

"A fight with her husband left her with amnesia that conveniently cleared up right before his trial." Ben tossed the lid to the first box aside. "Sally's off drop-ping the charges against Mitch Kruger as we speak, and I'm going to start digging through these documents to get some background." He shook his head. "It's a shame we can't keep him a little longer. I can't help but feel he's getting away with something."

"You'll want to talk to the detective on the case and the folks at the crime lab," Jack said. "We need them to take a fresh look at the evidence."

"Yes, sir."

Jack placed his hands on his hips and took a breath. "I don't need to tell you that there's blood in the water," he said. "The media are circling. I need to know what the hell happened. I need to throw them something."

Ben nodded. "Yes, sir." He needed to get Sally of-ficially assigned to the case. That was part of their arrangement, and this was the perfect opening. "You know, I was thinking it might be helpful if Sally helped me conduct this review."

Jack shook his head. "I went over this with Sally earlier, Ben. I want an independent review. A fresh set of eyes."

"Oh, I understand that, sir. It's important that you feel you're getting an honest analysis of the case." Ben shrugged. "I just thought that if time is of the essence, and it seems that it is, then it's going to take me a while to get up to speed with this case. But if Sally were to assist me, show me where to look and who to talk to, I might be able to get somewhere, quickly."

Jack folded his arms across his chest as he consid-ered this, his brow creased in thought. "So you think Sally should help in the investigation?"

"It's clear to me that no one in this office knows

or cares more about this case than she does," he said. "I think she could speed up the investigation significantly."

Jack let out a breath. "But your report would be independent, correct? That's a sticking point with me. I need an unbiased review of this case. It helps that you're an almost complete outsider."

"Absolutely, sir. You have my word."

The older man paused again, then nodded slowly. "All right. That makes sense. Have Sally partner with you on the investigation side, but I want that analysis to be completely independent, got it?"

"Yes, sir."

Ben smiled to himself after Jack left the room. He'd upheld his end of the bargain, and now Sally had to uphold hers. Wouldn't she be pleased.

"He came in and interrupted us. He actually walked right into my office as if we were standing in the hallway, and said he would review the files. He was so smug about it, too. You would've thought he was a knight in shining armor!" Sally punctuated her statement with a fork and then viciously speared a ketchup-soaked French fry on her plate. "Of course Jack agreed because, what, like he has *any* free time these days to review my files."

Tessa took a sip of seltzer water from her straw and nodded at Sally's plate. "Can we talk about how you're the only person I know who eats French fries with a fork and knife?"

"How am I going to get through this, Tessa?" Sally continued, her eyes beginning to sting. She rested her fork on her plate. "I've worked harder on this case than any other. I thought I was doing everything right. And now?" She swallowed the tight knot that had worked its way into her throat. "I could lose my job."

"Oh, honey." Her friend leaned forward to grasp her hand. "I promise you won't lose your job. You're too damn good at it. Besides, we all have those loser cases, the ones we take a chance on, only to come up short."

Tessa was being generous. She was one of the most skilled attorneys in the office and a genius with juries. Sally had been partnered with her a few times and had witnessed firsthand the way Tessa could read a jury, predicting which members would form a friendship, and knowing instinctively how to win them over. She was such a brilliant advocate that she routinely gave lectures to organizations in the Connecticut bar about jury psychology. Did she lose cases? Sure. But when jurors voted for acquittal, they sometimes apologized to her personally afterward. Sally was confident that whatever Tessa imagined her "loser" cases to be, they paled in comparison to this debacle.

"This is more than a 'loser' case, okay? My murder victim held a press conference."

"This is where I remind you that we're bureaucrats. We're lowly cogs in a wheel on a big justice machine. You're not the only one who decides to bring a murder case to trial." She removed her hand from Sally's to absentmindedly brush a crumb off the table. "That evidence must have been pretty darn compelling, for Jack to agree to go to trial without a body."

Sally had thought so. Now she didn't know what to think, other than that the instincts she'd always trusted had been horribly wrong. "The evidence was good." She reached for her glass of lemon water and finished it off. "It doesn't matter anymore. Let's change the subject."

"Okay." Tessa set her fork down beside her plate and softened her gaze. "How are things going? How are you feeling?"

That hadn't been the change of subject Sally had hoped for. Tessa was the only other person in Sally's life who knew that she'd been undergoing fertility treatments for months, trying to conceive her first child. The only other person who knew she'd been successful. "I don't want to jinx it," she said quietly. "So far, so good."

"Any nausea? Fatigue?"

Sally shook her head, not wanting to confess that even though she was early in the pregnancy, the lack of symptoms troubled her. "Not yet, but who knows? Maybe Mr. X just has great genes."

Mr. X was the man of last resort, the final reproductive frontier. The anonymous sperm donor. He was the concept to which a woman turned when she wanted a family, but the men she'd met were complete duds. When a woman spent so much of her youth heartbroken over men who were more interested in the size of her trust fund than the content of her character, she reached a breaking point. For Sally, that point came last year, when she'd walked in on her fiancé, Michael, with another woman.

She didn't understand her luck. She was repellant to decent guys and syrup to creeps, and she'd spent more than enough time around men who'd treated her poorly. Ben, for example. She'd once allowed herself to believe she'd fallen in love with him. He'd gotten what he wanted from her, and then he'd been purposefully cruel. Broke off contact. Saw other women. Treated her as if what they'd shared had been nothing. Seeing him again reminded her of how foolish and naive she'd once been.

Well, no more. She was done. She wanted a baby and she would have one, but she'd just eliminate the middleman, so to speak. In a way, the decision was liberating. No more heartbreaks like the one she'd experienced with Michael. No walks of shame after a one-night stand, or waiting for a phone call that would never come. No more! She'd turned thirty-five over the summer and decided it was now or never. Insurance covered most of the treatments, and she had nothing to lose except the painful fear that she'd live out the rest of her life alone.

Sally knew nothing about her sperm donor except his education level, where he'd attended school, and that he lived in a different region of the country. She had a copy of one of his baby pictures, but he hadn't submitted a photo of himself as an adult. Mr. X, the man who would be the father of her child because she was finished with men and had completely lost hope of ever finding one she trusted enough to make a baby the old-fashioned way, was an enigma. But thank goodness for reproductive technology.

She bit her lip. She didn't want to talk about Mr. X. He was the white flag she was waving at her future. Yes, she appreciated his help, but he sort of depressed her, too.

"The doctor says it's probably too early for symptoms, and that I should feel grateful for any day I wake up and feel like eating breakfast." She looked at Tessa's large gray eyes. "But you know? I worry. I do. I worry about being too happy and getting too attached. I feel like I've been swimming upstream. I thought I was having a baby with Michael, and look how that turned out." The memory was still painful. "I just want something to go my way for once. Perfectly and easily my way."

"Oh, honey." Tessa grasped her hand warmly again, between hers. "It will. I want this for you, too."

Sally squeezed her friend's hands before gently pulling back. "Anyway, I haven't been thinking about it much since I found out last week that I was pregnant, because I have this trial. *Had* this trial." She twirled her straw around in her glass. "What am I going to do?" She brought her elbow to the table and rested her forehead on her hand. "I'm so finished. Ben is going to find something, and he's going to ruin me with it. I just know he is."

Tessa arched her elegant brown eyebrows. "What makes you sure he's out to get you? I met him, and he seems like a nice guy. Straightforward."

"Ben is not nice," Sally informed her. "If his picture was in a dictionary, it would be filed under 'nice, antonyms.' He is the anti-nice, and now he's my co-worker. Oh, and he's reviewing my file, and he's going to ruin my life. Et cetera." She paused. "He wants me to stop sneering at him. He says that I need to give him a second chance."

Tessa raised her eyebrows. "You held out on me! A second chance—what's that, like a date?"

She shifted in her seat. Suddenly, there wasn't enough air in the room. "It's not a date. It's more like blackmail."

Tessa chuckled. "Blackmail? Yeah, right. A man

who looks like Ben McNamara can blackmail me that way anytime."

Sally felt an odd flash at her friend's light remark, a twitch that felt something like jealousy. She tugged at the diamond stud in her right earlobe. No, not jealousy. She'd have no reason for that. The feeling must be protectiveness. "You wouldn't like Ben. Besides, you should watch out for him."

"Oh? Why's that?"

"He likes brunettes." Sally refolded the cloth napkin in her lap. "He also likes redheads, and blondes, so…"

"Okay, I got it. He's one of those." Tessa grinned. "But, Sally, you're acting so funny about all of this. Since when have you been intimidated by anyone? We've worked together for years, and you've never struck me as someone who gives a damn what others think."

She didn't care what Ben thought. She was certain of that. She also wasn't about to rehash their entire history right now, just as she and Tessa were finishing up lunch. They needed to get back to work, and things with Ben were complicated. They'd dated for three months, during which time she'd fallen completely in love with him. It could have been a happy ever after, until he'd gone and betrayed her.

She felt heat creeping up her neck. "I prefer to work with people with integrity, that's all."

Tessa dabbed at the side of her mouth with her napkin, then opened her purse as the check appeared. "You're not going to lose your job."

Sally shook her head. "You don't know—"

"You're not going to lose your job because you're too clever for that. Lunch is my treat, by the way."

Tessa slid a credit card over the check. "Considering the day you're having, it would be unconscionable for us to go dutch."

Sally barely registered the gesture. "What do you mean, I'm too clever?"

"I mean that if Ben's going to review your file, you're going to review Ben's. You're going to be his partner on this. You know that case. You know the weaknesses and the strengths better than anyone else. If you don't trust him, then don't let him out of your sight." She shrugged as if it was truly that simple. "It's not like this is a formal peer review. All Jack wants is a second set of eyes so that he can put some spin on it for the press. The way I see it, you stand your ground, supervise Ben while appearing to just be helpful, and you come out looking like a hero."

"How do you figure?"

"I know you. You didn't make a mistake on that file. I also know the crime lab, and they triple-check everything. So I'm thinking that you're either looking at some kind of terrible scam or publicity stunt by Mr. and Mrs. Kruger, or you're looking at something very grim."

Her words settled against the bottom of Sally's stomach like a brick. "You think—"

"You know exactly what I think." Tessa leaned closer and dropped her voice to a conspiratorial whisper. "I think that if the forensic evidence shows that someone was murdered in that house, then someone was murdered in that house."

"Yes." Sally nodded slowly. "Someone was murdered, and we just got the wrong victim."

She ruminated on this idea as they walked back to

the office. The wrong victim—was it actually possible? Her head ached.

Before she reached her office, she stopped at the little closet of an office where Ben would be working. This was the worst office in the building, hands down. She sort of pitied him for it. He was sitting at his desk, absorbed in some kind of reading material. Her files. "Hey," she said.

He looked up, and her traitorous heart kicked. "Hey."

Sally cleared her throat. "The judge granted the motion, so Mitch Kruger will be released from prison."

Ben nodded solemnly. "Okay. Thanks for keeping me informed."

She ran her tongue into the corner of her mouth. "There are food trucks out by the park if you haven't had lunch. I've already eaten, but I wanted to tell you."

He glanced out the window and then gave her a vague smile. "Maybe later. Thanks."

She felt as if she was having that dream where she was caught naked in public. A flush crept up her chest, and she turned to leave.

"Hey, Sally?"

She glanced back over her shoulder. "Yes?"

"I got permission from Jack to include you in this investigation. We're good to go." He gave her a half grin that made her think sexy things that she shouldn't be thinking. "You'll have to let me know your availability. I'll find the perfect place."

She glowered at him. So dinner with Ben was really going to happen? "Whatever," she said. "But don't expect me to have time for dessert."

She didn't wait for a response before turning and

leaving the room. *Dinner with Ben.* After ten years, this was really happening.

She would have scolded herself for entering into such a corrupt bargain at a time of weakness, if she wasn't so horrified by the shiver of excitement that the thought sent through her.

Chapter 4

Ronnie slid the glass door shut behind her and stepped onto the back patio. More leaves had come down last night, red and yellow ones that littered the cement. She didn't know a thing about leaves, or what kinds of trees these came from. They were pretty, though. She swept them off to the side with her foot to create an open space. Then she shook a cigarette from her pack, placed it between her lips and lit it with the old purple lighter she'd found at the bottom of a drawer. She took a drag, inhaling the smoke.

The lighter barely had enough fluid in it. James had probably been using it to light candles and incense. The kid was weird about things like that, all his candles and scented things. He was lucky he hadn't burned the house down yet. She flicked the cigarette butt with her thumb, sending a shower of ashes to the ground.

She hadn't been exactly honest with Mitch about her smoking. He'd be upset. She hadn't smoked since James was a baby. Back then he'd giggle and grab at smoke rings as she blew them, but she'd stopped when he'd developed pneumonia. Quit cold turkey. *Because I care about my family. I fight like hell for my family.*

This past year was no different. This was fighting like hell, *going through hell,* if she was honest. She'd enjoyed Vegas when she and Mitch made a long weekend of it fifteen years ago, but now she saw it was a dump. The lights and sounds of the place exhausted her, and Vegas was no fun unless you had the money to play. Turns out you needed a lot more money than the amount she'd had to hide out comfortably. Steak dinners? No way. Drinks at fancy bars? Out of the question. After she got her new ID set up, she'd found a job waiting tables ten hours a day, and she was still lucky to be able to afford a take-out pizza every now and then.

She took another drag of the cigarette. *Small price to pay for keeping your family together.* She had to keep reminding herself of that. Ronnie was a family woman. Without her husband and her son, she had nothing, and she'd thought of them every day during that long eleven months in virtual isolation. It was nice to be home. Nothing beat that.

The handle of the sliding glass door clicked behind her, and she dropped the cigarette to the ground, stamping it beneath her heel. Seconds later the door slid open, and James poked his head into the cool air. "Mom? What are you doing?"

"Getting some air, sweetie."

He hated when she called him that—she could see it

in his scowl and the duck of his head. But she couldn't help it. She loved that kid, and she was glad he'd agreed to move back home. "Wanna join me?" She held out her arm in invitation.

He hesitated, but then stepped outside. Sniffed. "You're smoking." His tone was accusatory.

She rolled the cigarette beneath her shoe before picking up the remains and tucking them into her pocket. "Don't tell Dad."

James turned his head away, but kept an eye on her, studying her with a sidelong gaze. "You haven't smoked since I was little. Smoking will give you cancer."

She loved teenagers. She'd worked as a nurse at the high school for over ten years, and they'd never changed. Every one of them walked around as if no one had ever known anything before they came along. "Is that right? So that must be why they call them cancer sticks."

She'd missed him, the sound of his voice, their conversations together. When he was a baby her only goal had been to kiss him a million times, and then he'd grown into a sullen teenager who'd stopped telling her where he was going, and with whom. Then her goal was to get him to confide in her, just a little, as he used to. In the months she'd been alone, she'd had plenty of time to think about James as he used to be, back when he'd rushed home to tell her about his day.

She leaned across the space between them to pull him closer, tousle his hair and wrap her arm around him, but he stepped out of her reach.

Ronnie swallowed the tension in her throat and let

her arm fall uselessly at her side. *Shrug it off. No big deal, the kid needs some space.* He needed lots of it.

The wind rustled the trees, sending a shimmer of yellow leaves to the ground. They stood breathing in the cool air for a few minutes. Ronnie hadn't expected to be happy to be back in this climate after those months in the desert, but she'd missed the unpredictable weather. There was a certain romance in rainfall, and she missed the trees.

"It's weird that you're back here," James suddenly offered. His head was still turned so as not to make direct eye contact with her. "I thought you were dead. How could you run away like that?"

His voice trembled, his emotions barely restrained. He'd always been a sensitive kid. Ronnie patted her back pocket, where she'd stashed her cigarettes, and then thought better of lighting up in front of him. He was right, and she should set a good example.

"I didn't run away," she replied in her best mom voice. Calm to the verge of impatience. "I've told you, I was very confused. I'd had a terrible shock." She leaned a shoulder against the side of the house and watched him. "I only regained my memory a few days ago, and what did I do?" She waited for a response that didn't come. "James, what did I do? What did I do when I regained my memory?"

He shifted to his other foot and looked as if he desperately did not want to answer her. "I don't know—"

"I came right home. As soon as I regained my memory, I came home to you and Dad. It was like I woke up, and in a flash—" she snapped her fingers for emphasis "—I knew where I belonged."

He continued to stare out at the backyard, at the

edge of the property where the neighbor's clothesline was coming into view as the tree that normally shielded the properties from each other shed its leaves. Ronnie sighed and edged closer to him. He'd barely come near her, except to offer a stiff hug. He was probably in shock, and who could blame him? This was all just temporary. She wanted to tell him everything, to explain what a sacrifice she'd made for the good of the family. *If you only knew what I've been through, James. What Dad and I did to protect this family from falling apart.* But that was it: teenagers only *thought* they knew everything.

"I missed you," she said softly. "I'd take back the past year if I could. I missed you so much."

The hard lines of his shoulders relaxed, and he finally spared her a direct glance. "I missed you, too, Mom." He turned away again.

It was a start.

He scuffed his foot across the cement, scraping at a leaf. "Dad hates me, you know. 'Cause I was going to testify that I thought he killed you."

Ronnie's heart clutched. She'd understood when she'd left that she'd be making certain sacrifices, but she hadn't fully appreciated how her absence would affect her son. "That's not the way it is with your dad." She tried to keep her voice even. "He understands. You were confused. Everyone was."

The look in James's eyes sent a chill through her. "You don't get it. He's never going to forgive me. I helped send him to jail."

She rubbed her tense jaw. Sleep had been eluding her for days, and when it came, she often ground her teeth and woke with a splitting headache. "He'll come around. We'll get back to normal." She paused. "Well, as soon as that prosecutor stops nosing around."

Her shoulders tightened just thinking about the interview at the prosecutor's office yesterday. Ronnie could tell by the way Sally Dawson had looked at her that she had it out for her and Mitch. There was nothing for her to find, of course, but that was beside the point. She could make their lives hell. She could tear apart their family, ruin everything for which Ronnie had sacrificed.

"She's not gonna do anything, Mom." James sighed. "She probably just has paperwork or something to fill out."

"I don't think so." Ronnie's fingers itched for the cigarettes again, but she caught herself in time. Months of chain-smoking, and now she was home and required to be on her best behavior. "She's not going to let it go. She thinks something happened here."

James stiffened. "*Did* something happen?"

"What?" Ronnie studied his figure, awkwardly settled in place, looking as if he was leaning while standing straight up. "No, of course not. Just an argument that got a little out of hand, that's all." She paused. "But I'll tell you, I saw a different side of your father that night. A side of him that frankly scared me to death."

Her son's eyes were fixed on her now, watching intently. "Did… What did he do?"

She wrapped her arms around her chest as a breeze blew past them. "It wasn't what he did. It was that I saw what he was capable of doing when pushed into a corner." She took a deep breath. "The first thing I told him when I came home was that I don't ever want to see that side of him again. He swore I wouldn't. That's the only reason I agreed to stay here, and it's the only reason I pressed you to come home." She shivered, running her hands up and down her arms. "But I worry about what will happen if that prosecutor keeps pursuing this case, James. I really do."

"What do you think will happen?" His voice was barely a croak.

She thought about it, but concluded by shaking her head. "I don't know. But I know your father, and he's never going back to jail."

Ben gripped the wheel as he pulled into the parking lot at the courthouse, wondering what the hell was wrong with his car this time. He'd just had new tires put on, and the car was handling poorly, veering off to the side of the road. He parked at the end of the lot and got out, slamming the door shut behind him. Piece of garbage, this car. He checked the tires. That explained it. One, two—no, *three* flat tires.

Ben knew he was making a mistake when his brother, Nate, had offered to sell him his car, but he had just come back home and the price was right. The clunker had been nothing but trouble, and Ben fought his mounting suspicion that he'd been sold a lemon. A broken side-view mirror, a mouse nest under the hood, a strange humming noise every time he went above fifty miles an hour, and now three flat tires. He and his little brother were close, but next time, he'd trust his gut. He pulled out his cell.

Seven-thirty, and Mike wasn't in the repair shop yet. He spoke to the voice mail. "Mike. Ben McNamara. Hey, listen—you just replaced four of my tires two days ago, and three of them are flat. I'm at my office, and I'm not paying for a tow. Call me when you get this." Damn.

He and Sally were meeting the detective on the Kruger case at the crime lab in a couple hours. Now he'd have to ask her for a ride. Part of him was irritated, and the other part couldn't believe his luck. That would be the same part of him that couldn't stop thinking about her, and thinking too much about Sally was dangerous.

No sense overthinking the attraction. She was a cute girl with great legs—legs that looked strong and capable, suggesting she could hike a mountain as easily as she could track bargains in a department store. But lots of women had nice legs, and Sally's happened to come with a high maintenance trifecta of designer clothing, manicures and temper tantrums. He'd been burned by difficult women before, women who demanded fresh flowers on a regular basis and jewelry on special occasions. Women whose egos filled the room, and who thought they were worth the migraine. They were never worth the migraine.

Not that Ben was looking to settle down just yet. Not at any point in this lifetime. He'd realized a few years ago that he wasn't marriage material. Maybe because the thought of being tied to one woman for the rest of his life made him itch as if he'd been wrapped in wool. Maybe because he'd once imagined himself to be the marriage type, and then reality had proved him so very wrong. There was some comfort in loneliness and in knowing that he wasn't responsible for anyone but himself. God knows he'd had times in his life when he could barely handle even that much responsibility. He was done with relationships, finished

with one-night stands. In his mind, the simple elegance
of being alone was sadly underappreciated.

Ben ran his hand along his tires, looking for nails
or pieces of glass, but came up empty. He straightened again and sighed, turning his thoughts back to
Sally. He'd asked her to give him a second chance,
and maybe it was time for him to do the same for her.
He admitted he wasn't perfect—hadn't he been running from his own mistakes for most of his life? Out-
wardly, he'd been a success by any measure. First in
his class at Columbia Law, then a prestigious job on
Wall Street, where he'd met and fallen in love with a
woman in marketing. He'd worked hard for all of it,
and then he'd gone and drunk it all away.

He'd started drinking in high school, after his father
died. A shot of vodka here and there, just to sleep at
night without dreaming of his dad disappearing below
the surface of the lake for the last time. Even now the
memory of that moment was like a fist to the gut, and
Ben still didn't dare answer the question he'd posed a
thousand times: What kind of person watches his father drown? But he'd stood by and watched him sink
like a rock into the grainy, dark depths of the water, not
fully believing his father was capable of something as
human as death, not knowing what to do. Ben's cow-
ardice had killed his father, and that was a burden he
wouldn't wish on anyone.

The drinking helped at first, but over time the smol-
dering guilt intensified to a blaze that couldn't be ex-
tinguished, not even temporarily, with one drink. And
so he'd taken two a night, then three. He'd measured
his life in shot glasses, then lost count of the drinks
and began to measure his life in mistakes. One-night

stands. Drunken brawls. Missed deadlines. He'd nearly lost his job, and nearly killed his fiancée.

Ben's jaw tightened. So Sally liked to shop, and sometimes she acted like an indulged child. He'd stood by and watched his father drown. What gave him the right to be so damn judgmental?

He'd made plenty of mistakes, and he regretted what he'd done to Sally. She'd been different, and he'd realized it right from the start. He'd never had to work hard to attract women, but Sally made him want to work. He'd bought her coffees before their morning contracts class, and he'd asked to review her notes. Beneath her sparkle and veneer, she was effortlessly smart, and he'd found it fascinating. At first he'd been interested in the chase. She was a challenge, nearly untouchable, and he'd wanted to win her attention.

For months, he'd worked hard to prove himself worthy. He'd followed her like a lost dog, slowly and deliberately working to earn her trust, and then once he had it, he'd violated it. She'd been hotter and sexier than he'd imagined, and after they'd dated for a few months, she'd told him she loved him. He'd panicked. He could have formed a meaningful relationship with her, or at least told her the truth. Instead he'd taken the coward's way out, hopping right into bed with a different classmate, someone he barely knew, trying to convince himself that he didn't feel anything for Sally. Because in those years, his lost years, numbness was the only feeling he could handle.

He trekked across the parking lot toward the courthouse. She hated him still. He could see it in the way her eyes narrowed in his presence. He supposed he should feel flattered that she thought about him enough to maintain such hatred. He'd often thought of her, too, even halfway around the world, but his thoughts had been different. While she probably imagined some form of horrific revenge, he'd thought of apology. What he would say, if he saw her again, to make her realize he wasn't the monster she thought he was. Not anymore.

He climbed the stairs to his office and unlocked the door. The place seemed to have shrunk since yesterday, with all the Kruger files scattered across the floor. Once upon a time he'd had an office with a view of downtown Manhattan, and now he had a converted janitor's closet. The room even smelled vaguely of bleach.

At least he was close to home. His family lived less than an hour away, and his mom had been recently diagnosed with Parkinson's. For the first time since enlisting, Ben could go home for a weekend if he wanted, or if his mom needed his help. Being so close made him feel grounded in a way he hadn't for as long as he could remember. Even if it wasn't glamorous, there was something reassuring in the familiar.

He heard a rustle behind him and turned to see Sally standing in the doorway, her lithe figure backlit. Ben was relieved to see that she was dressed in a white blouse, a pink cardigan and tailored brown pants. Her blond hair was smoothed into place by a thin headband. Today's look was elegant. No bare legs, thank God. He needed to be able to think straight.

"Detective Maybury is meeting us at the lab at nine," she announced. "We'll have to take separate cars. I'm meeting my parents after work. They're taking some cooking class where they make crusted goat cheese things, and then they invite me over for dinner and I have to tell them how delicious their flan is." She took a breath. "It can be exhausting. They get so needy about it, and I don't even like flan, you know? It's something with the texture. But I have to go, because they're my parents and I need to be supportive, and anyway, I promised to help my mom move some boxes of books that she's donating to charity."

A smile tugged at his mouth. Nice that she was talking to him, at least. "Good morning, Sally."

Her cheeks reddened, and she lifted her hand to cover her bare throat. "That was a lot of information."

"You were on a roll. I didn't want to stop you." He powered on his computer and opened the blinds. "Have you been here long?" He suspected he already knew the answer. She was jittery, as if she'd been pounding cups of coffee for a few hours.

"I got here at six. I couldn't sleep." She tilted her head. "I'm not actually experienced in this sort of thing. This media attention. Some reporter said that I'd been placed on administrative leave pending an investigation into my competence. That was on the front page of *The Journal*." A line appeared between her eyebrows. "I called him to chew him out. I don't know where he got that information. A correction will be made online, but there's nothing he can do about the print copies. I'm *mortified*."

Ben let out a sympathetic sigh. "I can't say that I blame you, but we're going to figure this out, Sally. Your good name will be cleared." He frowned. His computer was accusing him of not shutting it down properly. "But we can't take separate cars. I have three flat tires."

She smirked. "What, were you driving through a nail field?"

"Funny. I just had new tires put on. I suspect shoddy workmanship." He typed in his computer password. "I thought I knew the reputable places, but I may have been mistaken."

She was studying the pictures he'd stacked on his bookshelf. Mostly they were ones he'd taken while traveling, but he had a photo of some of his buddies in Afghanistan. He'd hang them at some point, when he had more time for interior design. She was looking intently, not even bothering to hide her interest. "Are these your friends?" she asked.

"Were. Two of them were killed by a suicide bomber. The third lost his legs." He couldn't talk about it without the words clogging his throat.

She was quiet for a moment, and ran a fingertip across the glass. "That's really sad," she murmured. "I'm sorry. I'm…I'm glad you're okay."

She picked at the ends of her hair, and he looked away. She was glad he was okay? That made one of them. He'd felt nothing but gnawing guilt at his survival since that day. He should have been with them. Who was he, to have been spared? They were good, decent men who'd deserved to come home, while he'd entered the military because he'd had nothing to live for. He should have taken their place. He coughed and pretended to be interested in the error message that continued to pop up on his computer screen.

She wasn't satisfied with the silence. "Why did you come here, Ben? Why Bedford Hills?"

"I grew up in this area of Connecticut. I wanted to come back."

"But it's so different from the city. And then being in a war zone." She set the pictures down again. "Bedford Hills is quiet. You're going to be bored here."

"There's nothing boring about murder victims coming back to life."

She was studying him, her heart-shaped lips relaxed as she seemed to look at him for the first time. Sally was soft today, almost vulnerable, and he thought about how it might feel to pull her into his arms and protect her. A foolish thought from someone who should know better. Sally could look after herself. She may not have factored into his decision to return home, but there was nothing boring about her, either.

She scrunched her forehead and chewed her lower lip, as if thinking about saying something. They both jumped at the sound of her cell phone.

"Sorry." She looked down and made a face. "Wait. I have to take this."

She ducked out into the hallway. The number that had come up belonged to James Kruger, Mitch and Ronnie's teenage son. She hadn't talked to him in a few weeks, but they'd exchanged numbers at one point in the investigation.

"Sally Dawson."

"Attorney Dawson? It's James Kruger." His voice sounded tight with anxiety. "Can we talk?"

"James. Good to hear from you. Yes, of course we can talk. What's on your mind?"

"In person," he added. "I'm downstairs."

She looked at her watch. He'd rolled out of bed to meet with her this early? This had to be pretty important. "Yes. Sure. Come right up and I'll meet you."

They clicked off. She knocked on Ben's door. "We have a special guest. James Kruger."

His eyebrows shot up, and he rose from his chair. Sally tried not to watch too intently as he slipped his arms into the sleeves of his black suit jacket. Another designer suit—Gucci, if she had to guess. The man was impeccably dressed. Distractingly gorgeous, and well dressed. These thoughts would do her no good.

"Just give me a minute," he mumbled, leaning back toward his computer. A series of chimes rang out as he tapped on the keyboard.

"Whatever." The nonchalance of her response belied her sudden and inexplicable interest in his strong profile and angular jaw. He hadn't worn his glasses today, and for some reason that made his gaze appear even more intense than usual. She thought of how it might feel to be the subject of his scrutiny, to feel her stomach flutter as he undressed her with his eyes. *Dangerous thinking, indeed.*

She stepped back into the hallway and pretended to examine a flyer on a corkboard. *Look, someone's selling a barely used washing machine—interesting.* There was something decidedly unsexy about large household appliances. She'd seen plenty of washing machines in her lifetime, and not a single one had made her swoon. Then Ben entered her thoughts unbidden, shirtless and glazed with sweat, laboring over a washing machine. Turning screws and lifting sides and just being manly about it, with his broad shoulders tensing with effort, his biceps tightening. Her head felt a little light.

No. She'd vowed that she would be professional today. Yesterday she'd allowed her emotions to get the best of her, and that was understandable, given the day's developments. But today was about professionalism and reining in her overactive imagination. No more sneering at Ben. No more being rude. He'd done her a favor by convincing Jack to involve her in this investigation, and maybe he wasn't a complete snake. Maybe he was trying.

Her attempt at professionalism was quickly challenged when he brushed past her in the hall. He smelled mouthwatering, and how was it possible that in all these years, she'd almost forgotten how hot he was? Except more so now that he had the upright posture of a military man and the strong, confident stride to go with it. As they walked down the hall, he led the way, stopping only to allow her to pass through doorways first.

No sneering and no leering. But she did check out his backside. Just a quick look, more accidental than deliberate. *Shoot,* she lamented. His rear end was perfect, which meant she might accidentally end up stealing another look, and that was completely unprofessional.

This had to stop. This was *Ben.* She still couldn't believe he'd had the nerve to ask her to dinner after all these years. Who did that? Confident seemed like an understatement. Arrogant, perhaps?

She smoothed her hair as they came to the reception area. *Professionalism.* Besides, she was in no position to become involved with Ben, or any man, for that matter. Her hand flew to her abdomen. Might as well put such dangerous thoughts out of her head. Even if it had been a depressingly long time since she'd been intimate with a man. Even if Ben had once treated her to the best sex of her life.

Good God. Professionalism was in short supply this morning, wasn't it?

James Kruger was in her line of vision as they entered the area. His gaze was darting nervously around as if he'd just wandered in and didn't quite know where to go. What did he have to be so worried about? His mother was home safely, after all.

She'd never known James to dress up, and he hadn't changed. He wore a black hooded sweatshirt that was fraying at the seams. She wouldn't try to guess what substances had caused the several obvious stains on the front. His jeans weren't torn, at least, but worn thin at the knees and stringy at the bottom edges. His light brown hair was long enough to fall into his eyes, and Sally fought the urge to groom him, reaching up instead to brush aside her own nonexistent bangs. The silver ring in his bottom lip was new. They'd had a discussion the last time they'd met about what might be appropriate to wear to court. Nothing on his person made that list. He was dressed for comfort, and must be feeling agitated.

"James." Sally took his awkwardly offered hand. "Good to see you. This is my colleague and partner, Ben McNamara."

"Pleasure." Ben shook the young man's hand warmly, and Sally couldn't help but observe a change in James's eyes. He was interested in Ben.

Poor kid just learned his father hadn't killed his mother, and he was probably desperate for a stable male role model. It made sense that he'd be interested in a clean-cut man who exuded confidence and stability.

Sally gave James a smile and touched him gently on the shoulder. "Let's go talk."

They walked to a small meeting room lined with bookcases that held old law reporters. Some of the volumes curled at the spine, and the room itself smelled vaguely like dusty paper. Sally pulled out a chair for James and then seated herself beside him. Ben sat across the table from both of them, but his eyes were fixed on the teenager, a touch of concern creasing his forehead.

"Have you seen your mom yet?" Sally kept her voice gentle, knowing this was tricky territory. James had been set to testify against his father in his mother's murder trial; the family dynamic had to be complicated.

James's face was dark, but he nodded. "I'm back home now."

Sally started at the news. "Oh. That's wonderful, James." She wasn't certain she meant it. "So you and your mom. Is your dad home, too?"

His jaw tightened. "Yeah."

A silence extended for a moment before Ben spoke. "What brings you here, James?" He had both hands on the table and he leaned forward, looking every bit the sophisticated older brother. "You seem like you've got something heavy on your mind."

The teenager met Ben's gaze and then looked toward the door, almost as if he was considering running. But he stayed in place. "I had to talk to you, Attorney Dawson. You've been...nice to me."

"That's easy." He looked so broken that Sally wanted to lean forward and take his hand. "I like you, James."

"She's like that," Ben added. "She's the kind of person you can trust. A good person."

Sally spun toward him. Was he mocking her? But no, she saw by the look on his face that he was completely serious, possibly even sincere. Her heart rose higher in her chest and she murmured a barely audible "Thank you." She wasn't quite sure how to take the compliment.

"Yeah," James agreed. "I mean, and you have to keep secrets, right? Like, if I tell you something, you can't say anything?"

Oh, no—what was he hiding? She winced. "Not exactly. It's a little different because I'm a prosecutor. I'm an attorney, but I'm not *your* attorney."

His face scrunched as if he was in pain, and then he brought his elbows to the table and rested his head in his hands, his long fingers threading through his hair. Something like an agonized groan came from his throat.

Ben and Sally exchanged a quick glance.

"Hey, buddy." Ben's voice was low. "You need to talk. You can trust us."

Sally started to correct him, but stopped when Ben held up his hand as if to say *Trust me*. She sat back. If he thought he could get the kid to talk…

James eyed Ben suspiciously from below his tangled hair. "What if it's about a crime? Do you have to, like, report it?"

Sally stiffened. "Are you going to confess to something? Maybe you should get a lawyer—"

"No." James sat a little straighter in his chair and released his hold on his hair. Some of the hair remained standing. "No. I don't want a lawyer, and I need to tell you this." He took a deep breath as if bracing himself. "I know you questioned my mom about her disappearance."

"How do you know that?" Sally asked.

"Because she told me. She wanted to know if you'd questioned me, too. I told her no, and she said that I shouldn't talk to you. That talking to you would piss off my dad." He brought his hands to his lap and slid them inside the sleeves of his sweatshirt.

"So why are you here, James?" Ben had fixed his gaze on the teen, and now Sally saw a hint of suspicion in his eyes where warmth had been only moments before. "Do your parents know—"

"My dad killed someone." James looked Ben straight in the eye. "He killed someone, and he's going to get away with it."

The statement thrust Sally back against her chair. She'd suspected as much, but she didn't have anything to go on, and the evidence they had was lousy. Ronnie Kruger's DNA was on a carpet, but Ronnie was very much alive. Without a body, they couldn't even begin to think about opening another murder case against Mitch Kruger. "Why—what makes you so sure your dad killed someone?"

"Because I saw the body." His voice was calm, a contrast to his anxious mood when he'd first sat at the table.

"Wait." Now Ben was out of his chair, and pushing back his jacket to rest his hands on his waist. He looked seriously intimidating, pacing like a panther in a cage. "You saw a body? This wasn't part of the report."

"I know," James admitted. "I've never told anyone this before."

Sally wanted to grab him by the shoulders and shake him. He'd seen the body? Why in the world hadn't he mentioned this minor detail? "James." She covered her face with her hands and tried to gather her thoughts. "What, exactly, did you see?"

"I saw my mother."

"But it *wasn't* your mother." Ben had stopped his pacing and was standing near James, his legs wide, his hands on his waist again. He looked as if he was deciding whether he should pick James up and hurl him out of the office, chair and all. "Your mother is alive. You're living with her."

"I know. I know my mother's alive, but I could've sworn I saw her on that carpet." He rubbed his forehead with one sleeve-covered hand. "I can't explain it. I saw a woman's body. She was definitely dead." He shook his head, the pain of the confession erupting across his face. "It was horrible. I don't know who she was."

Sally placed a hand gently on his arm. "If you think your father killed someone…you need to speak with the police about this. Maybe you can help us figure out what really happened that night."

He shook his head, glowering at the table. "I don't know anything. I told you, I thought it was my mom. That's not why I'm here, anyway."

"Then why are you here?" Ben sat on the edge of the table, crowding the teen's space. An old intimidation tactic.

But James ignored Ben now and looked straight at Sally. "I'm here because I'm telling you I know for a fact that my dad killed someone." He paused. "And if you keep pushing this case, he's going to kill you, too."

Chapter 5

Sally stood so quickly her chair fell over. She didn't seem to notice as she scrambled backward, away from the youth. "No. No. That's not true."

James blinked at her as if he didn't understand. "I just told you. My dad killed someone. A woman." He shook his head. "You don't know him the way I do. He'll do anything to stay out of prison."

She stood by a bookcase, as if she didn't know where she was anymore, and Ben felt something protective surging through him. He fought the desire to carry her out of this room and bring her somewhere safe, settling instead for placing himself in between her body and James. "I think you need to tell us the truth about what you saw that night, kid."

He rubbed his forehead again. "Yeah, I know. I will. I just… I didn't lie. You—the police—everyone knew my dad killed her. Thought he did."

"Maybe you didn't lie, but you hid the truth of what you saw from us." Sally's voice was tighter now, and her arms were folded across her chest defensively. "You told me that you had been at a party that night and that you'd snuck into the house and gone to bed. Then you said that the next morning, your mom was gone and your dad was acting suspicious. You said he'd removed the area rug in the living room the previous night without explanation, and that the house smelled like bleach."

"Yeah, all of that is true. It's just...I left out a part where I came home from the party. I came in and I saw her. She was lying facedown on the rug. Blood everywhere." He chewed on the edge of his sweatshirt sleeve, pulling on a thread with his teeth. "I thought it was Mom. Now I don't know who it was."

Ben mumbled a curse. Was this kid for real? He'd neglected to inform the prosecution that he'd seen a woman's dead body in his living room. He'd "just left out" that part? Ben bent over and placed his hands squarely on the table, bringing his face within inches of James's. Time to get up close and personal with this punk, and he wanted to be close enough to watch him sweat. "How the hell do you neglect to tell the cops that you actually saw what you believed was your mother's body in your living room? What the hell kinds of drugs would you have to be on for it to sound like a good idea to keep that little secret to yourself, huh?"

The kid flinched and looked away. Ben's stomach sagged. "Wait a sec. Were you on drugs?"

Sally slumped into a chair. "James. Oh, God." She balled her fist and kneaded at her forehead with her knuckles. "All right, let's hear it. What kinds of drugs were you doing that night?"

He shifted in his seat. "Just a little weed. And I had a couple shots of tequila." His eyes widened. "That's it, I swear. And it's not like I was hallucinating. I mean, I know what I saw."

There was a long pause, and Ben heard Sally inhale deeply. "So you didn't tell us that you saw the body because you were high and drunk at the time, and you thought…what? That we'd press criminal charges against you for marijuana use or underage drinking?"

"I didn't want to get my friends' parents in trouble. I was at their house."

Ben snorted. "How considerate. You realize that you've been helping your father get away with murder, right? I can't speak for Sally, but I'm pretty sure a stoned teenager would have been the least of her concerns." He raked his hand through his hair. Sure, he'd been a teenager once, too, but that didn't mean he'd ever understand the weird reasoning that went into some of their decisions.

"You must have been terrified." Sally said it quietly but intently, staring at James with eyes that had softened. "You thought your father had killed your mother, and you thought you saw her body, but if you told us the truth, you knew it would come out that you'd been engaging in illegal activities that night. You thought you'd end up in jail, too."

James swallowed and nodded slowly. "Yeah, I figured you would catch my dad anyway, and if he knew what I saw, I didn't know what he would do to me."

Ben groaned loudly. "Forgive me if I don't exactly care about all of that."

Her eyes grew huge. "Ben—"

"Sorry, Sally, but this sympathy of yours is crap. Complete crap. This kid has been concealing information in a murder case. Now we're investigating how it is that a woman we thought was dead could turn up alive right before trial. How much do you want to bet that Junior's testimony—*honest* testimony—could have saved this office from this embarrassment?" He spun to face the kid again. "I don't care how much weed you smoke. For future reference, if you see a dead body in your living room, you tell the cops about it. Got it?"

James blinked a few times and glanced away. "Got it."

Sally shot Ben a look that warned him off, before saying, "What happened after you saw the body? What did you do?"

He swiped under his nose with his sleeve. "I ran. I thought I'd go get my dad, and maybe he could call the cops." James spread his hands wide on the table. "I thought it was a burglary or something. Dad was at work. Supposed to be."

Ben remembered reading that detail. Mitch Kruger had been scheduled to work late at the hardware store, but had called in sick at the last minute. "You could've gone to a neighbor," he noted. The homes in the Krugers' neighborhood were far apart, but the hardware store was farther.

"I panicked." The youth hung his head slightly. "I wasn't thinking. I just thought that I needed to find my dad."

"So what did you do?" Sally asked.

"I took my bike to the hardware store, but Dad wasn't there. I didn't want to go home." There he went again, rubbing his forehead. "I called his cell phone and he wouldn't answer. Then he finally picked up. He was talking like there was nothing wrong, and he told me to get home right away." James's eyes were haunted as his gaze jumped from Ben to Sally. "He was home. He told me he'd called in sick. I mean, don't you see? He was home the entire time. That's when I knew. I knew he'd killed her."

Ben pulled out the chair across the table from James and sat down. "How long would you say it was from the time you first came home to the time you heard from your dad?"

He shrugged. "Maybe two hours. It took me a while to get to the hardware store, and then, like I said, I was walking around. I didn't know what to do. I thought it was the drugs. Paranoia, you know? I just kept thinking that I had to wait. I had to wait, and then my head would clear up and I'd know what to do." He balled his hands until the knuckles turned white. "But after that phone call, once I knew what had happened…" He made a hissing sound through his teeth as he fought to maintain control. "I still didn't know what to do."

Ben couldn't decide whether to believe him. He appeared distraught, but then again, it was incomprehensible that the kid would have hidden this information in the first place. Were they supposed to believe that he'd seen what he believed to be his mother's body, and then neglected to mention it? That didn't sit well with Ben. "And what's your point in coming here now, James? To scare Sally off this case?" He laughed drily. "In my mind, that makes you a suspect." After all, James could be trying to hide something by tossing threats around. If he was lying about seeing the body, what else could he be trying to conceal?

"I didn't do anything." James's voice was surprisingly calm. "I mean, yeah, I did some weed, but I've been straight since then. You can ask anyone. I didn't hurt anybody." He swept his sleeve under his nose again and looked at Sally. "My dad's bad news, that's all. I don't know who he hurt or why, but he killed someone, and he's gonna get away with it. If he sees you coming around, asking questions…" His voice trailed off. "I don't want you to go missing, too."

Sally's mouth pressed into a line, and she nodded tightly. "All right. Thank you. I appreciate you telling me all of this."

She stood to signal that the interview was over. Ben and James rose, and Ben walked the kid outside the office, gesturing to Sally that she should stay in the conference room. She didn't argue. She wrapped her arms around herself and watched them, her brows tightly knit.

James looked over his shoulder as Ben followed him out of the state's attorney's office. "You don't need to follow me."

"Oh, yes, I do," he replied evenly. "You just delivered a threat to my partner. I'm making sure you leave here without any trouble."

"I was trying to help her," he retorted. "I was doing a favor."

"You let me be the judge of that. Keep walking, kid."

Ben followed him to his car, a beat-up blue Honda coupe with a dented passenger's side door, and stood with his arms folded across his chest while James climbed inside. Ben grabbed the edge of the door with his left hand before James shut it. He leaned in closer, his right hand braced against the roof. "From now on, if you have anything else to say about this case, you say it to me. That means no more threats to Ms. Dawson and no more remembering about other dead bodies you saw in your living room. I don't care if you suddenly remember where you saw your dad stash the corpse. If you have anything else to say about it, you tell me, not her. Understand?"

The teen swallowed and stared at the steering wheel. "Yes, sir," he mumbled.

Ben stepped back and shut the car door firmly. Then he watched as the kid backed out of the parking space and sped away. When he was sure he was gone, Ben walked back to the office. He couldn't say for sure if James had been lying again, or for the first time. If he was lying, he was a hell of an actor. The body language was spot on—the way he met their eyes when he told the story, his anxiety about his previous half-truth.

The fact was, Ben couldn't be sure whether he could discredit that surprise meeting as an orchestration by a troubled teen. Until he could, he had to take the threat seriously. Taking it seriously meant he had to do whatever he could to protect Sally from the Kruger family.

Sally was standing beside her desk, tapping her pen rhythmically against a stack of papers and staring out the window. A landscaping truck had pulled up beside the park and unloaded several employees with leaf blowers. She could only faintly make out the steady mechanical sounds, but she found the loud drone almost soothing to her nerves. By the time she heard

Ben's voice in the doorway, she had completely lost track of how long she'd been standing there.

"I'm talking to Jack," Ben declared with authority. "I want you off this case."

She let out a strangled laugh. "You don't get to decide whether or not I'm on a case. Being partners means if you're on this file, then so am I."

He shook his head. "Nope. Not anymore. If James Kruger is right, his father killed someone, and you could be in danger if you continue to pursue your investigation."

Sally rolled her eyes and let out a melodramatic groan. "Don't tell me you actually believed him!"

Despite her protest, a part of her had turned to ice at James's words. She knew him well from the investigation. They'd had several long talks about the case and his mother's disappearance, and he'd confided in her about other family dynamics. By all appearances the Kruger household was normal, but below the surface ran an undercurrent of chaos.

James's parents had fought constantly, he confessed. They'd eloped as teenagers when Ronnie became pregnant, and while she'd ultimately returned to school to become a nurse, Mitch Kruger blamed his son for holding him back and tying him to a woman he didn't love. James had told Sally that he was a mistake, the kid who never should have been born. He'd cried while sitting in the very conference room they'd just left. He was a hurting, confused young man, but he was not malicious. If James told her that she was in danger, he was telling her the truth—at least as far as he understood it.

But Ben didn't need to know all that. He didn't need to develop some hero complex about her, so better to play it cool. Besides, there was no way she was going to be edged off this case now. If James had seen a woman's body in his living room...well, that changed everything.

"I'm not going anywhere, and there's not a damn thing that you and Jack are going to do about it." She grabbed a notebook and some pens and a few scattered files. "We're supposed to go to the crime lab, and you don't even have a car. Ergo, you need me."

His brows drew together. "We need to rethink this partnership," he said softly. "You can't take any chances. It's not worth the risk."

Warmth crept across her cheeks at the display of concern. For years, Sally had been fighting the impression that she was soft, flighty and undeserving of her position. Ben may have been battle-tested in a war zone, but she had plenty of scars of her own. She'd risen through the ranks based on merit, and she'd earned every single promotion and show of faith from her superiors. The last thing she needed was for Ben to plant a suggestion in someone's mind that her life was in danger, and to have her removed from this file for good. Sally cared about all her cases, but this one was special. She needed to see it through to completion. She had something to prove.

She paused to tilt her head at him. "It's not like that, Ben. James Kruger is sensitive. He fears his father, that's all. Anyway, I prosecute violent criminals. That's what I *do*. So now I'm supposed to be afraid to prosecute them because they might get angry about it?" She scoffed. "It's my job to not care what they think."

"But this is different." He set his jaw. "There's something wrong here."

"And what do you care, Ben?" The words came out in a flash, riding the tide of anger that swept through her. "Since when do you care so much about who's threatening me or what cases I work on? You spent nearly three years in law school making it clear how little you think of me, so why the sudden change of heart?"

His mouth tensed, but he didn't say a word. He just stood frozen in place. Sally's frame trembled beneath her clothing. She wished she could be honest with him and tell him how terrified she was, without fearing that he'd use her own words against her to push her off this case. But she couldn't trust Ben with her feelings.

She pulled on her coat and marched up to him. "We're going to be late. Are you ready to go?"

He looked conflicted as his gaze darted to her face. "This isn't done yet, Sally."

"You keep telling yourself that," she replied as she turned off her light and stepped out into the hall. "In the meantime, I'm going to do my job."

She'd taken only two steps when he fell into pace with her. "Wait. It's not about you or me, remember? We're a team now."

She brought her shoulders back and lifted her chin, but didn't verbalize a response. They walked in sync down the hall, their footsteps falling at the same time and in the same rhythm. She could feel Ben's tall presence beside her, and for the first time, she felt grateful that she'd been given a partner despite her protests.

Chapter 6

The lights on the BMW convertible flashed as they approached. Sally cleared her throat. "I should warn you, I'm a terrible driver."

Ben sucked in a breath. "Nice car." The vehicle was gorgeous. Sleek black exterior with gray leather seats. A convertible wasn't a sensible choice for the climate, but he wasn't about to complain.

"It's a rental," she explained as she opened the door. "Some guy rear-ended me at an intersection. It wasn't my fault," she added.

"Is this part of you being a terrible driver?"

"More like unlucky. The string of vehicular homicides makes me a terrible driver." He must have made a face because she started laughing. "I'm kidding! Geez." She slid into the seat as he opened the passenger door. "But seriously, buckle your seat belt."

She wouldn't need to tell him twice.

Ben started to climb into the car, but stopped. Had she been transporting small children? The seat was positioned only inches from the dashboard. He leaned in and pulled a lever to move it back, but was only partly successful. He sighed and climbed in, folding himself nearly in half. Then he fastened his seat belt.

She backed out of the space and pulled onto the street. They drove in silence for a few minutes. Thanks to the warning Sally had given him, Ben was hyperalert to her speed and the position of the vehicle on the road. She drove with something close to passion, throwing her entire body into each curve and every shift of gear. She used her turn signal to switch lanes, and she checked her mirrors. Sally wasn't a bad driver, just a fast one. A very fast one. His right foot reflexively jammed the nonexistent passenger side brake pedal more than once before they reached the highway.

"Now that James claims to have seen a body in his living room, we'll test that claim with the science," he said. "The way I see it, that was the foundation of your case."

"No body. Science is all we had to go on," Sally agreed. She regarded him out of the corner of her eye. "You can move your seat back, you know."

"I'm fine," he said.

He kept his gaze forward. The black ribbon of highway was damp from the morning rain and spattered with red and gold leaves. As they drove, the compartment filled with Sally: her sweet smell and the humming under her breath, as if she'd forgotten she wasn't alone. He couldn't place the tune. He listened for a minute or so, but then she stopped.

"What did Jack say yesterday?" Her voice sounded uncertain. "I mean, when you suggested that I help you?"

Ben kept his face turned toward the road. "I told him that if he wanted an answer quickly, I needed someone who was familiar with the case. He agreed."

She smoothed a hand over her hair. "So Jack must not think I messed up too badly if he's willing to let me help with the investigation. He must suspect that something more is going on here."

Ben shifted slightly in his seat, suddenly feeling as if he was sitting naked on pinecones. "I think he agreed that he needs an answer quickly," he said softly.

"Oh," was her soft response.

Ben felt her disappointment in his gut. "Look, it doesn't matter what Jack thinks or doesn't think. We've got a kid who says that he saw a body in his living room. Let's focus on proving or disproving that for now." He didn't want her to worry about losing her job when there were a hundred more important things to worry about. Her life, for example.

"We should talk to the detective about any Jane Does," she said. "We've been keeping an eye out, hoping that Ronnie Kruger's body would turn up." She laughed drily. "I guess she did, didn't she? But if anyone else has been found, we need to know about it."

"Yes, ma'am."

She slowed suddenly and narrowed her eyes to stare at an empty cardboard box on the side of the road. Then she sped on without comment. Ben studied her. "Uh, everything okay?"

Her cheeks grew pink. "Yes, fine." She tucked her hair behind her right ear.

She didn't offer an explanation, but Ben wasn't about to let that slide. He ran an index finger beneath the thick shoulder strap of his seat belt, loosening its hold. "Let me guess—you lost a cardboard box and you thought that was it? Or maybe you're moving and in need of boxes." He sat up straighter. "If you're moving, I can give you some of my boxes. I'm in the middle of unpacking, and I've got enough cardboard to move a thousand designer handbags."

She tightened her lips. "You're bad at guessing."

"Cardboard box rescue, then? I could tell you're a Good Samaritan." He grinned when she shot him a look. She was fun to tease.

Sally shook her hair and focused on the road, shoulders bunching up around her ears. "An elementary school friend of mine found a litter of abandoned kittens in a cardboard box once." Her face pulled into a frown. "I just think about it sometimes."

"So you were looking for kittens in that box?"

"No." She glared at him and pursed her mouth. "I wasn't looking for kittens."

He shifted to face her fully. "You were looking for abandoned kittens." He laughed from the bottom of his belly. "That's adorable. Do you always do that when you see a cardboard box on the side of the highway?"

She sighed and tightened her grip on the steering wheel. "I told you. I wasn't looking for kittens."

Their conversation lapsed into silence again. He didn't know what she was so uptight about—he liked that she looked for kittens in cardboard boxes. He suspected he could spend a lifetime with her and be continually charmed by the little surprises that comprised her personality. His pulse quickened as he thought back to the first semester of law school and the nights they'd shared together. He'd lusted after Sally from the second he first saw her in their contracts class, dressed in designer clothes but talking with their classmates as if she was one of them. He'd quickly learned that she wasn't. She was bright and dynamic, with a dramatic streak that any reality television show executive would fall over himself to capture. She could be sweet or haughty, and either mood had turned Ben on.

Then he'd gotten her alone. In his apartment. They'd had sex in the galley kitchen, her on the countertop, her long legs wrapped around his waist. He'd been sober for a change. They both had been, but he'd told himself that whatever they'd shared had only been casual. They'd continued dating. He'd treat her to dinner, lingering for hours over coffee and conversation, and then they'd go somewhere to have mind-altering sex. That was the pattern, and it worked just fine for him. Then Sally had gone and told him that she was in love with him.

Looking back, he figured maybe he'd shared similar feelings, but at the time, he'd panicked. He'd drunk himself into oblivion that night, then the next day seduced a classmate who'd been coming on to him—all to prove that he hadn't felt anything for Sally. Feeling anything for her would leave him raw, exposed and open to pain. He'd already had too much pain.

He swallowed the tightness in his throat. The years he'd been abroad, in the middle of a war zone, he'd thought about Sally Dawson, hot and sweet and pressed against his body, or whispering some shared secret in his ear. He'd crafted an apology note a hundred times, but each draft fell flat. How was he supposed to apologize for the hurt he'd caused her? He'd spent so much of his life trying to numb his senses—how was he supposed to explain that he'd wanted to shame her for making him feel something for a change? Now the sight of her humming quietly to herself dragged to the surface the ache he'd long ago tried to drown.

"Sally." He scratched his eyebrow, not knowing where to start. "I appreciate that you're okay with us being partners on this case." As difficult as it was for him to look at her and to be reminded of his past in-sensitivity, it must be a hundred times worse for her.

"I'm not okay with it," she replied brightly. She reached for a dial on the dashboard and turned up the heat. "I don't like having a partner, and I don't need one. Even if I did need or want one, I'd prefer to part-ner with someone I could trust. But it's not up to me." She gave him a withering smile. "We have a business arrangement, that's all."

Her nonchalant delivery knocked him back against his seat. At least she'd stopped humming. "I don't bite." Damn, he sounded injured, and that wasn't what he'd intended. "It's been a long time since…you know." *Since we had the hottest sex of our lives on my counter and then I stopped talking to you.* "Since law school."

"Has it? Seeing you again brings it all back like it was yesterday. Funny how that happens. Besides—" she swept one long, elegant index finger across the corner of her mouth "—you're lying about not biting. I've been bitten by you before, and I'll be damned if it happens again."

His forehead tensed, but he didn't respond. He'd enlisted in the marines knowing that he'd be sent to war, part of him hoping he'd be punished for what he'd done. He'd hated himself enough to want to die. If she wanted to hate him, too, she was entitled.

He settled back against his seat. She didn't want to talk about it, and any apology would go unheard. Maybe another time. "You know, you're not a half-bad driver," he said. "You just have a lead foot."

She clung to the steering wheel, robbing her knuckles of color. He was looking out the window as if they were on a pleasant Sunday drive and she hadn't just given him a piece of her mind. Was this his new angle, that he was going to take the insults? Disappointment tugged at her. Not fighting back took all the fun out of it.

She had a hundred angry things to say to Ben about their new and weird partnership. For starters, how dare he? How dare he come back into her life in this way after humiliating her all those years ago? She was embarrassed to admit how hard she'd fallen for him in law school. He was charming, smart and funny. He'd listened to her as if she had something important to say, and she'd bought it. As soon as she'd confessed her feelings, he'd jumped into bed with another woman. Even now, her face grew hot and her pulse beat an angry staccato in her chest at the memory. He was the type of person who used others and abused trust, and she'd never let him forget that she was onto him.

"I don't have a lead foot," she grumbled, needing to release her anger in some way. "I'm going the speed limit."

Then she looked at the speedometer. Scratch that; they were traveling at almost twenty miles per hour above it. Okay, well…she conceded nothing. She eased off the gas pedal.

"And what gives you the right to say anything about my driving?" He wasn't her boss, and he was sitting in her rental car, all smug and self-satisfied and talking about how she drove too fast.

How *dare* he?

He continued to not respond, to sit and stare out the window. As the seconds dragged into minutes, Sally's pulse stopped its angry sputtering and slowed to a normal pace. Maybe he was thinking about the few choice words she'd broken off for him a few minutes ago. Ruminating on her sharp rebukes and backing off with his tail between his legs. Somehow, she doubted it.

Ben shifted again to face her. "I agree with you."

She started. "You do? About what?"

"This case. I think there's much more than meets the eye." He was animated, gesturing with his hands as he continued. "This is a murder investigation, and you had lots of eyes on these facts. Everyone agreed that the case could proceed to trial, even without a body. You have blood on a rug that matches the alleged vic's blood, and a suspect who looks like he was covering his tracks by disposing of the rug and cleaning up blood on the floors and walls. As of this morning we even have a son who's ready to testify that he saw his mother's body." Ben frowned. "Once I started to dig into the notes you'd prepared, I understood why you brought this case. All of the signs point to Ronnie Kruger's murder."

"Exactly!"

"Except she's not dead." Ben reached up to rub at his temple. "She's not dead, and we have to start over.

Toss that assumption out the window. We need to find something new by coming at the case with a different perspective," he said thoughtfully. "Once we stop assuming that Ronnie Kruger was murdered, we'll finally see what really happened."

Sally stole a glance at him as she exited the highway. His face was relaxed, and his hands rested on his legs. Huge hands with strong, capable fingers. She thought about those hands on her bare skin, how it would feel if she pulled over to the side of the road, stopped the car and eased herself into his lap. How she might respond if he tucked those hands under her sweater, slid them deliciously up her back....

Now her pulse was skyrocketing again. She needed to get a grip. Ben McNamara was a heartbreak wrapped in sexy packaging. She was *so* finished with heartbreak.

Silence hung heavy between them until they pulled into the parking lot for the Connecticut Forensic Science Laboratory, and then walked through the lot to the front desk. "We have an appointment with Fritz Kilburn," Sally informed the woman sitting at reception.

"I'll let him know you're here," she replied with a stony smile, and picked up the phone. "You can have a seat." She pointed to a cluster of chairs and a small end table in the corner of the room.

Ben and Sally wandered over to the spot but didn't sit. She fidgeted with one of her earrings as they waited, listening to the echoes of the vast, empty space. Then the door opened, and police detective Dan Maybury stepped through.

"Detective." Sally rushed toward him, relieved to be in the company of a person with whom her relationship was blissfully uncomplicated. "Glad you could make it."

He was young for a police detective, maybe in his mid-thirties, with dark brown eyes and light brown hair. They hadn't spoken yesterday, but Sally could see from the circles under his eyes and the seriousness of his face that the sudden turn in the Kruger case had weighed heavily on him, too. She gestured to Ben. "This is Ben McNamara. He's helping me to investigate this case. Damage control. You know how it is."

The men shook hands, and then Dan returned his gaze to hers. "What the hell is going on with this, anyway? Is Ronnie Kruger a zombie?"

Dan didn't mince words. Sally sighed and placed her hands on her hips. "Do you want to sit down? Because this morning I got a visit from the son, James Kruger, who now claims to have seen a body in the living room."

Dan rubbed at his eyes. "Can he explain how that body bled Ronnie Kruger's blood?"

"I didn't get the impression he was a forensics expert," Ben said. "Although he seems to know a little bit about illegal chemicals."

"He was high," Sally explained with a sigh. "And a little drunk. He'd been smoking pot and doing shots of tequila."

"Perfect," Dan said with a roll of his eyes. "We love eyewitness testimony from stoners."

"Sorry I'm running a little late."

They heard the voice behind them and turned to see Fritz Kilburn come out to the reception area with a genial wave and a smile. He was a compact man with thick glasses and short, spiky hair that looked more white than blond in the glaring light of the lab. After completing introductions, he led them back to a conference room where he'd set up a series of boards containing evidence that would have been used at trial.

"We have a problem, Fritz," Sally began.

"Tell me something I don't know," he replied. "Looks like it's back to square one, with a lot of blood on an area rug and...well, that's it, really. We don't even need to worry about the missing persons report."

"Not for Ronnie Kruger," Ben noted. "But we need to consider other missing persons and Jane Does."

Dan folded his arms as he thought. "I've watched for Jane Does. I don't even know where to begin with missing persons. What are we looking for, exactly? Someone with Ronnie Kruger's blood?"

Sally chewed her lower lip and tried to ignore Ben, who was standing close to her side again, his broad figure hovering like a shadow. "Let's start with blood. James Kruger thought he saw his mother in the living room, and we know we found a fatal amount of blood spilled on that area rug."

"How do we know that?" Ben's voice was thrillingly close to her ear. A wave of prickles dashed across her skin.

"Here." Fritz gestured to a manila file, then shuffled through the contents as he spoke. "We begin with an area rug covered in a huge stain. Tests confirm that this stain is in fact dried blood."

He spread several eight-by-ten pictures across the table. Each photograph featured the notorious area rug, with the progression of photos moving from the folded rug being discovered in a brown Dumpster to the crime lab, where it was spread on a tarp. "With a smaller stain," Fritz continued, "you can experiment with recreating the area of the stain to determine how much blood was lost. With this amount, we use old-fashioned math. First we weighed a clean area of the rug and compared it to the weight of a stained area the same size. A little subtraction and we know the weight of the blood on that carpet sample. Once we have that, we can calculate how much blood was saturating that sample, and then multiply the result by the area of the entire stain."

Sally arched an eyebrow and glanced over her shoulder at Ben. "Got that?"

"I'll trust your calculations, Fritz," he replied. "How much blood do you calculate the victim lost?"

"About four liters. A fatal amount."

"Gunshot?" Ben leaned sideways, propping himself against the wall with one arm.

"That's what the spatter patterns on the wall show," said Fritz. "Mitch Kruger scrubbed it after the crime, but a little luminol exposed them."

"We know it was fatal, and we know it was Ronnie Kruger's blood because the lab ran DNA tests," said Dan.

"Except it couldn't have been Ronnie's, because she's alive," Sally said.

"Maybe she harvested her own blood somehow." Fritz stared into space, lost in thought. "She could have saved a series of smaller donations to fake her own death."

"She *is* a nurse," Sally mused. "But she works at a high school, so she wouldn't have access to blood collection materials."

"That also leaves us without a motive," Ben said.

"Why would she fake her own death and then wander back into town? As a suspect in her disappearance, her husband wouldn't have been able to collect on a life insurance policy."

"He may not have been able to collect without a body, either," Sally agreed. "Not for years. James Kruger thought his mother was lying on that rug, and we found Ronnie's blood. Is it possible that she would share her DNA with a relative? A sister, maybe?"

"Only an identical twin," Fritz replied. "But she doesn't have one." He twisted his mouth to one side as he thought. "Come to think of it, I don't remember ever hearing much about Ronnie's family. Does she have any living relatives?"

"In Pennsylvania." Sally thumbed through the photographs of the area rug. "A very strict family with religious roots. Ronnie was pregnant out of wedlock and her parents disapproved, so she and Mitch left the state. That was almost twenty years ago, and I don't think they've spoken since. Her mother and sister refused to return our calls, and her brothers were little help."

"A sister?" Ben's interest was piqued. "We need to find her."

Sally sighed and turned to face him. "Not a twin, Ben. It doesn't fit." She spoke slowly, as if he was missing something obvious.

He shook his head. "I know that. But James saw a woman who looked like her on the living room floor. Allegedly," he was quick to add. With this case, they couldn't take anything for granted. "A sister might have similar hair or features. Come to think of it, did you find any hair on the rug?"

"Sure." Fritz shrugged. "Ronnie's hair, Mitch's hair, James's hair, dog hair. Nothing that tells us anything."

Ben stepped closer. "What about foreign hair? Any strands that couldn't be identified as belonging to an immediate family member?"

"Yes." Sally nodded, and Ben detected a mounting excitement in her voice. "Yes. That's a good idea. Let's take a second look at that evidence. This time, we should check for hair that may have come from a relative of Ronnie's." She exchanged a glance with Ben. "If the family was estranged, it's unlikely a relative would be there under normal circumstances, right?"

Fritz furrowed his brows. "Okay. We'll take another look at the rug."

"And we'll take a closer look at the relatives," said Dan. "Try to locate the sister. We didn't have any reason to dig too deeply the first time around, but it makes sense."

"Great. Okay, this is good." Sally spoke to herself more than anyone else. Then she glanced at Ben, her brown eyes wide and soft. "That was a good idea."

God, she was lovely, and his heart quickened at the sudden change in her tone. His back straightened, but then he shrugged. Better to play nonchalant. He couldn't exactly claim any victory here. Not yet. "It's just a possibility."

"A good one," she stressed. "This could be what we overlooked the first time around."

"We're still missing a body, Sal," he said. "If you're thinking that we could bring a different case based on forensic evidence, I fear you're going to be disappointed. Pardon the term, but I expect Jack will be a little gun-shy about these cases from here on out."

"I know." She approached him and leaned back against the long table on which Fritz had displayed the photos. Ben mirrored her position. "I don't know if this will come to anything, and DNA evidence will take weeks to process. But it's a good start. There are all these things we didn't consider because we thought we were looking for Ronnie Kruger."

He tried not to focus on the warmth radiating off her body as she sat so close to him. He looked at the floor, the dull gray tile spotted with shards of white and black. But his eyes wandered to her brown, sensible-heeled shoes, and the fact that if he allowed himself to look, he could make out the outline of her shapely legs below her pants. He brought his eyes back up to stare at the gory crime scene evidence Fritz had so helpfully displayed around the room. Nothing sexy about that.

"You thought you were looking for Ronnie Kruger," he repeated, "and that's why you didn't consider following up on these other leads. Ronnie's absence was a distraction." He stood up again so that he could look at all three of the professionals at once. "A red herring to draw your attention away from a real crime. And maybe that's why Ronnie Kruger disappeared in the first place."

Chapter 7

They remained at the lab for several more hours, giving Ben a tour of the forensic evidence. By the time they returned to Sally's car, it was after five o'clock.

"My vehicle should be back at the lot," he said as he opened the passenger door. "I got a message from the mechanic that whoever changed my tires hadn't replaced the old valves, so that's how I wound up with three flats."

"What?" Sally wrinkled her nose. "Was that to save a buck?"

"Apparently." Ben had been tamping down his disgust all day, but he'd give the mechanic a piece of his mind. "Thanks for the ride. It won't happen again."

"See that it doesn't." Her tone was almost light.

Ever since he'd suggested they look for a relative of Ronnie Kruger's, Sally's manner toward him had taken something of a shift. Gone were the sneers, pointed glares and general haughtiness. Instead she'd started looking to him when offering her opinion, as if to gauge his response. It was almost as if she'd started to see him as a true partner. He was nearly afraid to move for fear of disrupting a delicate balance.

Sally turned the key in the ignition and then sat for a moment, blowing into her hands.

"Cold?" Ben reached forward and turned on the heat. Warm air blasted from the vents.

"Thanks," she said.

They locked gazes for a moment, but she broke contact, pushed the gearshift to Reverse and backed out of the space. "Interesting day," she said. "Do you think you have enough information now? You know...for your report?"

Ah, there it was. The report. That's why she was laying on the charm, because it suited her right now. He swore he felt his heart drop. "Not yet," he admitted. "There are too many unanswered questions as far as the forensic evidence goes." He shot her a glance and noticed the worry line creasing her brow. "I told you, I'm on your side with this. Ronnie Kruger's disappearance forced you to look at the case a certain way. You couldn't have anticipated this twist." He leaned toward the window.

"So that means you're going to report that I exercised appropriate judgment under the circumstances, right?" She was animated now, and there was more than a tinge of hopefulness in her voice. "You're going to tell Jack that I can't be blamed for Ronnie Kruger being alive?"

Ben forced a dry laugh. "Yeah. That will probably

be my report, though I may use different words." He massaged his temple with his index finger. "I'll also tell him that according to James Kruger, there was a murder, after all. Maybe Jack'll allow us to continue the investigation."

"Here's hoping," Sally said brightly.

Boy, had her mood changed. She was humming to herself and tapping her fingers in rhythm on the steering wheel. She seemed so happy all of a sudden. Something twisted in his gut. He couldn't blame her for feeling relieved at the conversation they'd had with Fritz and Dan. The forensic evidence was strong, but subject to human interpretation. It required context, and it appeared the investigators may have simply placed it in the wrong context to begin with. Now they could return to the evidence with fresh eyes and a fresh theory, and discover something new. "Bringing Mitch Kruger to justice for a murder that he actually committed would go far in restoring the office's reputation in the eyes of the public," Ben mused.

"Yes, it would. I just worry that our hands will be tied until we find a body. Jack won't be likely to support another case brought purely on forensic evidence. At least, not against Mitch Kruger." She slapped the steering wheel forcefully. "It makes me so angry! To think that Kruger could get away with murder because he managed to do a good job at hiding the body."

"We can't discount Ronnie yet," Ben noted. "If there was a body, what was her involvement in the cover-up? She disappeared for almost a year, and I'm not buying the amnesia story. I wasn't born yesterday."

"Yeah, I know. I'm not buying it, either."

He leaned his head back against the seat, pulling his

hands to his stomach. A knot in his gut still told him that Sally was in danger. "I can't forget what James Kruger said this morning. That if you keep poking around, Mitch may try to silence you. You need to talk to the police about that."

Even in the fading light of dusk, he saw her throat tense. "I have nothing to tell the police. You know that. There have been no threats, and they're not going to do anything based on one person's speculation." She ran her fingers through her hair, scattering honey-blond waves that plummeted softly around her shoulders. "There's no sense in either of us worrying about it. Not now."

But her admonition went unheard. The threat stirred something fierce in him. They were partners, and that status made him feel extra protective of her, responsible for her safety. Besides, he owed Sally for any hurt he'd caused in the past. Protecting her was a way to make his stupidity up to her, to turn a new leaf. Keeping her alive and safe would be a do-over. He owed her that much. No matter what she said or how she warned him off, he would be keeping an eye on her. His military training would come in handy for that.

Her cell phone rang, and she glanced down at the number. "Oh, shoot. It's my parents. I completely forgot I was supposed to meet them for dinner." She picked up the phone from where it sat balanced on the center console, and placed it on her lap.

"Goat cheese crusted stuff," Ben mumbled. "I remember."

"Well, considering how late I am, this is probably my mom calling to find out whether I'm lying dead in a ditch somewhere." Sally looked over at him. "Can you block your ears for a sec? I have it programmed with the Bluetooth system in the car."

"You want me to…what? Put my fingers in my ears?" He tilted his head. If they were stuck in this vehicle together for a hundred years, he was confident he'd still never manage to predict the things that came out of her mouth.

"Just, you know, cover them," she replied casually. "Like headphones, but with your hands."

He did as asked and felt completely ridiculous. Covering his ears succeeded in blocking the sound of absolutely nothing as Sally spoke with her mother.

"Hey, Mom. I'm not dead, I just forgot about dinner. Work has been a little crazy." *And Wednesday night dinners with my parents are easily forgotten.*

"Hi, sweetie. Oh, yes, we saw the news. Was that your case where the dead woman was really alive? It's like something out of a crime show."

Her mother would know. She had the elegance of Jackie Onassis crossed with a passion for violent crime shows. Sally shot Ben a glance to see if he was listening, but he looked disinterested. "Yup, that's my victim. Turns out she's been in Vegas. With amnesia."

"Oh, honey, that sounds like bull—"

"Mom!" Sally shook her head as Ben started laughing. "Don't talk like a trucker. I have a coworker in the car with me, and you're on speakerphone. I have to drop him off at the office, and then I'll be over for dinner. Give me about an hour."

"An hour? Oh, honey." There was a pause. "Why don't you just bring him over?"

She and Ben exchanged a glance. Why not? *Because*

I'd rather eat shards of glass seemed like a rude thing to say, and the truth—that she'd planned to tell her parents she was pregnant—seemed much too messy. "Oh, I don't know...."

"Sally, we have more food than we know what to do with. It's dinnertime—just bring him over."

She felt itchy all of a sudden, and like she was trying to maneuver through a minefield. That would teach her to use Bluetooth when her mother called. "Mom, I just don't..." She eyed Ben and lowered her voice. "I'm sure he has plans." She pleaded with him silently to decline the invitation. Ben McNamara at her parents' house? The thought was too awkward for words.

But Ben flashed her a brilliant smile. "I'd love to stop over for dinner, Mrs. Dawson." He gave Sally a little wink. She felt every muscle in her body tense, and focused on biting her tongue.

"I thought you might!" her mother continued. "You must be hungry after working all day. Are you a lawyer, too?"

Oh, God, this was going to be *so* painful. "Yes, Mom, he's a lawyer, too." She didn't need to know that he was a former law school classmate, a certified hottie and a shameful part of her past all wrapped up into one devastating package. "His name is Ben."

He was grinning at her as if he'd just scored some major victory. Damn it.

"I'm new to town. Well, back after a long hiatus," he continued, laying it on thick now. No doubt enjoying himself immensely. "I just came back from tours in Iraq and Afghanistan as part of the Marine Corps. I was a lawyer for them, but we're all combat ready. I know my way around a gun." He beamed at Sally, so clearly pleased with the way she was fidgeting in her seat, as if she were sitting on rows of nails.

The tone of her mother's voice became subdued. "You're a real hero, Ben. Well, I'm honored you'll be joining us for dinner."

You have got to be kidding me. Ben was *not* a hero. Ben was a womanizer who'd broken Sally's heart. He was reason number one she had sworn off men, with her former fiancé following only as reason number two. She'd fallen in love with Ben, and he'd done nothing but abuse her feelings. But she bit back the acerbic words. He would be joining her for a family dinner now, and there was still the outstanding report he had to write. She may as well save all the awful things she had to say until that report was written and her job was officially safe.

He leaned forward in his seat, fighting back a laugh. Was he laughing at her mother? Sally felt a fierce protectiveness begin to swirl in her chest. Her mom might be a little on the nutty side, but no one criticized her unless they were family, and Ben was not family.

"Hey, Mom, this all sounds great," she lied. "We'll see you in twenty minutes or so, okay?"

"Okay, honey. Ben, we'll have a hot meal ready."

"Sounds delicious. Thanks, Mrs. Dawson."

Sally disconnected the call and spun toward him as he broke into a loud fit of laughter. "What the—? Are you laughing at my mom?"

He shook his head and rubbed his eyes. "Oh. No." He settled back into his seat, still chuckling. "No, I'm laughing at you. That look on your face. Priceless."

She glared at the road, her knuckles white on the steering wheel. "This counts as the dinner. I'm now forced to drag you to dinner with my parents and fake being a gracious hostess. I hope you're happy."

"Is this you being gracious? I couldn't tell."

"Yes, I'm being quite gracious," she snapped. "And I ask that you please not embarrass me in front of my parents. They're good people who mean well, and they don't have an eye for charlatans."

"Charlatans, huh?" A note of hurt registered in his voice. "Well. You've seen right through me. But fine, I promise to be as unembarrassing as possible, and maybe I'll even border on presentable." He turned his head. "And this will count as our second-chance dinner date. It saves me a few bucks, anyway."

She didn't bother responding. His little joke didn't merit a reply, and she was too angry to say anything nice.

Her parents' house was built in the Georgian style, with a gray stone exterior and a long driveway that passed through a sprawling lawn. Ben whistled under his breath as they approached and he saw the front of the home lit by spotlights. Sally brushed her hair back, feeling suddenly very self-aware. She hadn't grown up in this ostentatious house, but hadn't been raised in a home that would pass as modest, either.

Her parents were wealthy, and while she'd never complained about it, she knew that it affected the way others saw her. She'd dated far too many men who showed an interest in her because they'd made certain assumptions about the size of her trust fund. She'd hoped to find someone who didn't care about all that. Not someone independently wealthy, necessarily. Someone with character who would care about her for who she was, not what she came with.

Too bad, so sad, she thought wryly. She shouldn't feel sorry for herself when others had so much less—didn't she see that reality each day at work? Broken families, poverty, abusive relationships. If the worst thing that happened in her life was that she never found her soul mate, she'd be lucky. She had Mr. X, her mystery donor who was giving her a family. She'd be fine.

She pulled her coat tighter around her frame as they walked up to the door. "I half expect an English butler to greet us," Ben quipped, though Sally thought she detected a hint of anxiety. "What do your parents do?"

"My dad is one of the founding members of Hamilton Dawson. He was in research and development for years."

"Yeah? For what? Was he building a better virus?"

"Again with the assumptions."

Sally inhaled the cool fall air. Ben's eyes grew huge at the sight of the house. Everyone's eyes were wide when she brought them to meet her parents. He might act immune to a lot of things, but not to the smell of money. "Dad started off developing artificial flavors. He was responsible for creating a pretty convincing strawberry-vanilla combination, although my favorite of his is chocolate mint mocha." She rang the doorbell and listened to the chime echo through the great house. The door would be locked, and she'd forgotten her key.

"Artificial flavors. You mean for candies?"

"Candies, sodas, fruit drinks, medications, you name it. I call this the house that junk food built. He also developed natural flavors, but I'll let you in on a secret." She leaned closer conspiratorially. "The natural part of those flavors is that they are made from secretions in a beaver's anal gland."

He recoiled. "Wait…what?"

The door swung open. Her father was standing alone, his tall frame backlit by the crystal chandelier hanging in the foyer. A blessedly warm gust escaped and hit her, and for the first time Sally realized how cold it was outside.

"Hiya, sweetheart!" He stretched out his long arms and gave her a warm embrace. Sally exhaled. She might be an adult, but there was something about a bear hug from her father that left her weightless, like a child without cares. "Ar-r-r, it's cold outside! Come in, both of you."

Sally and Ben obliged. She wondered if she should have mentioned to Ben that her father spoke in his own language. "Hiya's" and piratelike "ar-r-r's" were only the beginning. He was quite expressive with his voice, and she often regretted that he hadn't made use of his creativity to write novels instead of developing flavors.

"Daddy, this is Ben. We work together." That about summed up the parent-friendly parts of their relationship.

The two men exchanged a manly handshake. She'd expect a full rundown from her father later, when he'd tell her whether or not Ben's handshake had been at all limp, clammy or awkward. She was guessing he passed. The two men were built similarly, with broad shoulders, strong arms and a confident lift to their chins. Ben, like her father, was a true man's man. "I understand you served in the marines," her father said.

"Yes, sir. I served as part of the Judge Advocate General's Corps."

"You served in JAG?" He nodded. "I served in the marines myself."

"Oh?" Ben looked at Sally. "You never mentioned that."

"It doesn't usually come up in conversation," she replied. "Look, if you two are going to talk about marine stuff, I'll go help Mom in the kitchen."

"Dinner's on the table," her father replied. "Let's go eat before it gets any colder."

Ben felt as if he'd walked into the mouth of a beast. He'd been swallowed and digested by the massive gray architecture of the impressive home, along with original oil paintings and tapestries, and random pieces of silver cutlery that probably served a function, but that function escaped him. So this was where Sally came from? He'd always known she was rich and spoiled, but he'd never actually imagined what that would look like. She probably didn't have to work ever again, if that's what she chose. Yet she'd gone to law school and taken a high-stress, low-pay job in the state's attorney's office. The thoughts flitted across his mind, and he simply registered them without analyzing their significance.

Sally's father was over six feet tall and still muscular into middle age. He led them into a dining room that the family probably considered intimate, but in reality was almost as large as Ben's apartment. A great stone fireplace at the far end of the room held a roaring blaze. The table was long and wooden, draped with white linens and set with china, silver and crystal. He suddenly regretted seizing the opportunity to make Sally squirm. He was out of his league.

A woman who had to be Sally's mother entered the room, a warm smile on her face. Her blond hair was the same soft shade as Sally's, but cut to her chin. She wore a button-down blue shirt and a gray skirt. And pearls. She was wearing pearls to dinner in her own dining room. He was *way* out of his league.

As if she sensed his discomfort, Sally turned to him with a smug smile and arched her eyebrow as if to say, *Look at what you just got yourself into.* She didn't need to say anything out loud. He got the message, all right.

His own family was squarely middle class. After his father died, his mother had remained unmarried until recently. His new stepfather was a nice guy, but no millionaire. His mother had raised him and his brother on her own, on the modest salary she'd received as a middle school math teacher. He'd earned scholarships to go to college, and had taken out loans to go to law school. Life had changed a few years ago, when his uncle had died and left him and his brother with sizable trust funds. Ben would inherit that money next month, when he turned thirty-five. Beyond buying a better car and renting a nicer apartment, he had no idea what to do with the cash.

He itched under his shirt collar. He'd had some exposure to this kind of wealth when he was working on Wall Street, but he'd never become comfortable around it. He owned designer suits, but they were almost as old as his law degree. Being here, surrounded by fancy clothes and silverware, being in the company of people who'd had every advantage in the world... He straightened his tie, wondering if they could sense how much it had cost him, and how many seasons ago he'd purchased it.

"This must be Ben." Sally's mother raced over to

give him a hug, startling him. "I'm Lana, and you've already met Hank."

"Yes," he said, grateful she had withdrawn from the embrace. Those things always sent his nervous system into overdrive. "Thanks for having me over. Dinner smells delicious." He couldn't identify the aromas in the room, but his mouth was watering. He hadn't realized how hungry he was.

Lana waved one hand and squeezed his upper arm with the other. These Dawsons were touchy-feely, weren't they? "Really, it's our pleasure to have you here. We enjoy meeting our daughter's friends."

He was relieved to see that Sally didn't start foaming at the mouth when her mother referred to him as a friend. That had to be a good sign. She simply smiled that tight smile that didn't quite reach her eyes, and said, "Mom. Let's eat."

"I should get you a drink," said Hank. "Wine? Beer? We have a full bar."

Ben had managed to not touch a drop of alcohol in years, and no matter how uncomfortable he was, he wasn't about to give in now. "Just water is fine."

Dinner, as Lana and Hank explained it, was handmade ravioli stuffed with butternut squash and dressed with a mixture of pine nuts, sage and melted butter. "We get the butter down the road at a little farm," Lana said as she piled ravioli onto Ben's plate. "We know the farmer, and all of his cows are grass-fed." She sent Ben a knowing look. "It makes such a difference."

He wasn't sure what to make of that; every form of butter seemed as good as the next to him. But obviously Lana took some pride in the grass-fed cows. "Sounds perfect." Yes, that was the right response—

he could tell by her smile. "It must be nice to live so close to a farm like that. Local produce is…popular."

Popular? He'd just hit rock bottom.

"The farm," Sally chimed in, "is half an hour away, not down the road. The only thing down the road from here, businesswise, is a designer shopping center and a Starbucks." She picked up a fork and jabbed at her salad. "Mom and Dad travel for their ingredients." Her words were pointed, but the look she gave them was affectionate.

Hank put his hands up as if in surrender and laughed good-naturedly. "We're taking cooking classes," he said. "Sally's right, we've been traveling to find the right foods to create our meals. It's all for fun, to spend time together. The classes were my idea. Lana accused me of not knowing how to boil water, so I had to invest in a little help."

"It's been so much fun," Lana gushed. "We have the classes every Tuesday night, then on Wednesday we make the meal by ourselves." She shrugged, seeming embarrassed. "It's a luxury, I know. But we're semi-retired now, and we figure we need to spend the time together while we still have our health." She reached out and squeezed Hank's hand.

"Mom is semiretired from charity," Sally explained as she reached for a glass of water. "She's a director on the board at the children's hospital and volunteers her time with an animal rescue nonprofit."

Sally looked uncomfortable, but Ben couldn't tell whether it was from her parents' open displays of affection or something else. His presence, maybe. But he realized now how wrong he'd been about her. She'd come from a perfectly normal, loving family. They had money and yet managed to be down-to-earth. She'd lived a charmed life, indeed. Still, she was crumpling her napkin in her lap and seemed disinterested in her food.

Well, if she wasn't going to eat, he would. The ravioli practically melted on his tongue, and the broccoli with lemon that they served as a side dish was cooked to perfect firmness. They served a butternut squash risotto and handmade bread rolls with an entire bulb of baked garlic soaked in olive oil for dipping. Dessert was a good, strong coffee and individual raspberry tarts. Funny, but when he'd accepted the invitation to dinner, part of him had expected meat loaf.

Throughout the meal, Sally was nearly silent. She'd chime in now and then to correct her parents or tell them that she didn't want to talk about work, but overall she looked miserable. So miserable, in fact, that he seriously regretted pushing for dinner the way he had. Lana and Hank were pleasant and gracious, and welcomed him openly, but Sally was unhappy, and she was the one he'd have to deal with in the morning. He shouldn't have teased her like this.

They said a quick goodbye at the end of dessert, with Sally giving the excuse that it was nearly ten o'clock and they both had to be at work in the morning. They walked to the car and drove down the driveway in silence, and Ben had the impression that he'd done something very, very wrong at some point that evening.

"I tried to be on my best behavior." He cleared his throat and looked out the window as the Georgian home slipped from view. "Your parents are very…" Affectionate? Gracious? Culinary? "…pleasant."

She made a noise like a hiss and turned on the heat. "They're all right."

All right? She'd grown up in the Cleaver household, but with millions of dollars. "You're really lucky to have a close family." Loving parents who made her meals and enjoyed spending time with each other.

"Hmm," was her response. "Sometimes I think they just have me over to rub it in my face. How happy they are." She sniffed, but she wasn't crying. Just sniffing. "They were quiet about it tonight, but normally I'd hear the lecture about how I'm not getting any younger, and do I really want to go through life on my own, without a partner? They're great, but they really want me to settle down. Ever since…" Her voice trailed off.

"Ever since what?"

She was quiet for so long that Ben wondered if she was ever going to answer his question. Then, just when he'd given up, she said, "Ever since my engagement blew up in their faces."

The weight of that answer settled between them. Sally had been engaged? He hadn't kept track of her, but the news was surprising. "I had no idea you'd been engaged."

"It was so brief. Whirlwind romance, then he proposed and we were supposed to be married three months later. It was barely enough time for me to plan everything."

"Why the rush?" He realized he may have just overstepped his boundaries, but he didn't care. He wanted to know what had happened. The intensity of his need to know was surprising to him.

She withheld her answer for a few moments, pressing her lips together. "I was pregnant," she said at last, her voice barely a whisper. "We got engaged, and I started to plan the wedding. Then I lost the baby." Her voice quavered with still-raw pain.

Ben didn't know what to say. "I'm sorry," he finally murmured.

"Thank you." She sniffed. "I mean that, by the way. You don't know how many people have told me it was for the best, or that it wasn't meant to be. Especially after I caught him in bed with another woman two weeks before the wedding." Sally swept a finger beneath one eye. "He was all wrong, and I guess I was with him because I thought I couldn't do any better, but that was my baby. I still wanted that baby."

Ben chewed on the realization that someone as beautiful as Sally could think she was somehow unworthy of a decent man. There was something tragic and infuriating in that, but just as he was about to pass judgment on the cheating bastard, he thought about the way he'd moved on from Sally himself. If she thought she couldn't do any better than a man who treated her like garbage, did he have something to do with it?

His forehead tensed. "I am sorry, Sally. You deserve better than that."

She eyed him. "So? What's your baggage? I showed you mine. Seems only fair."

He hadn't expected they'd be sharing so much of themselves tonight. He had a number of skeletons in his closet that could be marched out. He chose the first one that came to mind. "Since we're on the topic of broken engagements, one of my closest friends is marrying the woman I was supposed to marry. The wedding's next week."

If he'd thought he'd come to terms with that, he

thought wrong. Even now the emotion closed around his larynx.

"What?" She took her attention off the road for a bit longer than he was comfortable with, to glance at him with her huge, expressive eyes. "Your close friend? That's awful!"

"It's been over six years since we broke up. *I* was awful," he added. "I'm the one who screwed up."

"That sounds kind of harsh. What could you have possibly done?"

He thought back to that night, clear as if it was yesterday. Didn't he hear the crunch of metal each time he turned a key in the ignition? Didn't he still always brace himself for a repeat of that evening? "I almost killed her," he said quietly. "I hit a tree while I was driving her home. I'd been drinking." And then, as an afterthought, he added, "Her name's Karen."

He couldn't read Sally's expression in the inky darkness of the vehicle, but he knew what her silence meant. Judgment. This was the moment that would vindicate her low opinion of him. He was reckless. A drunk. Not to be trusted. She didn't need to say anything, and he didn't need to hear it. He'd looked in the mirror many times since that night and thought the same.

"She's lucky to be alive. We both are," he continued. "We were arguing again, and I was over the legal limit and lost control. She had a few broken bones. I walked away with some scratches." He tightened his fists until his palms hurt. "That's what kills me. I was the one who should have paid. I was the one who almost killed her. And I walked away."

Sally was still quiet, not saying anything, not audibly breathing. The headlights of the vehicle ripped through the darkness ahead, but did nothing to illuminate the space between them. He'd made a mistake all those years ago, and while the scratches and scrapes and broken bones had healed, talking about it still felt raw, like nerves on fire. Like something bubbling painfully up from his gut. Healing never came. It never had. Karen had forgiven him, and he'd pretended to accept her forgiveness. Then he'd enlisted in the marines in the hopes of finding salvation through death. Two of his buddies were killed by a roadside bomb in Afghanistan. Another lost his legs. Ben was unscathed. Brutally, unfairly unscathed.

"I could have killed her," he said. "I could have killed someone else."

He thought about that each morning when he woke up and decided not to drink. He'd spent his life prior to that night thinking about time in terms of weeks and months, sometimes years. Now life was one day at a time.

"Are you going to the wedding?" Sally's voice sliced through his thoughts. "You said your friend was getting married, so I thought…I wondered if you were going."

She kept her eyes on the road, her face inscrutable. People had heard him talk about the accident and then asked him questions in voices tinged with condescension, pity or judgment. Sally's voice was clear and quiet. Beautifully untainted with anything but curiosity.

"Yes," he replied. "I was invited, and I said I would go." He sighed. He could focus on their happiness to get through the event. Pretend he wasn't watching his chance at forever walk down the aisle.

If he'd been a betting man, he'd have wagered that answer didn't satisfy Sally, but she had the decency to not ask a follow-up question. His disaster of an engagement wasn't high on his list of favorite conversation topics.

She swung into the parking lot at the office and dropped him at his unimpressive car. At least the tires appeared to be fully inflated. "Thanks for the ride, and for dinner," he said as he climbed out of the warm BMW into the crisp October night. "You're officially off the hook, no more obligations. I hope you don't have a long drive home."

"It's not too bad. I live out in Avon, on the lake. I need to live on the water," she added as if that was a natural thing to say. "I'm a Pisces."

He knew little about astrology. "What's Pisces, the fish? I'm a Scorpio." He paused. "Where do scorpions live? Under rock ledges? Creepy places? I may need to find some new real estate." He stood looking at her, one hand clasping the car door. James Kruger's warnings played over in his mind. "I should follow you, make sure you get home safely."

She waved a hand dismissively. "I'm fine, really."

"But James—"

"It's nothing, believe me. I have a top-of-the-line alarm system." She adjusted her seat belt. "It's late. We both need to go home."

He hesitated. "Be careful, Sally. Call the police if you see anything strange. Anything at all."

She gave a small smile and a wave as he closed the door. Ben checked to make sure that his car had four inflated tires. Then he climbed inside and blew his breath into his hands, waiting for Sally to leave the parking lot and drive safely away into the darkness. He turned the key in the ignition and turned on the radio, flipping the station to a late-night talk show. He didn't know how long he sat there, waiting for his heart to calm its rapid pulse. So much for keeping his head down and making a fresh start. So much for proving he was a better man than the one she'd known in law school.

His gut churned as he backed the car into the evening, kicking himself for his honesty. He'd made a mess of his life, and he'd just stirred that mess up and shown it to Sally. So much for trying to settle their past. Some people were beyond redemption, and the sooner he accepted that about himself, the better.

Chapter 8

Mitch was angry again. Ronnie could tell from the way his boots struck the kitchen tile. Mitch was as transparent as lake water. No, not lake water. Sunlight penetrated lake water at an angle, and the murkiness stopped it before it got too deep. Lakes held secrets. Mitch did not.

She sighed and flipped through her magazine. It was the new issue of her favorite celebrity gossip rag, and she'd been looking forward to it all week. Funny how attached to particular magazines she'd become while living in Vegas, mostly isolated from the world. Sure, she'd talked to people at work, but she'd needed to maintain a distance, and that meant she'd hidden herself away each night instead of going out for social gatherings.

Her ritual had been to finish her shift, which usually ended around ten, stop at the convenience store for a cup of burned coffee, a pack of cigarettes and a gossip or fashion magazine, and walk the three blocks to her motel. She'd smoke and read, dozing off after midnight. The ritual that had begun as the pathetic act of a lonely woman soon came to possess meaning and its own comfort, because walking to a convenience store, buying a magazine and reading in bed for hours was the first ritual she'd claimed for herself since she met Mitch.

His footsteps halted in the kitchen below, and she heard the refrigerator swing open. Mitch. Everything was always about Mitch, and had been since the day they'd met. What does Mitch want to eat for dinner tonight? What does Mitch want to do this weekend? Does Mitch like this blouse on her? How about that skirt? She'd been devoted to him, and she'd never questioned his devotion to her. She'd been a damn fool.

No more.

Ronnie calmly turned the page. She liked this feature, the one where they compared pictures of celebrities in the same clothes and asked which one looked better. *I could do this. I could follow celebrities around and take their pictures.* How did one get to be a member of the paparazzi, anyway? She'd need a good camera, and from there it was probably a matter of knowing who liked to frequent which frozen yogurt stand or bistro. Those photos sold for thousands of dollars.

In high school, she'd won an award for her photography. At one point she'd dreamed about going to art school. Then she'd met Mitch and gotten pregnant. By the time James was old enough for her to return to school, art school was out of the question. Not that being a school nurse was the worst career in the world, but it wasn't her first choice. She'd done a lot of settling.

The refrigerator door slammed shut. A year ago, Ronnie might have jumped at the sound, but not today. Not anymore. She wasn't afraid of Mitch. She sighed and turned the page as his angry footsteps plodded up the stairs. If James wasn't out at a friend's house right now, she'd have reminded Mitch that he wasn't the only person who lived in this house and to please be considerate. But since James wasn't around, she didn't care how much noise Mitch made.

"Thought you'd at least have made dinner," he snarled as he entered the bedroom.

He was wearing that stupid green polo shirt the hardware store required him to wear. She supposed he was lucky his old boss had been gracious enough to offer him his job back after he'd been released from prison.

I told you, she'd said. *I told you to trust me, and that everything would be all right.*

And it was all right, just as she'd promised. He was upset about spending so much time in jail, and that was fair. She'd had no idea, really. She would've come back sooner if she'd known. They didn't think the police would move that quickly. He didn't believe her, though. He thought she'd stayed an extra long time in Vegas out of spite. He still thought she was punishing him.

Maybe he was right.

"I didn't have time," she replied with calculated indifference and a flip of the page. "Anyway, I had a late lunch. You know I can't cook when I'm full."

Never could, and the handful of times she'd tried, the food came out limp and unseasoned, and Mitch had complained.

If Mitch revealed his moods in his footsteps, he wore them on his face with even greater transparency. She could see out of the corner of her eye that it was awash with shadows—cloudy and cold, as if a storm could erupt at any moment. "You contact the school yet?"

He wanted her working again, now that she was home. Earning her keep. But Ronnie had decided she'd earned a vacation. She still had some savings from the job in Vegas. "I was so busy." She sighed. "Must've slipped my mind."

She kept her gaze pinned to the magazine. Some controversy surrounded the celebrity adoption of a child from an impoverished nation she'd never heard of, but her eyes stopped short of registering the images. Her muscles were pulled tight, her entire body preparing a fight or flight response as Mitch stood stock-still, looking as if he could kill her with his bare hands. He'd be sorry if he did. She'd given her attorney a letter to open in the event of her death, and Mitch knew it.

His lips barely moved when he spoke, the words filtered through clenched teeth. "You can't sit around the house all day. We can't afford it. I thought I made myself clear."

"Perfectly," she chirped. "But I'm just getting back to my old life, and I need to ease into things. Don't you think it would look strange, in light of my recent amnesia, if I simply walked back into the high school and asked for my old job? Besides, I don't care what you say anymore, Mitch." She closed the magazine and laid it in her lap, folding her hands demurely on top of the deodorant ad on the back cover. "And I thought I made *that* clear."

He wasn't the only one who was angry. She should've known better than to trust him with her dog. Poor Pookie. She'd been looking forward to seeing him, and all Mitch would tell her was that he was gone. *Got sick,* he'd said, though that was clearly a lie. Had he let him out the back door? Dropped him off along the highway somewhere? She couldn't even think about it.

Mitch's breath came in loud huffs through his nostrils, and he stood facing her, hands clenched in large fists. He had massive strong hands. She'd found them attractive at one time, then she'd feared them, and now she regarded them as impotent. Her gaze narrowed. "I did some cleaning today. I noticed that you kept a picture."

His face registered surprise, then rage as his hazel eyes turned dark. "You went through my things."

"You're a fool," she snapped. "How many times did I tell you? Eliminate all traces of her. If anyone finds something, they're going to ask questions."

"No one's going to find anything." He turned away from her and loosened his belt, sliding it through the belt loops with one slick movement. "The cops have given up."

"That prosecutor hasn't." Ronnie tossed the magazine on the bed and pulled her knees up, forming a tent with the sheets. "James said he spoke with her. She was asking him questions."

Mitch stiffened. "What kinds of questions?"

"He wouldn't say. Just that she made it clear she was still watching us. Watching you. He didn't even want to talk about it, but he came back to the house looking like he'd just seen—" She stopped. She'd been about to say "a ghost," but that seemed tasteless. She folded her arms across her chest. "This thing isn't over. You're risking your life by holding on to souvenirs. This is your problem, Mitch, and I'm not going to jail. Fix it."

He changed his clothes slowly, as if he'd forgotten he wasn't alone. When he was finished, he dropped his work shirt and pants into the laundry basket and turned to her for the first time in several minutes. His tone had changed. "I'll get rid of everything. I promise."

She lifted her shoulders and reached for the magazine. "Good idea. But you don't need to worry about the photograph." She flipped through the pages and found the place she'd left off. "I already burned it."

"Big news," Sally announced as she stepped into Ben's office. "And I do mean *big.*"

"Emphasis on big," he said as he swung around from his computer. "I got it." But he sent her a smile that lit up the office.

Since last Wednesday night, when Sally had dropped him off at his car, they'd spoken only about the Kruger case, and even those conversations had been limited. She knew he was busy working on a report for Jack that would detail the strength of the forensic evidence, and Ben had led her to believe he saw this as a once-in-a-lifetime fluke of a case. The stars had aligned improperly, and investigators hadn't had reason to examine other evidence. She'd been trying to leave him alone so he could complete his work quickly, and she'd focused on her other cases in the meantime. But she couldn't quite explain why her stomach sparked at the thought that she finally had an excuse to speak with him. She smiled as their eyes met, and she saw that he felt it, too.

Maybe this fondness was simply what partners felt for each other. A shared dependency on the other's strengths, a shared mission. She told herself that it didn't mean any more than that. They were working together and getting along. That was the arrangement, after all. He would share a draft of his report with her and give her an opportunity to respond, and she wouldn't sneer at him. She was finding her promise easier and easier to keep.

"I got a call from Dan." She couldn't contain the bubble of excitement rising in her voice. "He's been trying to locate Mary Ann Hennessy, Ronnie Kruger's sister. Well, that turns out to be a tall order. He called her brothers, and they said that Mary Ann left town a while ago."

"Let me guess." Ben folded his arms across his chest and lifted an eyebrow. "Did she vanish about a year ago?"

Sally nodded. "You got it. It was a planned departure. Apparently Mary Ann sold her house, quit her job and moved to Hawaii. With a *mystery lover,*" she added with inflection.

"Who doesn't have a mystery lover?" he said. "I'm waiting for the big news. You made some promises, so it's time to deliver."

"You can't interrupt me. It's complicated." She took a breath as he watched her with piercing blue eyes, and her heart scampered. His good looks helped nothing. "No one's heard from her since. She hasn't kept in touch, but then no one has reported her missing."

"Because her move was planned," he said. "They

just assume she's lousy at keeping in touch, which doesn't seem to be out of character in this family."

"They're not close siblings, and there seems to be some bad blood. Something about an inheritance," Sally agreed. "So no one has questioned her disappearance or her mystery lover. Just like they didn't seem concerned when Ronnie vanished."

"There's nothing like family," Ben said with a grimace.

Sally wondered whether he had firsthand experience with painful family dynamics, but now wasn't the time to ask. Then again, *no* time was the time to ask about such a subject. Despite sharing stories about their failed engagements, they didn't have a relationship outside this case and work, and there was no reason for her to take such an interest in strictly personal matters.

She swallowed. "Anyway, this was a lead that was dropped during the investigation. We knew that Mary Ann had moved and that she wouldn't return phone calls, but investigators weren't interested because things were heating up around Mitch Kruger." Sally shrugged. "He had disposed of a bloody area rug, and his son was set to testify against him. There didn't seem to be any reason to pursue an estranged sister. Until now."

"Ah. Is this the big news I've been waiting for?" Now she had Ben's undivided attention. He leaned forward in his chair and gestured for her to have a seat. "I'm listening."

She caught his eye dipping lower as she sat in the chair and crossed her legs. The look was over in a flash, but her pulse kicked again. "So Dan said that our meeting on Wednesday got him thinking about the sister for the first time. Mary Ann may not have returned our calls because she didn't know anything, or didn't want to be bothered. In either case, she wasn't a person of interest, and we received enough information about the family from Ronnie's brothers." Sally gripped the chair seat and leaned forward. "Fritz called me this morning. He went back over the evidence investigators vacuumed from the rug after it was abandoned. Sure enough, your hunch was correct—they identified several long blond hairs that didn't fit Ronnie Kruger's DNA profile, but that matched a relative." She arched her eyebrow at him and waited as the revelation settled.

A smile slowly spanned his face. "Like a sister?"

"Exactly."

"So let me get this straight." Ben rose from his chair and wandered toward the front of his desk. "The crime lab has evidence that potentially places Ronnie Kruger's estranged sister at the scene of the crime—a sister that no one has seen or heard from in almost a year."

Sally nodded. "You got it."

He ran a hand over his face. "So we're looking at an investigative failure here," he mumbled. "Dropped leads, unexplained evidence."

"It looks like that. The significance of the evidence was missed. Everyone was focused on the blood and the domestic dispute. But it gets better. Or worse." She sat back in the chair. "On the night Ronnie Kruger vanished, Mary Ann boarded a plane to San Diego. The last anyone's heard of her was when she used her credit cards. In *Vegas*."

"You don't say." Ben stood transfixed. Then a smile, slow as honey, spread across his face. "Okay, this…

this is potentially big," he agreed. "I think we have ourselves a real case, Sally."

She flushed with pleasure. "I *know*. Mary Ann could be the body we're looking for, not Ronnie."

"Ronnie may have assumed her identity. Of course, to do so, she may have killed her." He drummed his fingertips on the desk. "But can we prove it for a fact?"

"Ronnie will stick with her amnesia story. She may claim it was coincidence that her sister has apparently been spending money in Vegas, and we don't have anything stronger than that." Sally looked at him. "But we have that hair. It places Mary Ann at the scene. And Dan is trying to gain access to her credit card statements for the past year, to see where she was spending her money. If our hunch is right that Ronnie was the one using it, that will tell us a lot about what she's been up to."

"This is something," Ben agreed. "Either Mary Ann gave her credit cards to her estranged sister—" he made a face as if he'd just eaten something sour, to indicate that this theory didn't work for him "—or Ronnie took the money, and Mary Ann didn't stop her."

"And if Mary Ann didn't stop her, it's because she *couldn't*," Sally said gravely. "That means that when James Kruger saw a body on the rug that he thought was his mother, he may have been looking at his aunt."

Ben returned to his chair, crossed his arms across his chest and looked deep in thought. "This is nice work, partner," he said. "Now I'm wondering if I need to delay my report a little longer, to leave our friends at the police department some time to follow up on these leads."

Sally felt as if a heavy weight had just fallen off

her shoulders. "I'm relieved. I'm not going to pretend I'm not. I've been replaying every detail of this file in my mind, wondering where we went wrong. If it turns out that Ronnie and Mitch have been covering Mary Ann's murder, they've been doing a hell of a job of it."

"None of this explains why Ronnie's blood was on the carpet," Ben said. "There's more to this story, and I feel like we're only scratching the surface. This is a strange, strange case."

Sally nodded in agreement and remained seated in the chair. She had other files to attend to, but had more to say to Ben. She'd been thinking about their discussion in the car on Wednesday night. Her engagement had been an admitted disaster, and she could see that in hindsight. At the time, she'd gone nearly out of her mind with grief, convinced that her broken engagement signaled the final barrier to the future she'd always wanted with a loving husband and children.

She'd ultimately accepted that a husband wasn't in her future, and with a clearer head she'd taken her desire to have a baby into her own hands. She was finally gaining control of her life, and while she felt empowered by that, she was confident she'd never be able to attend her ex-fiancé's wedding to another woman. To see him getting what she'd once so desperately wanted: love, and the chance at forever.

She cleared her throat. This was a delicate matter, and she wasn't quite certain how to broach it. "You know, I've been thinking a lot about what you said last week, about this wedding for your friend." She began slowly, watching for Ben's response. His angular face remained unmoved as he watched her. "I think that if you're going…I don't think you should go alone.

Look, I owe you a dinner. A real dinner, not one with my parents."

She didn't know whether or not he had a girlfriend, but she'd gathered from their conversations that he was single—maybe even resistant to relationships. Still, Sally knew how she'd feel if her ex was getting married, and she assumed Ben would be grateful she was showing concern.

She couldn't have been more wrong. His face darkened and he set his jaw, muttering only a terse, "That's not your business."

The sudden change hit her like a slap. "Um, you *made* it my business. You told me what happened." *You confided in me,* she wanted to say. *I thought it meant something.*

"It was a late night. We were sharing, and I felt sorry about your ex-fiancé, and the baby, and I said too much, that's all." He unfolded his arms and shrugged his shoulders. "You don't need to worry about it."

She'd gone out of her way to show her concern, and this is what she got for it? "I'm trying to be nice. Your ex-fiancé is marrying one of your close friends." Her voice slipped, regrettably, into a bit of a growl. "I won't pretend to know what it's like to be in your position, but I know what it's like to feel betrayed. I wouldn't have gotten through my breakup without my friends, but in your case, your friend is the one getting married. If you were going to the wedding alone, I was going to offer to go with you. For support. That's all."

He stared at some spot on his desk, and after a long period of silence he said, "We're colleagues. Partners. Not friends."

Sally blinked back a sting of humiliation. She'd

been foolish. She rose. "I—I promised to be decent to you," she stammered. "I was only trying to be decent."

She spun and marched toward the door, feeling shame coating her like a heavy wool blanket. Her instincts about him were right. He was unable or unwilling to let anyone get too close. He deserved to go alone to this wedding, to see the woman he'd once loved profess her love for someone else. Every measure of his pain was reward for the pain he'd inflicted on others. He was still the same Ben. She was naive to believe he'd ever become anyone other than who he was.

"Sally. Wait."

He called from behind her, and she turned to see him standing behind his desk, his hands limp at his sides, his gaze fixed on her. "Don't go."

He couldn't stand the pity in her eyes when she'd asked him about the wedding. All that silence in the car, and now, a week later, she returned with this? Who did she think she was, to *pity* him? He wasn't so broken that he deserved that.

He gathered his reserve and reminded himself to keep his cool. If they'd had this conversation early last week, he would have brushed her off as being snobby, or thinking she knew what was best for him. But right now he saw that despite the proud lift to her chin, her nose was already red. She wasn't thinking she knew what was best. Well, maybe she was, but that thinking came from a place of concern. He'd asked her to be decent to him. He couldn't blame her for trying.

"I shouldn't have snapped at you," he said. "I wasn't prepared to talk about this today." Or any day.

She half turned, as if still weighing whether it was

worth it to stay and hear him out. Her hands were clutched in fists. God, she was going to cry, and it was going to be his fault. He ran his palm across his face. "I wasn't planning to go to the wedding. I responded, but then as it got closer…" He let his voice trail off. He couldn't go. He couldn't watch one of his friends marry the woman he was supposed to wed. He'd been a masochist at one point, but he couldn't be that way forever.

Sally folded her arms across her chest. She hesitated, dragging out the silence, and then said, "You should go, Ben. It's closure."

And punishment. "They won't miss me."

"Not for them, for you. So that you're not always wondering about it."

He looked away from her, thinking about the many hours he'd spent imagining the event, and how happy Karen would be to marry someone else. Someone kind and decent. "You're probably right." The admission still felt heavy against his chest. He hated that she was likely right. "I can bring a guest. You're…welcome to join me."

Sally was unconvinced, punishing him with a stony stare and a stretch of silence. He didn't mind most silences. This one was painful. "It's tomorrow," he continued, desperate to hear words, however ineffective. "Four o'clock, in Bedford. I have new tires now." He smiled feebly. "I could drive. I responded for a guest already. A mystery date." His smile felt more like a grimace. "You'd be having the fish."

"I hate fish," she replied. "It makes me feel itchy. Unless it's salmon."

Her tone was cool, but she was smiling faintly as she said it. She was teasing, giving him a hard time.

Thank God. "Yes, that would be strange if you ate fish. You are a Pisces, after all. But I think it's salmon." He exhaled. "If it's not, I ordered the steak. I'll switch with you."

"So you ordered the steak for yourself and the fish for your mystery date?"

Was she asking him to explain his rationale? "I thought most people liked fish. I figured it was a friendly food for a mystery date."

"You hadn't planned on me."

Her words were underscored by the intense gaze of her beautiful whiskey-colored eyes. The look crept up on him and sent the blood rushing from his head. Was this a pity date, or did Sally have something else in mind entirely? He was hoping it was the latter.

"No," he agreed. "I hadn't planned on you."

Not at all.

Tessa's jaw nearly hit the ground. "You're going on a date. With Ben." It wasn't a question. "You've been holding back on me, Sally!"

"I haven't held anything back," she replied. "It's not a date. It's just a favor."

Her voice was calm, but her palms were sweaty and her heart was doing jumping jacks. She wanted to believe her own words. She did. But she also wanted to believe that there was something more between her and Ben. She wanted to believe it so much that it scared her. Two competing desires—one to remain uninvolved with Ben, and the other to become very much involved—waged fiercely within her.

"It doesn't mean anything," she continued, whispering the words as they walked out into the cool autumn sunshine. "Remember Mr. X? I read in a woman's magazine that the worst time to enter into a new relationship is when you're pregnant by donor sperm." She would be wise to remember that. "I'm done with men. *Done*."

"Oh, come on now." Tessa waggled her eyebrows suggestively. "Would you ever consider it?"

"Consider what? Dating *Ben?*" Sally scoffed. "You're hilarious."

"But why not? He's hot, and he seems smart. Yesterday we were in the kitchen together, and I kept staring at his hands. Have you seen his hands?" She measured in the air. "Huge."

"Yes," Sally mumbled. "I've noticed."

"Big strong hands," Tessa continued with a grin.

Sally's shoulders tensed. What did she care if Tessa was talking about Ben's hands? It wasn't as if they were a private body part. Then again, if her friend had noticed his hands, maybe she'd noticed other parts of him, too. His eyes, or his smile. Maybe she'd flirted with him. Sally was caught by a flash of jealousy that she had no business feeling.

"I love military men." Tessa sighed. "They're so... large."

Sally bit the inside of her cheeks and said nothing. Her hands hurt from being balled so tightly inside her coat pockets. Ben was hot and large and all of it, but he was also coming dangerously close to being a friend, and she didn't talk about her friends like that.

She hit the keyless entry button for her car and saw the lights flash invitingly. "I was thinking we could go—" She froze when she saw the web of splinters across the glass. Her breath snagged in her lungs. "Someone smashed my windshield."

She took a step closer but was brought back by Tessa's firm grip on her arm. "Stop right there. I'm calling the police," she said. She was already dialing.

Within minutes, a squad car had arrived and two officers were assessing the damage. A group of curious onlookers from the office were watching from a distance. "Seems like someone took a bat to your car," said one of the officers. "You have any idea who would do this?"

Mitch Kruger, Sally thought, remembering James's warning. "You should check the surveillance footage," she replied through chattering teeth. "I wouldn't know."

She looked over and saw Ben's large figure ambling out of the building. He approached faster as he seemed to realize what had happened, nearly breaking into a run. Sally ignored Tessa's whistle under her breath.

"Sally," he said, pulling up next to her. "What the hell happened?"

"Someone smashed my windshield." She couldn't stop her teeth from chattering, and she pressed her hands deep inside her coat pockets, trying without success to keep from shivering.

"Kruger?" he whispered.

"They have to check the footage. This could be random for all we know."

Ben raised an eyebrow, making it clear that he didn't believe that to be the case. "Random? Your windshield just happens to get smashed when the police detective gets a lead on the Kruger case?" He shook his head angrily and scratched the back of his neck. "I don't think so. Kruger knows that you're pushing this case. You're keeping it open, and he probably knows that the police have been interviewing relatives about Mary Ann Hennessy. He wants you to back off."

"We don't know that." Sally's voice sounded shrill, but her nerves were frayed. It was just a car, so why did she feel so *violated?* "We can't just assume. You know that."

"I don't know anything like that." His voice was hard, his face etched in shadow as he straightened his spine and looked down at her with concern. "No more chances, Sally. You need to talk to the police about what James Kruger said, and you need to make sure you're never alone. I'm serious."

She nodded mutely as his words struck home. "I'll tell them. But I'm fine. I am. My address is unlisted, and Mitch doesn't know where I live."

"Sally, he knew enough to recognize your car," Ben said gravely. "Why don't you stay somewhere else tonight?"

"That's crazy talk. I'm not in any danger."

"This is that guy who was accused of killing his wife, right? Sally, you told me he has a gun collection." Tessa came up behind them and wrapped her arm around Sally's shoulders. "Ben's right. Better to be safe. You can stay with me tonight. I have a guest bed." She gave her a one-armed hug.

"I don't know—"

"You could be in danger," Ben insisted. "Stay with Tessa tonight. Tomorrow, you'll be with me. We'll figure out where you should stay tomorrow night."

His words were heavy with meaning. Sally fought to keep her traitorous knees from softening. She could claw his face for suggesting that she needed someone to decide for her where she should spend the night. Or she could hold her tongue and let this play out, decide whether she liked the bed he'd choose for her.

"My sleeping arrangements don't fall within the purview of our partnership," she replied. "I'll stay with Tessa tonight, and I'll decide for myself tomorrow whether it's safe to go home."

She noticed him open his mouth and then bite his lip, as if he was fighting the urge to say something. She didn't care. She had a mind of her own, and most of her instincts told her to steer clear of Ben McNamara.

He came closer to her, his figure towering protectively over hers. "We'll talk about this tomorrow," he promised. "Wherever you stay, I need to know you're safe."

Something in his tone snagged her breath, and the heat in his eyes made her want to bury her face against him. Her head reeled. She was falling for him, hard and fast.

Her head told her this was no good at all, but the rest of her had all but given up fighting the attraction.

Chapter 9

Ben ran five miles around the park on Saturday morning to calm his nerves and sharpen his thoughts. The surveillance footage of the parking lot had been little help in identifying the person who'd smashed Sally's windshield. All they'd been able to see was a man who'd walked onto the property, his face shadowed by a baseball cap, smashed the car with a bat and ran away. Ben's stomach had been on fire for most of the night, burning as he thought about Sally being in danger, and the time he was about to spend with her.

They'd agreed she would stay the night at Tessa's, but that he'd pick her up at her own home. After his run, Ben spent a good part of the morning washing and vacuuming his car. His vehicle couldn't compete with Sally's BMW, but getting a rental would look desperate. He called her before he left his apartment.

"I hope you don't mind," she'd said. "Since this was so last minute, I'm just wearing an old dress I found."

Of course he didn't mind, and he'd felt the knot in his gut relax slightly. His heart had been racing since the previous morning at the thought of seeing Sally dressed up. Of being next to her at dinner, possibly dancing. Seeing her lipstick on a champagne flute. Knowing that the entire time he'd be playing the casual, detached date, he'd be thinking about what her skin might feel like beneath that dress. At least if she wasn't making too much of an effort at dressing up, he wouldn't have to try so hard to keep from doing something they'd both regret.

They worked together, and work relationships were never a good idea. Besides, there was something he liked about Sally. He felt lighter around her, and he couldn't ignore this protective streak he'd suddenly developed. He'd hurt her in the past, and now all he could think about was keeping her safe—from Mitch Kruger, and from himself. Sally was a sweet girl who deserved better than that, and the last thing on his mind was hurting her again.

Ben took more care than usual when dressing, though he kicked himself for it. Before he donned his jacket, he slipped on a shoulder holster and his .38 automatic. He had a bad feeling about Mitch Kruger, and he wasn't about to take any chances.

He followed the directions to Sally's house, trying to imagine what one of her old dresses might look like. Something frumpy? The girl didn't have a frumpy cell in her body, and he doubted she owned a stitch of clothing that would qualify. Sally would undoubtedly look beautiful and stylish in her old dress, but he was still unprepared for the woman who emerged from the modest home fronting Avon Lake: a woman with her blond hair swept up from her face, an elegant diamond necklace lacing her throat and a dress the color of the light blue sky at dusk adorning her body.

The dress had been made for her to wear it—for him, for that night—with each inch of the fabric caressing the voluptuous curves of her body. He nearly stopped breathing when he saw the swell of her breasts pressing against it invitingly. An old dress—meaning someone else had seen her looking like that before him? He didn't fight the jealousy that rose in his chest. God help him to exercise self-restraint tonight.

She slid into the seat beside him, flooding the car with her sweet perfume, and flashing a smile that stopped his heart. "Hi," she purred.

Somehow, he found his voice. "That's not an old dress," he mumbled. His collar felt tight.

"I swear it is." She spread her long fingers on her thigh and smoothed the material. "Do you like it?"

"You're going to detract from the bride." His admonishment was half-serious, but she beamed.

"You look nice, too."

He backed out of the driveway without a word and cracked open the window. The car was too warm.

The drive to Bedford took half an hour, but if Ben had worried about how to fill that time, it was needless. Sally had come prepared with an almost endless supply of funny stories about her parents and her siblings, or, as she called them, Hank and Lana and the kids.

"We had cocktail hour growing up. Hank had a bourbon, Lana had a highball and we had seltzer with a twist of lime. Every night."

His stomach hurt from laughing. This was the Sally he remembered from law school—the charmer who was underestimated and passed off as fluff, the engaging girl who spoke animatedly with her hands and lit up when she told a story. She was a born actress, he realized. A natural storyteller who did hilarious impressions of her parents and each of her siblings. She must be a hell of a litigator.

"What did you talk about? At cocktail hour?"

"Beaver anal gland secretions and how they can be used to make a delicious, all-natural vanilla flavor," she deadpanned. "Or algebra. There was a spectrum, and no topic was off limits."

"I know your secret mission is to get me to swear off all forms of flavoring," he said. "Natural, artificial. But you haven't considered the error of your ways."

"Oh?"

"What becomes of your family fortune if everyone stops eating that stuff?"

She grinned. "I'm not trying for everyone," she answered. "I'm trying for you."

He might have imagined the suggestion in her voice, added it as a sort of wishful thinking. Then she made a pretense of leaning to reach something, and brushed her fingers against him. His body stiffened in response. Every part of it. She flashed another flirty smile. She knew exactly what she was doing, and he had the thrilling suspicion that she was trying to seduce him.

The Gilmore Estate was set in the rolling hills of Litchfield County. He'd worked summers here during high school, doing landscaping work, mostly. The estate was picturesque any time of year, but now the fall foliage was a spectacular mixture of vibrant reds, yellows and oranges that rippled over the hills like a blaze. They parked in a gravel lot and made the short walk to a large tent in back of the sprawling white manor. Rows of chairs were set to form a makeshift chapel. The altar itself was decorated only with white pillar candles, but the tent sides were raised so that the brilliant leaves on the surrounding hills were visible.

Ben gripped Sally's elbow as they walked. Mostly because he was a gentleman and she was wearing impractically high silver heels, but also to feel the soft warmth of her skin. To remind himself that he wasn't alone. He was glad she'd come.

"How long has it been since you've seen them?" she asked softly when they'd taken seats in the back.

"A few months," he said, trying to keep his voice quiet. "They've been together for years now, and I've always known. I made peace with that long ago."

She peered at him with wide eyes, searching his face for something. "You loved her, and she's marrying your friend. How could you ever make peace with that?"

He hadn't invited her here to administer psychotherapy. To be fair, coming had been her idea, and he hadn't really invited her at all. He leaned away from the heat of her body, the scent of her perfume. Her concern. She was so concerned about him and his response to his ex-fiancé. He wanted Sally to stop it and just let him *be*.

More and more guests were filing into the area. People he didn't know, dressed in dark autumnal shades, reds and muted golds. Black. So much black, and this was supposed to be a celebration. They looked somber against the colors of nature. Sally's dress, by contrast, came alive in the candlelight, catching the flames in a rush of movement that made it appear as if she might melt and run downstream, or take off and fly. She had the right idea, to wear the color of the sky. All this darkness, and Sally wasn't afraid to shine.

"I made peace with this the same way you made peace with your ex sleeping with another woman," he replied in a voice that felt as if it had been wound too tightly. "It hurts, and then over time it stops. You move on, and you forget."

She furrowed her brows and then sat back in her seat with a little "humph."

"What?" He wasn't angry, just curious at the response. "What's that mean?"

"Nothing." She flipped through the little paper program they'd received from one of the ushers. "Like you said, I made my peace. I got over it."

"But?"

She folded the program and smoothed it across her lap. She'd painted her nails a light pink, like bubble gum. "It's just that I think that if you love someone, there's no getting over it. There's no peace to be had. That was a sign for me."

"What was?"

She turned her face to him, lovely and soft in the candlelight. "Don't get me wrong. When my ex cheated, I was devastated. I cried for days. But then it didn't take too long to stop hurting, and I realized that I'd been ignoring how wrong we were together. When I stopped hurting, I realized I'd never loved him in the first place. I was humiliated, but relieved." She raised one shoulder in a half shrug. "I like to think that love would last forever. Through mistakes and betrayal, even." She smiled. "Maybe I'm idealistic."

He started to say something to her, but a string quartet began to play, and she settled back to examine her program again. She clearly wasn't interested in hearing a response, and his wasn't necessary. He'd only been about to tell her that he'd like to believe in love, too.

He watched as the groom took his place at the altar. Ben felt a calmness about it, about watching his close friend, who'd swept in and taken the girl Ben had once loved. Thought he loved. Maybe Sally was right, and there was no getting over love. The groomsmen and bridesmaids filed down the aisle in a wash of more red and black, and Ben and Sally stood with the rest of the crowd as the musicians signaled the arrival of the bride.

He'd expected to feel a mix of anger and regret, or even the cold grip of despair as he faced a symbol of his lonely future. Instead, when Karen walked down the aisle with her father, gorgeous in a white gown, unblemished where her bones had broken and beaming at her groom, he felt content. And when Sally slid her warm hand into his and squeezed, he felt the truth of her words. He'd never loved Karen in the first place.

Sally scolded herself for being so morbid as to compare herself to the bride. Karen was stunning, with high cheekbones and a proud, straight nose. She could have modeled if she wanted to. She had gorgeous bone structure, and the dark brown hair that Sally had tried once in high school, only to find it made her look washed out and pale. Gorgeous chestnut hair that Karen had pulled only half up, allowing the rest to fall like silk threads down her back. Sally's stom-

Natalie Charles   *163*

ach rose and fell when she caught the way the groom waited for her at the altar. He was looking at her as if they were alone in the world. A tightness gathered in Sally's chest. She'd been scheduled to have a wedding day once, too, but no one would have ever looked at her like that.

Ben watched the ceremony with calm interest, but not the emotion she'd feared. Sally exhaled. She'd made a lot of jokes on the ride over to dissipate some of the awkwardness, but she knew that the night could have gotten ugly, and fast. She gave his hand another squeeze. She was glad she could be here for him, to be his friend. They were partners, after all, and it was sort of nice to have a work buddy. Someone who could shoulder some of the weight of her case.

Ben had changed. He wasn't the womanizer she remembered. He looked at her as if he was interested in her opinion, not in getting her to sleep with him, and that was a relief. She wanted to be taken seriously. She was a professional, after all.

She went to drop his hand and started when he held on to hers. Then he gave her a look out of the corner of his eye that she couldn't read. A shiver darted down her spine. She slowly broke the connection with him and avoided further eye contact, but she couldn't ignore the way her pulse was racing.

She pressed the fabric of her dress between her fingers and rubbed. Time to get a grip. Sally was feeding herself a bunch of trash if she thought she wasn't attracted to Ben. He was kind, strong and vulnerable at the same time. He had a smile that made her heart flutter and drew her to him like waves to the shore. He remembered her stories. He liked her crazy parents.

But none of that made it a damn good idea for them to get involved. They were just getting back to being decent to each other, to being friends. Moving into more intimate territory would only screw up their progress.

The bride and groom had written their own vows. Hearing them, Sally felt her eyes start to sting. They were such a cute couple, and the way he was looking at her… Sally sniffed and ran a finger beneath her eye. She'd spent way too much time on her makeup as it was, and she didn't need Ben to watch her shape-shift into a zebra.

He nudged her then, holding out a simple handkerchief. She accepted it without further acknowledgment and edged the fabric into the corners of her eyes. He was still watching her, she could feel it. Her body responded with prickles and shivers that skittered across her skin like a flash of electricity. She clutched the handkerchief in her fist, willing herself to not look back at him. To fight whatever urges passed silently in the space between their bodies.

Once the ceremony had ended, they stood in the receiving line and offered their warm congratulations to the bride and groom.

"Karen." Ben took her hands in his and offered her a soft kiss on the cheek. "You've never looked so happy."

"I'm so pleased you could come, Ben." Her tone was affectionate, her gaze soft.

"Ben." The groom wrapped his arms around his friend and gave him a few slaps on the back. "I haven't seen you since you got back, man. You look good."

"You, too, Matt." He pulled back to look his friend in the eyes. "You take good care of Karen, okay?"

The groom gave him another hug. "Will do, buddy. Thanks for coming."

Ben took Sally by the hand and led her along a brick path toward the cocktail hour at the estate house. He'd been so casual in his compliments to the couple that Sally wondered whether she should anticipate a breakdown of some sort. "You okay?" she whispered once they were out of earshot.

He bent toward her, wrapping his arm possessively around her waist. She didn't bother to brush it off. "Why wouldn't I be?"

"You seemed happy for them. Genuinely. I wanted to make sure you weren't putting up a brave front. You know, being all manly about it." She cleared her throat. "In case you haven't noticed, you lock your feelings away."

"And you wave yours like a banner," he said. "But I have a stunning woman on my arm, and it's a beautiful night. What isn't there to be happy about?"

Her throat locked tight against a response.

He skipped the cocktails and ordered a glass of tonic water. She had the same. They milled about in a crowded room with lots of people he didn't seem to know, eventually pressed into a corner by waves of perfume and cologne and exuberant conversations punctuated by inside jokes. Sally gripped her glass, the condensation dripping onto her fingertips. The atmosphere grew thick, and when he caught Sally fanning her face, Ben leaned in to whisper in her ear, "Let's get some air."

They stepped through a great row of French doors onto a slate patio that overlooked the sunset across the valley. The sun, a red bulb on the horizon, still cast a brilliant light on the hillside. "Autumn sunsets are always so bright," she observed, holding her drink out as if she could catch the rays. "They're nothing like the summer."

He was quiet, leaning one shoulder against a black lamppost that had just come on. He stared at her, his gaze pressing against her like fingertips. The air wasn't cool enough. Her skin was feverishly hot.

A breeze carried the sound of a band tuning instruments. "Karen and Matt love to dance," Ben said under his breath. He emptied his drink in one gulp. "Ballroom dancing. Karen's won awards."

Sally gazed up at him. Ben was so tall and broad, she couldn't quite imagine him gliding across a dance floor. "Do you dance?"

"Hell, no." The ice clinked in his glass, and he set it down on a circular glass table. He took a step nearer and Sally froze in place, not wanting to show that she'd noticed how close they suddenly were. "I don't want to talk about dancing. I want to talk about how beautiful you look." His voice was deep, edged in solemnity.

The burn on Sally's skin deepened and she glanced around, frightened that someone might have heard him. "Stop." The command came out as a weak murmur, more like an invitation to convince her why he should continue.

He cocked his head slightly, and a smirk played on his mouth. "That embarrasses you. That I called you beautiful."

"It doesn't. It's just not appropriate. We're colleagues."

His gaze danced across her face, lighting on her eyes before turning to her cheeks and finally settling on her lips. She licked them and heard his sharp intake of breath as he pulled closer, speaking into her ear so that she knew his words were meant for her alone. "Would you feel better if I told you that I find you hideous? Would that put you at ease?"

Her heart was flitting like a caged bird, and the brush of his breath against her ear sent a blaze across her skin. "Yes," she breathed. "It would."

He reached up to stroke the back of his fingers across her hair, tucking a few stray tendrils behind her ear. "Then I find you repulsive," he murmured. "And I haven't devoted an obscene amount of time to thinking about the things I'd like to do to you, given the chance." He swept his fingertips along her jaw, lifting her chin to catch her gaze. "Thoughts that would make you think less of me. Dirty, sinful thoughts."

He came still closer, to position his hips against hers, and she felt his arousal straining against his pants. Her lips parted of their own accord as she urged him to come still closer, aching to feel more of him. "You shouldn't think those things."

"I don't," he replied hoarsely. "I don't think about this estate, and how I worked here for several summers. I'm not thinking about where we could go to be alone."

His words agitated her pulse further, increasing its frantic pace. "There's…an antifraternization policy—"

But he only chuckled. "I don't care about that. You don't, either. You want me as much as I want you, Sally."

The gentleness of his touch unraveled her thoughts, sending them tumbling into a hazy mass. She wanted to deny the truth of his observation. Instead she reached up to stroke his chest, sweeping her fingers across the muscular expanse. She wanted him more than she'd ever wanted anyone, and nothing mattered but having him.

"Yes," she whispered. "I want you."

All sense of right and wrong had flown out of her mind a long time ago. He was hot and hard and his breath was tickling her skin, dulling her capacity for thought. He lowered his mouth to hers with a moan, pressing her back to deepen the contact between them. She reached up to thread her fingers in his dark hair, closing her eyes to feel the heat of his mouth and the eager thrust of his tongue.

"Anywhere," she gasped when she'd managed to break contact. "Now."

He led her around the estate to an arched doorway. The door, constructed of oak boards secured by iron nails, was unlocked. He knew it would be. It was always unlocked for events.

They stumbled into the cool shadows of the old wine cellar. The air was heavy with the scents of oak barrels and wine. The family hadn't fermented grapes here in almost a generation, but the stone walls still gripped the smell. At the far end was a temperature-controlled room for storage. They risked being discovered by the waitstaff or the sommelier, but most of the wine being served should have been moved to the reception by now.

Ben couldn't stop kissing her, couldn't break away from her soft lips and the sweet taste of her breath. She was electricity on his nerves. He brought her to rest on a long wooden table in the darkest corner of the room, and lifted her dress to her waist, parting her knees so he could stand between them. A low moan escaped her throat and threatened to make him lose all control before they'd even started.

"Sally," he whispered. She was unbuttoning his shirt and flicking her hot tongue down his neck. He gripped his hands in her silky hair and brought her mouth back up to his. "If you keep doing that, I'm not going to make it."

Her response was a deep, throaty laugh. Then she stopped as her hands came across his holster. "What's this? A gun?"

"Don't worry, I have a permit." He slid the holster off and rested it beside the table. He ran his lips lightly against her bare throat, his stomach tightening at her moan.

"Ben. You brought a gun to a wedding."

He raised his head to look in her eyes, cradling her jaw in his hands. "I wanted you to feel safe," he said.

She lifted her hands to meet his, and even through the shadows of the room he could see the fear she was fighting. She was wondering if he was going to use her and leave again, to betray her trust. He couldn't imagine ever doing that. His throat squeezed as he fought to answer her unspoken questions without saying too much. "You're safe, Sally. No one's going to hurt you." *Least of all me.*

He felt her relax against his hands. "I—I hate guns," she stammered.

"Then pretend it's not there."

He could barely see her in the darkness, but his other senses were heightened by the smell of her perfume, the heat and silk of her skin. She assisted him with her zipper, and he eased the top of her dress down to feel the achingly perfect weight of her breasts on his palms. He took them into his mouth, sliding his teeth across their plush surface, nipping gently until she melted in his hands, drawing her head back with a deep moan that shot through him like need.

As he mouthed the hard tips of her nipples, her legs quivered against his thighs. She locked him against her, sighing in approval. He held her tightly as he felt her body stiffen with pleasure, and brought one hand lower to stroke the sensitive inside of her legs.

Then his mind went blank. His fingers sought fabric and found only bare skin.

He moaned helplessly against her neck. "That is… the damn sexiest…"

His words sputtered as he touched her softness. She gasped and writhed her hips beneath his hand, urging him to touch her harder and deeper. Just when he thought she was about to find her release, she stopped him and fumbled for his pants.

Now. It had to be now. All of him, right now.

She was dizzy with need for him, desperate as she tore blindly at his pants. Finally she managed to free him. She gripped him and drew him to her. He obliged, pausing only momentarily to apply protection.

With slow, deep thrusts he filled her, made her gasp for breath. She leaned back onto the table and wrapped her legs around him, holding him to her, wanting him to never leave. She peered into the darkness but saw only the outline of his back as he drove into her faster now, the quick rising and falling of his body pushing her to the brink of pleasure.

Then she was over the edge, releasing all her tension, all the need she hadn't realized she had for him, giving herself fully to him. He stiffened and groaned out his own release seconds later. They lay entwined in the darkness, panting and gripping each other, melting until she no longer knew where he ended and she began.

The vibration of his laugh tickled her cheek. "Sally." That was all he said, but it was enough.

She lifted her fingers, finding his lips in the darkness. "I never knew wine cellars could be so hot," she whispered.

He smiled against her fingers, kissing them lightly. "We should go back. Dinner's probably starting."

She reached higher to clutch his thick hair in her fingers. "I don't want dinner, and my hair is probably a mess."

"That's fine with me. I want everyone to know what I just did to you."

"No. Let's go home. To my house."

He moved his mouth down to her wrist and nipped her skin. A sting of pleasure shot through her. "I don't want you to be home alone tonight."

She smiled as he kissed his way up her arm. "Good," she whispered. "I was hoping you'd say that."

Chapter 10

They ordered pizza and ate it in Sally's bed. Greasy pizza with a doughy crust and pepperoni, and she didn't give a thought to her eight-hundred-fifty-thread-count sheets or the fact that she had a kitchen table that was perfectly suited for such meals. Ben ate the pizza without his shirt on, his broad chest on full display. Sally liked that he had dark hair there that she could rake her fingers through.

"This is my favorite pizza," she confessed through a mouthful. "I haven't had it in months, though."

"It's great pizza," he agreed.

"Sometimes I miss New York style. You know, the thin crust and large triangular slices. But this is what I grew up on—small, square pizza slices."

"And pizza corners." He lifted a little triangle of crust. "Me, too. As far as I'm concerned, there's enough room in the world for square pizza."

She laughed and tucked her legs beneath her. "It's weird, I guess. Pizza corners. I don't know why they cut it that way."

He bit into the piece and chewed thoughtfully before delivering his verdict. "Best part of the pie."

She couldn't remember ever eating pizza in bed with another man, but being with Ben this way felt oddly comfortable. She could tell by the curve of his shoulders that he was relaxed and enjoying himself, too. They'd shared a delicious tryst at the wedding reception, and now they were sharing a delicious pizza. The progression was natural.

"I keep forgetting that you grew up around here," she said.

"That's right. Just outside of Bedford, not too far from the reception."

Sally flushed at the memory, then lifted a clump of melted cheese to her mouth. "This is so much better than the fish dinner that was going to be waiting for me," she mused. "But maybe not better than your steak."

"Maybe not," he said with a half grin. "But then again, everything tastes better when you're eating it in a beautiful woman's bed."

She sighed at the slice she held in her fingers. "I'll bet you say that to all the girls."

His tone took on a more serious note. "Just the ones I like."

If he was waiting for a response, she resolved to disappoint him. The man was such a flirt. All of this was for fun, she reminded herself. Not for keeps. Last time, she'd thought it was for keeps, and that had landed her with a broken heart and a boatload of humiliation. This time it was strictly recreational, and that was fine with her. He was sure to head for the hills once he found out about the baby.

She took a sip of her water, not wanting to dwell on the inevitable. She felt beautiful at the moment, and wasn't that worth savoring? "This is better than butternut squash ravioli with my parents, admit it. Or dinner in a stuffy restaurant. My idea of a dinner date is much better than yours."

He held up his palms in surrender. "You got me there. I never would've guessed you were a pepperoni pizza in bed kind of girl. I'd pegged you for an escargot and *fois gras* type."

She wrinkled her nose and pinched a piece of melted cheese between her fingers. "Gross. You must think I grew up at the yacht club or something. My childhood was pretty normal."

"I find that hard to believe. You had cocktail hour every night with your parents."

She shrugged and waved a hand dismissively. "They wanted us to grow up to be comfortable in social situations, that's all. It was part of teaching me manners." The irony wasn't lost on her as she popped her fingertips into her mouth one at a time. "And see? I'm charming and full of class."

Actually, she'd never done anything like this before. Pizza in bed. Without plates. Without napkins. In shorts and a T-shirt. With a hot, shirtless man. Every element about this was new, and she was fairly certain that she'd never relive this experience with anyone else, either. Sometimes people were just *right* to do wrong things with. Ben was right for a lot of wrong things, and as she licked her fingertips, she hoped he wasn't about to get serious on her and demand she find a napkin. That would pretty much end the party right there.

Handing her a napkin appeared to be the furthest thing from his mind. He was watching her with a look of pain, as if she'd just tortured him by cleaning off her fingers like that. "What?"

He didn't reply. Instead he placed his pizza into the box before sliding it off the bed and onto an end table. "You know what," he said as he crept toward her, his muscular body inching up between her legs. "You drive me crazy, and you know it. You always have."

When he brought his lips down to hers, she surrendered to his touch, easing herself back against the bed as he pulled her knees apart. She closed her eyes and sighed at the feel of him, the weight and warmth of his body. A chill shot down her side as she felt his lips trace the sensitive skin of her jawline, the delicious thrill of his breath in her ear. "Sally. All these years apart, and all of my best intentions, and here I am, right here at your mercy. Why can't I get you out of my head?"

Those were her thoughts exactly, but she couldn't respond as he pressed his warm lips against the spot beneath her earlobe. He wasn't waiting for a response to his question, and she no longer had one to give, other than to tug at the steel muscles of his arms, pulling him closer.

He ran his hands along her sides, shifting her shorts down in one quick motion. Sally brought her hands up across his back and closed her eyes to experience him better: his taste, his moans, the feel of his skin against hers. She heard the sound of a wrapper as he opened a condom. At some point he'd removed the rest of his clothing, and when he entered her, she was nearly aching with need for him.

He was slower this time, his thrusts hard, deep and controlled, his breath steady in her ear. She wrapped her legs behind his back and clutched at his shoulders, slippery with a sheen of light sweat. He felt perfect. They felt perfect together, and as she shuddered with the force of her climax, she tried to bury the very real fear in the back of her mind: that this was Ben, and all these feelings were nothing but an illusion.

They slept in the nude, her back snuggled up against his front, his arm draped over her side. Her hair tickled his nose. He brought his hand up to brush it away from his face. She sighed and shifted in her sleep at the contact, pressing her perfect little bottom against his pelvis.

He lay in her bed, in her expensive pink sheets, listening to her breath and feeling the heat from her body. Sally was every bit the sweet, smart girl he'd once pretended she wasn't. She was exactly who he'd hoped she was. The only difference was that now he was mature enough to appreciate her. Lying next to her, he felt larger than himself, as if she was the better part of him.

He stroked his fingertips up the length of her arm and across the slope of her shoulder. Even her skin felt expensive, as if she'd bathed in exotic oils. He pressed his lips to a spot at the back of her neck, beneath her earlobe, and heard her sigh. Seconds later, she glanced over her shoulder and gave him a smile. "Morning," she said.

"Good morning." Though it was almost afternoon.

She tensed her body as she stretched and yawned, then rolled over onto her back to stare up at him. Ben positioned himself on one arm, staring down at her brown eyes and bow-shaped lips. He could get used to waking up like this every morning.

"I'll make breakfast," she said. "Eggs and bacon okay with you?"

"Perfect."

She smiled and slipped out from between the sheets, darting quickly to a bathrobe slung over a chair beside her bed. She shrugged into the pink robe and cinched it tight at the waist, tying a double knot. Then she left the room without another word, closing the door behind her.

Ben yawned and sat up. His clothes were scattered around the room. He reached for his boxer shorts and T-shirt and pulled them on. The old Ben wouldn't have stayed the night. That Ben would have left after pizza, promised to call in the morning and promptly forgotten about it. He felt different now. He wanted to stay, and he wanted to tread lightly. He wanted to do whatever was right to avoid hurting Sally again or sending her the wrong message. He liked her a whole hell of a lot more than he'd expected.

But how to act now? What was *this,* exactly? It felt like more than a one-night stand to him, but he wasn't sure what to do about it. Ass backward, he thought wryly, running a hand through his hair. He'd slept with her first, and now he had to find a thread to follow, to figure out how to get back to where they should have been. They should've had a proper dinner, not pizza in bed. Pizza in bed was too damn casual, and nothing about what he was feeling was casual. His feelings were more in line with an expensive meal at a restaurant he could barely afford that served foods in languages he could barely understand. An impressive meal, to match his impressive feelings.

She was phenomenal. She laughed easily and said the right things. She worried too much about his feelings and didn't pass judgment for his mistakes. She'd held his hand at the wedding. *She'd* held *his* hand, and that just about killed him, right there. That after he'd been pretty much the worst person he could be to her, she'd cared enough to reach out and hold his hand, and to worry that he was hurting. No, he owed her a real date, with flowers and dinner at a table in a restaurant. He wanted to take care of her, to make her as happy as she'd made him. Because he was happy, as if he'd been freed of some burden. If Sally could forgive him, then maybe he could forgive himself.

He walked into the kitchen and paused in the doorway, taking in her home. The back of the kitchen was composed almost entirely of windows that overlooked Avon Lake. The water was glassy and reflected the vibrant autumn leaves that surrounded the lake. The house itself was more simple than he'd anticipated. Small, intimate spaces that contrasted with her family's austere mansion. Sally had preserved certain details, such as a wooden door on the wall that had once opened onto an icebox, and a deep, white ceramic kitchen sink. But the house wasn't dated or musty. She'd placed mirrors strategically to bring more light to the small kitchen, and she'd set a small bouquet of flowers in a blue glass vase in the middle of the wide kitchen table. Her home was bright and cheerful. Optimistic, even—something classic dressed up with modern flair.

"I didn't give you the tour last night," she said with her back to him, as if she could read his thoughts. "This was a vacation cabin, built in the twenties. Two bedrooms, two baths. The kitchen is new." She gestured to the white cabinets and light brown granite countertops. "My parents just about died when I first brought them here. Some of the walls were moldy, and the back porch... Well, let's not even talk about the back porch." She laughed over her shoulder and scooped coffee into a filter. "Mold, wood rot. That was the first thing to go. I took a sledgehammer to it. Very therapeutic, by the way."

Ben ran his fingers across the smooth, polished wood of the doorway. It looked like oak, a toffee color with the thick rings of an aged tree. "You restored this place yourself?"

He detected a hint of pride in her smile. "Not *myself,* exactly. I'm not handy with a table saw. But I can design and I can oversee, and I can whip a contractor into shape like that." She snapped her fingers. "It's been a labor of love, bringing this old home back to life. My ex never really understood." She poured water into the coffeemaker in a slow, steady stream. "He didn't want to live here. It's too small for a family."

Ben brought his hand down and leaned one shoulder against the frame. "You wanted a family."

"Yes." The answer came quickly. "But I'm glad we didn't have one together."

She pressed a little button on the coffeemaker that illuminated a red light, then brushed her palms down the front of her robe. She'd already set a carton of eggs and a package of bacon on the counter, and she had a cast-iron pan heating on the stove. A silver teakettle began to hum.

"How about you, Ben?" she asked as she cracked an egg into the pan. "Are you the family type?"

He came closer to lean across the breakfast counter, eschewing the wooden stools she'd set out. "Never really thought about it," he confessed. "My dad died when I was fifteen, but before that he didn't come around much."

"Your parents were divorced?"

"No, just hated each other." This wasn't something he talked about, mostly because hearing those words out loud wrought something inside of him. "The biggest problem was Dad had girlfriends. Lots of them, but I didn't figure that out until his funeral, when all these strange women showed up, sobbing like they'd lost the love of their lives. Maybe some of them had."

Sally didn't turn as she prepared breakfast, but he saw that her face had taken on a pained expression. "I'm sorry."

"About his extracurricular activities?" He tried to joke about it, but the words fell flat.

"About that, and his death at a young age. All of it. I had no idea." She looked back at him. "I don't mean to pry...."

"You want to know how he died." Everyone Ben told always wanted to know how his father had died. "He took me and my brother camping over the July Fourth holiday, and we went fishing. He'd been drinking a lot, and he wanted us to dare him to touch the bottom of the lake." Ben shrugged. "We did that all the time. Stupid dares. Just guy stuff. And I agreed that, fine, he should go touch the bottom of the lake and bring up some of the sand to prove he'd been there. I didn't care about it, but he wanted to do it."

Ben paused, remembering the shudder of the little boat as his father jumped into the water for the last time. Ben and his brother had looked over the side and watched him sink to the bottom, bubbles gurgling behind him. Then they'd waited. And waited. And eventually they'd realized that too much time had passed. "They didn't find him for a day," he said through a painfully tight throat. He shook his head. "I saw his body when they pulled it up. I wasn't supposed to."

He looked up. At some point during the story, Sally had turned to face him, leaning her back against the countertop. Her forehead was creased. "That must have been shocking," she said softly. "Drowning victims, they don't even look like themselves."

He'd fought for years to get the image of his father's bloated body out of his head, and he didn't want to think about it now. "I got over it," he said. "But it took a lot of self-medication to get there. I watched my father drown, Sally." A fist closed over his heart and twisted the organ in place. "I could have jumped in. I should have, but I waited."

She hesitated, then turned back to the stove to lift the pan from the heat. The kitchen was warm with the smells of bacon and coffee. The teakettle whistled. He waited for her to say the same things everyone always said: that he couldn't blame himself, he was just a child, his father wouldn't have wanted him to live with that guilt. But she didn't say any of it. Instead, she prepared two steaming plates of food and brought them over to him before turning to get coffee and tea. The silence was unexpected, but appreciated.

He sat in one of the stools, and she took the one next to him after handing him a cup of coffee. "You take it black with no sugar," she said. "I remember that."

From ten years ago? She had a good memory. He did, too, only when it came to Sally. She took her coffee with milk, and she never drank it when it was hot. She preferred to wait until it was lukewarm, and then she liked to drink it all at once rather than sip it. He'd never met anyone who gulped their coffee. Today, however, she was drinking herbal tea. That was new.

She wrapped her fingers around her mug and sat for a moment. "You're waiting for me to lecture you about your guilt, aren't you? You've probably been told that your father's death wasn't your fault, right? But that doesn't take away the pain. You feel what you feel, and it shouldn't be dismissed."

He considered her words before taking a bite of eggs. "You sound like you're speaking from experience."

She tilted her head. "I just know what it's like when people tell you how you should feel or what you should do about something. Those people almost always have their own interests in mind. I hate to hear you say that you blame yourself for your father's death, but who am I to tell you that you shouldn't? That would just be me telling you that your feelings make me uncomfortable and I don't want to listen anymore." She blew the steam over the top of her tea. "This may surprise you, but I've been told I'm unconventional. I don't always act the way I should, either."

She spared a glance from the corner of her eye, and

he smiled. "I've always been told that I'm painfully boring. Maybe we balance to normal."

They ate their breakfast in a silence that didn't feel uncomfortable. The eggs were slightly bland and the bacon was salty, and the coffee had a strong flavor like dark chocolate. Ben devoured everything on his plate, grateful for a companion who didn't presume to tell him what he should feel about something as complicated as his father's death.

Sally was startled when the phone rang. She looked at Ben. "It's Sunday morning," she mumbled. "No one calls me on Sunday." She reached for the phone and frowned at the caller ID. Bedford Hills Police Department. "Hello?"

"Miss Dawson? This is Officer Mark Rutherford from the Bedford Hills P.D. I understand your car windshield was vandalized on Friday, and I wanted you to know we made an arrest."

Perched on the edge of her seat, she felt as if her heart had overturned and spilled its contents. "An arrest?" she repeated. "Who?"

"Kid by the name of James Kruger. You know him?"

She slumped, bringing her head down to rest on her hand. Ben was watching her, but she didn't want to explain. "Yes, I know him. Did he confess?"

"We asked around and got an ID from a witness who saw him throw the bat away in the park. Wit saw his license plate. We made the arrest this morning. We're holding him downtown. Thought you might want to talk to him."

James Kruger had smashed her windshield. She

grappled with the news. Poor, misguided James. What did he think he was doing?

"Ma'am? You still there?"

She exhaled. "Yes. Still here. Look, did he say *why* he did it? Give any indication? It's just that I know him, and this doesn't seem like something he would do."

Now Ben had turned toward her, wrapping one muscular arm across the back of her stool. He dipped his head to study her, but she stared straight down at the countertop, avoiding his gaze. He was close, and right now it felt *too* close.

"He didn't say anything," the officer continued. "But he did seem concerned that you would find out. I wanted to confirm that you knew each other and that we weren't dealing with a potential stalker situation."

A shiver ran down her back at the suggestion that James Kruger might be stalking her. She was certain she would notice something like that. She knew him and his car, so wouldn't it be virtually impossible for him to watch her, hidden from view? "I don't think so," she concluded. "He was going to testify in a case I was supposed to bring. That's how we know each other. He's a good kid. I think he just made a bad decision."

"He resisted arrest, took a swing at an officer."

Sally groaned. This just kept getting worse.

"Bail hearings won't be until tomorrow, so he'll be locked up until then," the officer continued. "You're welcome to come down and scare him a little."

She tugged at her earlobe. She hadn't removed her earrings last night, and she twisted the diamond between her fingers. Maybe she would speak with him. Then again, maybe she should steer clear of James and take this as a sign that her impression of him was askew. He was more than troubled. He was a potential threat to her safety. "I'll think about it. Thanks for all the information, Officer. I appreciate it."

"You got it."

She hung up the phone and set it back on the countertop. Then she pushed a forkful of eggs around her plate and took a bite. They were cold already. Besides, she felt a little nauseous, as if the little life she carried was starting to assert itself.

"Are you going to tell me what happened just now?" Ben leaned closer, resting his forearm on the countertop so that his arms practically encircled her. He had no right to take such a possessive posture. They'd spent the night together, but last time she'd checked, they hadn't been the ones getting married yesterday.

She leaned slightly away. "The police arrested James Kruger for smashing my windshield," she said, her voice soft and constrained. "That's all."

"Huh." Ben sat back and took a sip of his coffee. "Call it a hunch, but I thought that kid was up to no good."

Her gaze darted to him. "Oh, really? Based on what? The stains on his clothes? His piercings?"

She'd known James for almost a year, and in that time she'd witnessed him traverse hell. His mother was presumed dead, murdered by his father, and James had been brave enough to testify for the prosecution. That meant he'd been homeless, orphaned, for all intents and purposes. Then his mother had suddenly come back to life, and whether she was guilty of some conspiracy or worse, he'd realized only last week that everything he'd come to believe was wrong. He was a confused teenager who'd made a terrible mistake when he'd attacked her car, and Ben didn't know the first thing about it.

"Calm down." Ben lowered his mug to the counter. "The kid made a threat against you. I know you feel protective over him for some reason, but I'm telling you, he's got problems."

She fumed silently. "You wouldn't know the first thing about his problems. He's in a holding cell. I think I'm going to go down to talk to him this morning."

"That's foolish," Ben grumbled as he took another gulp of coffee.

"Oh, really? Foolish?" Something danced up the back of her spine. Was he actually trying to control her? "Last time I checked, I'm a grown woman. I sure as hell don't need you approving my every move."

"Suit yourself." His tone had taken on a frostbitten edge. "The kid has directed a lot of anger toward you. By all means, you should go spend the afternoon with him in jail. Maybe invite him to dinner."

She grabbed her plate, still piled with cold eggs, along with her fork and mug, and marched to the sink. "You have no idea what he's been through. And you're one to be judgmental." She scraped the eggs into the trash and spun around to face him.

Now Ben was frozen in place, waiting for her to elaborate. His eyes had narrowed and taken on a dangerously dark appearance. "What's that supposed to mean? I'm one to be judgmental?"

She knew she was walking down a dangerous path, but it was too late to stop now. Even if she could, she wasn't sure she wanted to. How dare he come into her house, as nothing more than a casual fling, and ask her who she'd been talking to on the phone? How dare he walk into the kitchen and tell her about his father's death and compliment her cooking? How dare he treat this as anything more significant than what it was: A one-night stand? Two lonely people who got a little carried away and took comfort in the wrong way. How dare he string her along?

Sally prided herself on keeping an open mind, but she knew one thing for sure—she was not girlfriend material, and Ben was not boyfriend material. Last night meant less than nothing to her. The only man in her life was Mr. X. No more betrayal, no more disappointments and no more relinquishing part of herself to be more desirable to someone else. She'd decided months ago that it was time to be unapologetically herself, flaws and all. No more boyfriends or fiancés who could pretend to love her and then walk away. No more.

"Yes," she replied in a dangerous voice. "You're one to be judgmental. Who are you to stand in judgment of a young man—a *teenager*—who just learned that his father didn't murder his mother? I don't know why James did what he did, but I'm not prepared to pronounce him a bad person, or to say that he's clearly up to no good." She placed her hands on her hips, daring Ben to defy her. "You, Ben. *You,* who've made some giant mistakes in your life. Who are you to judge him?"

He didn't flinch. He didn't move at all. She wished he would stop staring at her in shocked silence. She was being rotten. He'd confided in her, and she'd turned around and used his confessions as weapons. Her words sounded like a betrayal even to her own ears, but there was nothing she could do to take it back.

He looked down, as if something fascinating had

materialized on his plate. She heard him exhale. "I think you should be careful who you trust, that's all."

"I didn't invite you here to give me lessons on interpersonal relationships," she said. "But since we're both sharing, you should know that I think last night was a mistake."

He sat in stunned silence, and her heart beat painfully in her chest. Then he rose and left the kitchen, leaving his dirty plate behind.

Sally crossed her arms and leaned against the sink, listening as he moved around the bedroom. A part of her wanted to extend the olive branch, run in and apologize for overreacting. Salvage the past two weeks with Ben and try to make something good come out of the past twenty-four hours. The rest of her knew that this was the right thing, to let him be angry as hell with her and walk out the door. They shared a misguided physical chemistry, that's all. Besides, they worked together. They should have thought harder about keeping their relationship professional, and she'd rather err on the side of hating each others' guts than getting too friendly. Hating each other was easy. Attraction was complicated.

He came back into the kitchen wearing the jeans and Columbia Law sweatshirt he'd found in his car the night before. He didn't just look angry; his face had assumed a mask of absolute fury, and he paused in the kitchen doorway, clutching the ball of clothing that comprised his tuxedo, and jingling his keys in his hand. He spared her a sharp smile that ripped through her. No doubt that was his intention. "Thanks for everything, Sally," he said. "You've always been a good lay."

Her body went rigid, her muscles contracting in a painful, white-hot rage as she watched him walk calmly out the door. She listened as he started his car and backed down her driveway, waiting until he was out of earshot before sliding to the kitchen floor and sobbing.

Chapter 11

A cold front had rolled in overnight, and the bright afternoon sun did little to soften the brusque air that swept across Sally's bare neck. She pulled her coat tighter around her frame. She'd been raised in a family of skiers, but if she had her way, she'd flee the Northeast after the leaves turned, and stay far, far away until spring. This was the time of year when her fingertips frosted over and her nose turned pink, and she found herself thinking bitter, self-pitying thoughts as she approached the police station.

A good lay. Was that all she was to him, even now? The cruelty of that pronouncement stung her. Here she was, about to be a mother, and she'd gone and lost her head over Ben McNamara. *Again.* She pressed her palm protectively against her abdomen. She was going to have to be better than this. More mature, more responsible. She was supposed to be moving past men and the pain of relationships, insulating herself from heartache. Yet now she felt that old familiar twinge in her chest. Worst of all? She'd have to face him in the morning. At work.

How mortifying.

Sally pulled her shoulders back and lifted her chin. She'd become involved with Ben again, and heartache was inevitable. She knew his type, and she knew *him*. Better to take her medicine, feel all the pain at once and move on with her life. One thing she now knew for sure: she wanted something lasting. The fleeting connection she'd felt with Ben last night, the intimacy of pizza in bed and meaningful conversation, made her long for permanency. She might never find a man who fulfilled that need in her, but that didn't mean her life was destined to be empty. Having a child, someone she could care for and love without fear of rejection, would go a long way toward making her feel as if her life was full.

Maybe Ben was right about James, she thought as she filled out visitor paperwork at the police station. God knows she was awfully good at picking the wrong men, the ones who hurt her and used her and failed to value her for who she was. But something in her told her that he was wrong. James had something different about him, that essence of someone who'd always had trouble fitting in.

Sally was aware of the many privileges she'd had growing up: loving parents, a big house and minimal cares about money. She'd chosen a profession based on a desire to make a difference, not a need to make money. She was fortunate in so many ways, and yet part of her understood what it felt like to be misunderstood. She'd heard the whispers that had followed her through school, replete with implications that she'd bought her way in. The blessings in her life had been cause for others to judge her as unworthy of her achievements, and she'd spent her entire professional life trying to prove herself not only competent, but exemplary.

Still, she couldn't afford to misplace her sympathies with James. Hadn't she done exactly that last night with Ben, and allowed her heart to guide her head? And wasn't she paying for it now?

Her temples were pounding with the pressure of too many rapid-fire thoughts. Yes, she was paying for her transgression. She was paying dearly.

"Counselor. Nice to meet you." The man who held out his hand stood over six feet tall and carried the air of someone all-American. Maybe it was the blue eyes and blond hair, or the fact that he could have just walked off a college football field. Rutherford, she read on his tag. He looked as young as he'd sounded on the phone. Cops were getting younger and younger. "I'm guessing you're here to speak with our mutual friend?"

"James Kruger, yes," she answered, still feeling oddly protective of James. She'd known lots of people who were in jail—it was part of the job description—but she'd never actually cared about any of them on a personal level. Now, as they walked through the station to the holding cell, she noticed the smells of body odor and fluids. Some of these people had been locked up since brawling in a bar on Friday night, and they wouldn't get to shower before the bail hearing tomorrow. She'd learned long ago to chew mints in court on

Monday morning to mask the odor, but to think that James was locked up here, unable to escape it…

She gritted her teeth. She was being too soft on him. The punk had broken her windshield.

Officer Rutherford opened an interrogation room and invited her to take a seat. Sally pulled out the cold chair and obliged. The table looked dirty. Best not to think about the kinds of things that went on in this room, or the sweat and tears that had been spilled on the Formica. Her nose wrinkled. Honestly, did no one clean this place? A little bleach would go a long way.

Footsteps fell in the hall outside the doorway. She lifted her chin, preparing to stare James down and make him sorry he'd ever messed with her. Then she saw him. A purple welt was starting to swell beneath his left eye, and his black sweatshirt was torn at the collar. Officer Rutherford had cuffed him, and he looked gangly and harmless, like a pathetic scarecrow. Sally sucked in a breath. "My God, James. What happened to you?"

He eyed her warily. "Some guy sucker punched me."

Officer Rutherford, gripping him by the shoulders, steered the kid toward the second chair and then pushed him into it. "Come on, Jimmy. Sucker punch? You've been picking fights right and left today. First with us, then with your roommates."

"I didn't do anything to him," he mumbled through clenched teeth, before looking imploringly at Sally. "I swear, he just hit me."

She swallowed, suddenly uneasy with her mission. She'd been set to give him a piece of her mind, and now the poor kid was getting punched by men who were probably twice his size. "Don't you have someone watching the cell? Shouldn't they prevent this kind of thing?"

Rutherford gave her a half smirk, as if he found her question adorable. She ground her fingernails into her palms, fighting the urge to give this condescending officer a piece of her mind. "Fifteen minutes," he said, more to James than to her. "I'll be watching the whole time." That last part was directed to Sally.

She nodded. "Our conversation will be private, I hope."

"Whatever." The young officer shrugged and walked out the door. James Kruger was small-time. She doubted the police would take any interest in a single word of their discussion.

As the metal door clicked shut, Sally released a sigh and directed her best disappointed face to the youth in front of her. He avoided eye contact, preferring to stare at a spot on the table. "You know," he mumbled.

"Of course I know, James. Why do you think I'm here?" She brought her fists to the table. "You broke my windshield. I thought we had a good relationship. I never thought you'd...violate my trust like that."

He swallowed hard and looked as if he was about to cry. He brought his handcuffed hands up to rub at his eyes, which were turning red at the edges. "I'm really sorry, Attorney Dawson," he sputtered.

Her shoulders slumped. She couldn't very well continue the disappointed-teacher routine *now,* when the kid looked like he was on the verge of sobbing. "Fine. Okay. You're sorry. But why in the world would it cross your mind to do something like this in the first place? What did I do to you, James?"

He sniffled again, triggering an ache in her heart.

Despite being eighteen years old, he was so young and vulnerable. Bait for bullies in the holding cell. No wonder they'd already punched him in the face, and she worried they'd do something worse. "You didn't do anything to me," he answered softly. "You were always nice to me."

"Then for God's sake, why would you smash my windshield?"

He gazed around the room, blinking back the tears that rimmed his irises. "I was hoping you'd back off on this investigation. I don't want anything bad to happen to you."

"Back off on the investigation? You mean of your dad?"

"Yeah." He sniffed. "He knows, Attorney Dawson. He knows that you're all trying to lock him up again."

"How do you know that?"

"'Cause I heard him talking to my mom about it. They know that the cops are digging around, and they know it's because you're mad that my mom's still alive."

Sally's throat tightened, though whether from defensiveness or the cutting truth of his statement, she couldn't be sure. She leaned closer. "James, listen to me. I would never, ever be mad that your mom is alive. Don't you realize this is the best ending possible in any kind of homicide investigation? It's something I always wish would happen when I spend day after day thinking about horrible endings. Having her come back to life is like waking from a nightmare."

He cocked his head, unconvinced. "Then what are you looking for, if not to lock up my dad again?"

She blinked. She'd never said she wasn't looking to

imprison his father. "James, you told me that you saw a body in that house on the night your mom allegedly disappeared. We have to investigate that."

He sat back in his chair with slumped shoulders. "I was stoned that night. I was seeing things."

"Is that what you really think? That you were hallucinating?"

His gaze swept across the table, and he continued to avoid her eyes. "No."

She exhaled. "I didn't think so." He sat in frozen silence, his posture as still as the thick air. "You know I'm on your side, James, right? I didn't come down here to upset you or to give you grief. In fact, I'm willing to drop the charges—at least as far as my windshield goes."

That got his attention, though the look he gave her from beneath his eyelashes was still heavy with suspicion. "Seriously?"

"I swear." She folded her hands in front of her and rested them on the table. "But I want you to stay out of trouble, got it? No more interventions where your dad and I are concerned. I can take care of myself."

He nodded slowly, not fully convinced. "Okay."

She bit the inside of her cheek, debating whether she should continue to press him. Their fifteen minutes had to be almost up by now, and the poor kid had another night in jail before his hearing in the morning. She wasn't sure whether she should burden him.

Curiosity prevailed.

"James." Her voice lowered to a whisper. "Tell me everything you know about your aunt, Mary Ann Hennessy. And we don't have much time, so talk quickly."

He blinked at her. "Aunt Mary? What about her?"

"She and your mom. Were they close?"

His eyebrows drew together as he considered the question. "Sure, yeah."

"How close? Did they talk on the phone, go shopping together, what?"

"Close. I mean, Aunt Mary had leukemia and Mom donated her bone marrow. They were close."

"How long ago did she have cancer? Was this recent?"

He raised one shoulder. "Five years ago, maybe. She used to come around a lot for visits, like, stay for the weekend, but then it stopped. There was some kind of argument, I think."

Now they might be getting somewhere. "An argument? When was this?"

"I don't know. A couple years ago?"

"After the bone marrow transplant."

"Yeah."

The doorknob turned, and Rutherford reappeared. "Time's up."

Sally's heart felt cleaved in half at the look of pure dread that passed over James's face. It was on the tip of her tongue to apologize to him for everything that had gone so terribly wrong in his life, because someone should. But then he rose and turned his back to her before her throat opened wide enough to allow the words passage.

Ben returned to his apartment and took a quick shower, but he didn't stay for long. He was too worked up to sit still, too angry to be alone with his thoughts. *Last night was a mistake.* He'd only been trying to help her, and no doubt she'd ignored him and gone off to meet with that kid. The woman was beyond help. Impulsive. Dramatic. He sped down the road, passing lazy Sunday drivers. She was five different kinds of impossible, and he'd been a fool to let his body call the shots the night before.

Ben didn't do relationships. They'd never ended well for him, and what was the point? Everyone died alone. The thought of being linked to someone else till death did them part, under penalty of law…maybe he'd believed in that myth at one point. It had its allure, like believing in Santa Claus or the tooth fairy. *Convince someone to marry you, and you'll never be lonely again!* Wouldn't that be nice, to find a soul mate, the person who fundamentally understood who you were and what you were about? But he no longer believed the hype. He'd seen too many marriages fall apart and too many relationships end badly. People betrayed you, or left you or sat back silently and watched you destroy yourself. He'd never known the loyalty and honesty that would make him believe that true love was possible. He didn't do relationships.

He could say it a thousand times, and that still didn't explain his fascination with Sally, or why he'd allowed himself to start believing at some point last night that he'd got it all wrong. That there was such a thing as true love, and he might be looking at his. And that was a ridiculous thought. A lust-drunk, impulsive, stupid thought, brought on by too many months in sexual isolation. He had physical needs, and his body could talk a good game, convincing his brain of things he didn't believe.

The car wound down a familiar row of streets to the place where he'd grown up. He immediately thought of Sally's parents' house, that massive stone atrocity. His parents' old farmhouse was quaint in comparison, even though the house was one of the most stately on Main Street. His mother had raised him and his brother alone, but she'd been fortunate to have a small trust fund to assist her, and his father's life insurance had covered some emergencies. She'd nevertheless stressed the virtues of financial modesty. Designer clothes? That would have earned him a lecture on the number of children who went without basic needs, such as breakfast, home heating fuel or winter coats. He'd splurged on expensive suits and designer ties, but that was with the money he'd earned out of law school, when he was working on Wall Street. His mom had never seen them.

He grimaced as the car tugged slightly toward the right of the road. The tires had been replaced, but they still weren't quite right. Mom would be proud of him for bargain hunting for car maintenance, he thought wryly.

His stepfather was away on business for a few nights. He rang the doorbell and tried the front door, but it was locked.

"Coming!" his mother's voice called from inside the house, and he heard the shuffle of her footsteps. "Ah, Ben!" She threw her arms around him and gave him a kiss on the cheek. "So nice of you to stop by."

"It's not really a social visit. I wanted to get to work on that ramp," he said.

His gaze lit on her left hand, which had curled into a permanent fist. He swallowed a lump in his throat. "How are you feeling, Mom?"

"Oh, fine," she replied brightly as if it was no big deal. "Let me get you something to eat."

"Maybe later." He still felt full from the breakfast he'd shared with Sally, or maybe he'd lost his appetite. "Like I said, I want to get started on the ramp."

She rolled her eyes and waved her right hand. He noticed she'd self-consciously tucked her left hand away from view, behind her back. "I don't know why you're so worried about this. It's not like I can't manage to get up the stairs anymore. I'm not an invalid."

Her clothes told him otherwise. She had difficulty dressing herself, and opted for sweaters that zipped in the front rather than ones she had to pull over her head. Her feet were protected by slippers because she couldn't tie or fasten her shoes by herself, but she refused to get anything with Velcro. She didn't want to believe she was a victim of Parkinson's, but that didn't mean the disease hadn't affected her life profoundly.

"I know you're not, Mom," he said gently, resting his hands on her upper arms. "But I want this to be ready just in case you need it, and this way I won't worry about you walking up those cement stairs in the winter."

He could see the answer didn't satisfy her, but she didn't argue. He kissed her on the cheek and turned toward the back door, where he would walk directly to the shed. He'd brought all the tools last weekend, and there was more than enough wood.

"You look different."

Her voice stopped him in his tracks, but he didn't turn to face her. "Yes, Mom, I'm eating enough." She was always worrying about stuff like that.

"No, that's not what I'm asking. You look like something is bothering you."

His shoulders tightened reflexively. "New job, settling back into civilian life. That's all." He gave her what he hoped was a reassuring smile over his shoulder. "Don't you worry about me."

She held his gaze, her own eyes warm with concern. "I always worry about you, Ben. You're my son."

Something in her tone touched a painful place in his chest. The part of her that always worried about him was probably the same part of him that always worried about her, and how much time they had left. He looked away, clenching and unclenching his fists just to have something else to focus on. "No need to worry."

He pushed open the back door and proceeded to the shed. He had the measurements already, and could do most of the cutting here. He had just cleared the area around the table saw when his cell phone rang. His pulse quickened as he saw the number. It was Sally.

"This is Ben."

"Ben?" she repeated in a voice that was slightly too high. She was nervous. That made two of them. "I'm sorry to call. You left some of your tux…pieces at my place."

Impatience rose in his chest, and he gripped the phone tighter. "I'm in the middle of something," he said. "Can you just bring them to work tomorrow?"

There was a long pause. "I shouldn't have said some of those things to you," she said. "That was wrong."

Hell, yes, it was wrong, he wanted to snap. Instead, he took a breath and set an eight-foot two-by-four on the table saw. "What's done is done."

"I'm apologizing here." Her voice was edged with a slight condescension. "You said something terrible to me, too."

A smile lifted his mouth as he realized how much

he missed Sally when she wasn't near. "I gave you a compliment."

"Telling me I'm a good lay is not a compliment."

"Even if it's true?" He smiled again at the icy silence of her response. "Fine, fine. You're right. I'm apologizing. Okay?"

"Okay." He heard her take a deep breath. "So, can I drop this stuff off to you? I'm running errands."

"Like I said, I'm busy right now."

"Oh? Doing what?"

Now she was getting nosy, but instead of the annoyance he would have felt with almost anyone else, he felt an odd pleasure pulse through him. "Working. On my mom's house."

"Oh."

"You're welcome to come over. Just throw on some ratty clothing, and don't bother wearing any makeup." He nearly laughed at the thought of Sally Dawson performing manual labor.

"Fine, I'll come over," she said.

The laugh caught in his throat. Damn. She was calling his bluff.

He gave her directions to the house, and she pulled up less than an hour later. To his surprise, she'd listened to him: her jeans were tattered at the edges and splattered in paint, and the sweatshirt she wore had a hole in the side. "You told me to dress down," she said defensively when she caught him eyeing her.

"I did. And you listened." He hadn't expected her to look quite so sexy. "You could set trends, you know. Tell me, is there any time when you look like a normal person and not a fashion model?"

She rolled her eyes, but her cheeks flushed charmingly. "Stop."

"Stop what?"

"Staring at me. Saying things like that." She waved her hands in the air awkwardly. "Making fun of me."

"I wasn't making fun of you," he replied solemnly. "I was being honest. I like you like this."

"Oh, yeah?" She cocked her head. "Like what?"

He scanned her figure with his index finger. "Like this. Relaxed in your favorite clothes. Your weekend jeans and an old sweatshirt. I'll bet you never let anyone see you in them—am I right?" He had the answer to his question when she sighed and looked away. "Yeah." He chuckled. "I'm right."

He stepped closer to her until their faces were inches apart. She let him approach, allowed him to invade her space. "I think you look sexy," he said in a low voice. "Don't get me wrong. I can appreciate the silk dresses and the high heels. In my eyes, you always look like the best-wrapped gift under the Christmas tree—the one I hope is mine, just so I can have the pleasure of unwrapping it. But this—" he reached out boldly to stroke the heavy cotton of her sweatshirt, pleased when he heard a sharp intake of breath at his touch "—*this* look isn't stiff and brand-new. This is worn and familiar. Classic. And I often get tired of brand-new, but I've never gotten tired of the worn and familiar."

He left his deepest thoughts unspoken. *What I wouldn't give for you to be a familiar fixture in my life.*

She twisted her mouth, her thoughts practically visible as she processed his words. "You're a sucker for nostalgia. Like your old car, and this old farmhouse."

He smiled. "Not much different from you and your

fixer-upper on the lake," he observed. "I'd say we both feel a connection with the past."

She raised her chin at the house. "It's a beautiful place. Has it been in your family for long?"

"Over a hundred years." He couldn't help the pride that came from that fact. How many families handed down homes anymore? "My great-grandfather James Prescott built the house himself."

"Prescott?" She snapped her gaze to his. "Are you related to Benjamin Prescott?"

"The Wall Street guru and local legend? Sure, he was my grandfather. I'm named after him."

This left her looking puzzled. "No offense, but I would've thought your family would be…I don't know. Living in the south of France or something."

"You mean rich?" He smiled and gave a quick shrug. "Between you and me, I guess I will be soon. I have a trust fund that my uncle set up when he died. But I don't have access to it until I'm thirty-five. Mom didn't want me to grow up to be a lazy, good-for-nothing silver spoon. She wants me to know the value of a dollar."

Sally's eyes widened. "I had no clue. Not that it matters." She shook her head. "It doesn't matter."

"How could you know, when I drive that old car?" He gave her a sly smile. "First thing I do on my thirty-fifth birthday? I'm going to buy a Porsche."

She was so cute, the way she turned her head demurely. Cute, contrite and rolling up her sleeves. "Anyway, I'm here to make up for my bad behavior. What are we building?"

He walked her around to the shed and showed her his plans for the ramp. She held boards in place while he hammered. She even cut a few herself. With a little instruction, she handled power tools fearlessly, and at the end of the afternoon, as the sun began to set, Ben had to admit that they'd accomplished much more together than he'd expected to accomplish alone. They stood in the front yard, admiring the modest beginnings of a sturdy ramp.

"How do you know how to build this?" she asked.

He shrugged. "I read about it. There are certain ways to calculate the rise so it's not too steep. It's just math."

"You're good with your hands." The words must have slipped out of her mouth before she realized what she was implying, because she immediately started to stammer, "D-don't get dirty thoughts about that."

"I'm a red-blooded man, Sally." He chuckled. "You know I'll get dirty thoughts any time a beautiful woman is around. They get downright colorful when she says things like that."

Sally's lips pressed tightly together. She nodded at the house, avoiding his gaze. "Is your mom going to come out to see it?"

"Maybe later. She's probably resting. She gets tired easily, and my stepfather has been traveling, so she has to do a lot of things for herself." He didn't want to have to explain that his mother was feeling self-conscious about the many things she could no longer do for herself, and had difficulty welcoming company, aside from close family and friends. She had so many parts of herself that she kept hidden these days.

"Oh." Sally shifted. "I'll go, then. It's getting late."

He wanted her to stay, but he wouldn't argue. He would make his mother something for dinner and head home himself. It had been a long weekend.

The moment of silence between them was penetrated by the sound of a door closing. Ben turned to see his mother approaching, wrapped in a knitted, cream-colored cardigan. Her hands were tucked into her pockets.

"Ben," she called in a warm tone that reminded him of happier days, "aren't you going to introduce me to your lovely friend?"

He stepped to his mother's side, reaching out a hand to steady her as she walked. She waved him off crossly. "I'm fine. Stop fussing."

"Mom, this is my colleague Sally Dawson. She was in the area and offered to help."

"Lovely to meet you, Sally. I'm Eleanor." She extended her right hand, which Sally gripped warmly. "Thank you so much for supervising my son today. I worry about him every time he fires up a saw, but it looks like he still has ten fingers."

Sally grinned. "Your son is a man of many talents. I had no idea he knew his way around a table saw."

"Takes after his father," Eleanor confided. "More bookish, though. What were those books you always had your nose buried in? Those detective novels?" She turned back to Sally. "He used to read them in bed with a flashlight."

Ben rolled his eyes. "Okay, Mom. Thanks. I'm sure Sally didn't come here expecting to hear about my childhood."

"Nonsense. I have to repay her in some way." Her eyes shone. "Stay for dinner. Both of you."

Before Sally could reply, Ben interjected, "She was just leaving. It's been a long day."

He thought he detected a flash of hurt passing across

Sally's face. Just as quickly as it appeared, it vanished. "Maybe another time, Eleanor," she said cheerfully.

"I'd like that very much." His mother turned to him and pulled him by the elbow. "You'll stay, though. I don't see you enough." She gave him a pat on the upper arm and headed back into the house.

Ben waited until his mother had closed the door behind her before he walked Sally to her car. She popped her trunk, momentarily disappearing from view, only to hand Ben a grocery bag stuffed with the rest of his tuxedo.

"I was in such a hurry," he said softly.

"I know."

She cleared her throat and looked uncomfortable. Suddenly Ben felt like an ass for declining his mother's dinner invitation for Sally. "You're welcome to stay for dinner," he said. "I didn't mean…I just thought you had to go—"

"It's fine," she said in a tone that made it clear she didn't mean it. "I'm pretty tired, anyway." She sniffed and opened the driver's side door. "I'm glad we were able to smooth things over. This is a good place for us to be. Teammates. Partners. We're just too…volatile any other way."

He nodded lamely as if he agreed. As if he hadn't been thinking just the opposite for the past few hours as they worked side by side. He couldn't be close to Sally without wanting to touch her. Being "partners" with her was some kind of a cruel joke.

"I agree," he said. "Let's keep it professional. Thanks for your help today. I know my mom appreciates it."

Sally nodded rapidly a few times before sinking into

the driver's seat. He waited while she fastened her seat belt and backed out of the driveway, his hands jammed into his pockets. She gave him a little wave as she set off down the street. The car was going faster than it should. The woman had such a lead foot.

He walked back into the house, greeted by the smell of garlic and basil marinara sauce simmering and pasta boiling. "Mom. You shouldn't be doing those things."

But she stood with her back to the stove, her arms crossed in front of her, leveling that same pointed look he'd received a hundred times. The one that told him he'd just screwed up. "All right, what did I do?" He sighed.

"I raised you better than to speak for a young woman," she said. "She wanted to stay for dinner. She likes you. A lot."

He didn't want to explain how complicated this thing was between him and Sally. He chose to duck the issue entirely. "You're right, I shouldn't have spoken for her. I'll apologize."

His mom made a sound like *harrumph,* but kept her eyes trained to him. "I know you, Ben. You're thinking this is complicated with you two. That's what you always think. You like this girl, but it's complicated, and you'll use that as your excuse to walk away. You know, you're not the first people to ever fall in love, but it doesn't come around very often." She tilted her head. "I've always preferred complications to loneliness. Maybe you need to think about whether you feel the same."

He ground his teeth, relieved when the water for the pasta bubbled over the side of the pot in a cascade of steam and hissing water. "Why don't you sit down," he said. "I'll finish dinner."

He had his back to her, and he didn't hear her move for several moments. Then he heard her sigh deeply in a way that told him she wasn't finished with the discussion, but only taking a break.

He tried not to think about the weight of her words as he drained the pasta into a metal colander in the sink, sending blasts of steam onto the kitchen windows. He returned the pasta to the pot, added some sauce and cooked it on the stove for a minute, his brain somewhere else entirely. He was thinking about Sally driving home alone to an empty house. He was thinking about her safety, and realizing that he wouldn't rest until Mitch Kruger was behind bars.

Chapter 12

Seven-eighteen in the morning. That meant that Mitch Kruger would be opening his garage door in six minutes, backing up his old pickup truck and driving off to work, just as he had each weekday morning for the past two weeks since Ben had started following him. *Trailing him.* Following sounded creepy.

Mitch Kruger was a physically fit man who looked to be in his forties, but was actually in his late thirties. Ben recalled James saying that his parents had been young when he was conceived, and James was only eighteen. In his mind, Ben had constructed Mitch Kruger to be a monster—a beast who frothed at the mouth and had biceps the size of thighs. Physical features that would coincide with his capacity for homicide, because Sally was right: Mitch Kruger had killed someone.

Ben couldn't prove it. Yet. But he'd received several

calls from Dan Maybury over the past few weeks, informing him of new developments in the Kruger case. Since the lab had identified hair possibly belonging to Mary Ann Hennessy on the infamous area rug, the police detectives had doubled their efforts to locate the missing woman, contacting her relatives in Pennsylvania and even looking for traces of her in Hawaii. They'd learned from the airlines that Mary had purchased a ticket to Hawaii and had boarded the plane to San Diego, but she'd never boarded the connection to Hawaii. Dan surmised that Ronnie Kruger had taken the flight in her place and had then taken a bus to Las Vegas. No one had seen or heard from Mary Ann in almost a year, as if she'd disappeared from the face of the earth.

Her family members had cooperated, at least. One brother had expressed some concern about her disappearance, but he claimed she'd been seeing someone before she'd left, and that the relationship had been all-consuming.

"Could've been a married man," Dan had explained. "This definitely sounded like a forbidden love of some kind."

Ben lowered the back of his seat so that he was barely visible in the vehicle window. Mary Ann may have planned to run away with this forbidden love of hers, but it looked as if something had gone wrong. The only question was whether the Kruger household had been her last stop.

As if on cue, the garage door opened, sputtering and jerking on squeaky wheels. Ben's pulse quickened the way it had every day so far. He knew what he'd been looking for the first time he'd followed Mitch Kruger:

some kind of clue or sign that Sally's hunch was correct, and that he'd murdered Mary Hennessy. That first morning he'd followed Mitch, taking note of his route to the hardware store. There were plenty of wooded areas on the way, lots of places where a body could be concealed and go unnoticed for a long time. Mitch had dumped the area rug on his way to work; he felt comfortable in this neighborhood, and may have left a body here. Now, as the routine stretched into weeks, Ben no longer knew what he was looking for. A slip up, or maybe a moment of carelessness. He waited for the truck to back out of the driveway and round the corner before he turned the key in the ignition and followed.

Officially, Ben was finished with his investigation. The report was completed and Jack had issued his approval. "Solid report," he'd said. "Looks like investigative error."

Ben supposed that was the only conclusion to draw. The investigators had missed the significance of certain pieces of evidence, most notably Mary Ann's hair on the area rug. The sisters lived in separate states and didn't speak to each other anymore; red flags should have been raised. Still, he doubted that there would be any repercussions. The police had been looking for Ronnie Kruger's body, and that had been a red herring.

Sally's job was safe. Not that they'd talked about it. For the past two weeks, they'd made significant efforts to avoid each other, and they'd been largely successful. Once they'd wound up in the kitchen at the same time, both of them with their coffee mugs in hand. They'd done an awkward dance, moving this way and that, each trying to give the other space, before muttering something about the size of the kitchen, and dropping their gazes to the floor.

So much for being partners. Ben had left a copy of his report in Sally's mailbox, just as he'd promised. He'd even waited twenty-four hours before turning it in to Jack, to see whether she would comment, but she hadn't. Everything between them seemed simultaneously finished and maddeningly unresolved.

He was no good at this courtship thing, anyway. What should he have brought a woman like Sally to indicate his interest? Flowers? Chocolates? Instead, he was hoping to bring her evidence of murder.

Ben followed Mitch from two cars behind. The pickup careened down the hill in front of him, approaching a scenic reservoir. What leaves remained on the trees clung to the branches in desperate brown clumps and spatters, shaking in the breeze. The day was cold, the ground covered in frost.

His spine straightened as the pickup turned abruptly off the road. This wasn't the usual routine. Ben tapped the brakes, his pulse kicking as he debated whether to turn around. Maybe Mitch had finally gotten wise.

He slowed his approach to the spot. The truck had continued along a dirt path that led deeper into the woods. If he followed Mitch now, he'd look suspicious. Ben swung onto the shoulder of the road and pulled the car to a stop. Damn, now what? Follow him on foot? The place looked empty. It was early morning in November, hardly the time most people would choose to visit the reservoir.

He slapped his palms against the steering wheel in frustration. Just as he was about to spin the car around and follow that same dirt track the truck had taken, the pickup came creeping out of the woods. Ben lowered himself in the seat, but Mitch didn't appear interested in him. He slowed the truck as he approached the main road, looking right and then left, and turned and drove the way he'd been heading.

The guy probably had to urinate, and here I was thinking he'd been checking up on a shallow grave.

Ben backed up the car and spun up the track. May as well check it out.

The route was riddled with lumps from protruding tree roots, and Ben clenched his jaw as the car careened from side to side deeper into the woods. He'd driven past the reservoir before, but never stopped to visit. Stone fences were common even in thick woods in this area—evidence of the region's farming past, and relics from a time when much of the forest land had been cleared for cattle. These, however, were dense, old woods that appeared to have been untouched for hundreds of years. As he drove through a grove of mature pines interspersed with bare birch limbs, he didn't see any stone walls.

A clearing appeared momentarily—a small parking lot. He pulled into a space and climbed out of his car. A large wooden guide post at the entrance to a trail directed visitors down five different paths, each designated by color. Ben scanned the parking area. Mitch must have come here, but the ground was too cold to reveal tire tracks. Ben followed the short, single rail fence that bounded the lot, looking for anything at all that would give him a clue as to why the pickup truck had pulled in here this morning. The morning air chilled his lungs, and the ground held firm beneath his feet. Something told him he might never know why Mitch had taken this detour, and that something began to eat at him.

A bright sun hovered just above the horizon, sparking a gleam on the ground that caught Ben's eye. It was something shiny, and as he drew closer, he saw it was silver. Not round enough to be a quarter. He pulled a tissue from his pocket and bent to pick it up, his heart pounding wildly as he carefully turned it over. It was a small oval-shaped locket, its clasp open to reveal an empty interior. That wasn't what he cared about. On the back, in elaborate script, were the initials MAH. Mary Ann Hennessy. He smiled.

Bingo.

Sally leaned over the sink to splash icy water on her face. The colder, the better. She cupped water in her palms and rinsed her mouth once, then twice. Her fingers trembled as she reached for a thin paper towel and blotted the moisture off her face. Then she straightened, catching a glimpse of her ashen complexion in the mirror. Balling the paper towel in her fist, she chastised herself for even caring what she looked like right now. There was no one to impress, and it was only a matter of time before everyone in the office realized that she'd been locking herself in the far bathroom stall and getting sick every morning.

"This will pass, honey," Tessa whispered from the next sink, eyeing her in the mirror. "I promise it will."

Sally groaned, not quite ready to stand upright. "How can this be worth it? How could I have wanted this?"

She closed her eyes and felt Tessa's hand on her lower back, rubbing in small circles. "I've heard that it gets better after the first trimester. How many weeks along are you?"

"Eight," she mumbled. Six more weeks until the second trimester. "Just kill me now."

She didn't wait for Tessa's response before stumbling out of the women's room and into the hallway. Keeping one hand against the wall, she slowly made her way, holding her breath as she walked past the kitchen, which promised the smell of freshly brewed coffee. Once she was safely in her office, she nearly dived into her desk drawer for the bag of peppermints, popped one into her mouth and sank into her chair. Her thoughts unwittingly turned to Ben.

He was going to find out she was pregnant, just as everyone else would. Naturally, he would wonder if the baby was his, and she'd have to explain that no, she'd actually been expecting before they slept together, but she'd neglected to tell him. A minor detail, really.

Her stomach lurched again. Her pregnancy wasn't any of his business, so why did all of this feel like a giant deception?

It wasn't as if she owed Ben anything, and they didn't exactly have an open, friendly relationship since they'd spent that night together, either. Nearly two weeks had passed since she'd helped Ben build the ramp for his mother. That night had been a mistake. There was no hope of being more than business colleagues, not with a baby on the way.

Sally kept to herself under the misguided belief that the awkwardness between them would diminish with each passing day. Rather than forgetting their shared night and settling into the casual friendship of coworkers, they became two people making great efforts to look as if they were oblivious to each other. She'd never been so aware of anyone in her entire life, and ignoring Ben was akin to ignoring a Tyrannosaurus rex in the room. At some point she was only fooling herself.

Sally rose from her chair and opened the blinds. She'd spent the evening before with her parents, packing up old books for a charity collection. She'd been supposed to do that a few weeks ago, but then Ben had accepted the invitation to dinner. He really shouldn't have done that. Now he was all her mother could talk to her about.

"What a nice young man," she'd said, her voice heavy with meaning. "Do you think he'll be over again sometime?"

"No," had been Sally's blunt reply. God, no. Never ever. "He's just a coworker."

"Really?" Her mother had arched an eyebrow in that knowing way that always made Sally's cheeks heat. "Because he looked at you as if he'd like to be a lot more than that."

For God's sake. She had never spoken with her mother about her love life, and she wasn't going to start now, especially when the man in question was Ben McNamara. How, exactly, would she explain that one?

Oh, well, you know how it is, Mom. We're both single and not interested in settling down. We had amazing sex in a wine cellar and then ate pizza in my bed. But it was strictly a one-time thing. Also, I'm pregnant by donor sperm.

Once again she'd chickened out on that last part, much too afraid to tell her parents she was expecting. Deciding to have a child was such a mature decision, and yet the thought of telling her mom and dad the truth left Sally feeling like a schoolgirl. They wanted her to find someone to marry, and she'd given up.

Sally rubbed her forehead. It wasn't even a one-time thing with Ben, was it? He'd broken her heart in law school, and then she'd gone back for seconds. There would be no third time. In this case, third time would *not* be the charm, it would be masochism.

And yet something about him drew her, and that made her feel out of control and desperate. She'd done her best to get over him, she really had, but in her misguided attempt to ignore him she'd succeeded in observing everything about him. She now knew the sound of his footsteps in the hall, and the sound of his laugh from three offices over. She knew he came into the office at eight-fifteen in the morning and that he always parked in the same spot, way at the back of the parking lot—she could see him from her window.

She knew he ate his lunch late and that he liked the food from the Spicy Thai truck down by the park. She overheard him talking to a coworker about his holiday plans—Christmas in Connecticut with his family— and how he'd spent the past weekend completing the ramp she'd helped him begin. By ignoring him, she'd managed to carefully catalog a host of interesting facts and tidbits, as if it was some dysfunctional dating ritual to know so much about her mate that she could calculate exactly where he would be at any given time so she wouldn't run into him. Which, by default, meant she knew his schedule. As if she were some crazed, creepy stalker. Which she was not.

Like right now, for instance, she'd have a clear path to go into the kitchen to grab a cup of coffee, except that her stomach couldn't handle coffee anymore. Just the thought of it… She closed her eyes to scrub her mind of the sensory memory. No coffee. No water, either. The thought of a big glass of water made her want to lose her breakfast…at least, it would have if she'd managed to choke anything down that morning. Tea sounded good, she decided. Herbal tea, preferably mint.

She settled at her desk minutes later with a steaming mug of peppermint tea and inhaled the vapors, feeling better already. She took a careful sip and waited for her stomach to settle down again. When she looked up, Ben's lean figure was darkening the doorway.

Her heart thundered and her gaze flew to the clock on her desk. Seven minutes after eight. He was early today. "Hello, Ben."

"Sally." He stepped farther into her office without waiting for an invitation. His eyes were lit with excitement. That scared her. "I have something for you."

She pushed her tea aside with deliberate slowness. "I'm afraid I'm not available for whatever help you're looking for. I have a full caseload, and now that you've finished your report on the Kruger case, it's time for us both to return to business as usual."

He cocked his head. "You're upset with me."

She started. "What? No. Why would I be upset with you?" She paused. "Are you upset with *me?*"

"No." He smiled disarmingly. "But I think we can both admit there's been some awkwardness between us lately, and last time we spoke, we'd agreed to be friends."

Yes, she remembered that well. She'd been half hoping that when she suggested they be friends, he'd look hurt or angry or give her some other indication that he vehemently disagreed with that path. He hadn't. She'd gambled and lost, and that had stung. "Fine, let's be friends." She smiled tightly. Friends who'd had hot sex. Nothing awkward about that.

"As a *friend,* I'm telling you that I'd love to help you with whatever little project you're about to propose, but I don't have the time. Sorry."

That was meant to be dismissive, and she'd just turned her eyes to her computer when he said, "I didn't mean I had work for you. I have a gift."

He was close to her desk, his waist hovering suggestively at eye level—was he doing that on purpose? She rolled her eyes at him and gathered her thoughts, trying not to reveal how breathless his unexpected appearance had made her. She should come up with something clever, some smart comeback that would let him know he was still on thin ice and he'd better tread carefully. "Whatever." She groaned inwardly. She was *so* lame.

"I'll take that as willingness to hear me out," he said, stepping closer to her desk.

He leaned forward and brazenly took her right hand from her tea, cupping it in his and dropping something in her palm. An electric current darted up her arm at the contact. "What—"

"Look at what I found this morning." He stepped back, taking his warm, strong hands with him and looking very pleased with himself. It was almost adorable.

Sally examined the necklace. It was silver and delicate, enclosed inside a small plastic bag, and her heart lurched at the thought that he'd actually gone out and purchased a gift for her. "I—I don't get it," she stammered, terrified that she'd have to remind him that they were a two-time thing only. Completely finished. "What am I supposed to do with this?"

"Turn it over." He gestured with his index finger. "It's engraved."

Her breath snagged in her lungs, but then she saw the letters. "MAH." She released a breath, feeling like an idiot. Of course he hadn't bought a gift for her. "I still don't understand—"

"Mary Ann Hennessy," he interjected. "Ronnie Kruger's sister. I've been following Mitch Kruger for a couple of weeks now, trailing him on his way to and from work, just to get familiar with his routine, see where he goes." Ben helped himself to a chair without waiting to be invited. "You can set your watch to this guy. He's backing out of his driveway at the same time every morning, only to return at the same time every night. Orderly doesn't begin to describe it. But this morning he threw me for a loop. He stopped at the reservoir, and when I investigated immediately after he left, I found that."

Sally knew she was staring at him. She probably looked as if she'd lost track of her faculties, with her eyes wide and her mouth hanging open as she tried to process this information. "You've been following Mitch Kruger," she said quietly. Then, "Wait a minute. You've been following Mitch Kruger?"

"Yes, I just told you that."

Sally placed the necklace on her desk blotter. "But *why?* I mean, don't you see how *insane* that is?" She rubbed at her temples with both hands. "You must be, what? Parking outside of his house? Following him to work?"

"Pretty much."

"Ben." She leaned forward and drilled her index finger against her desk to make a point. "Stalking a suspect? That's something *crazy* people do. Unless they have a warrant, in which case it's something the *police* do. Not us."

He leaned forward, undeterred. "And why not us, Sally? Why not? When the police have bungled this case and made it clear they aren't going to go any further without a body? Why can't we do a little investigating of our own?" He shrugged. "I haven't broken the law. I've just observed anything that anyone else could have observed."

"First of all, there's no 'we' about any of this. 'We' aren't investigating, *you* are investigating." That was number one, but she was so distracted by the flurry of thoughts in her head that she hadn't thought ahead to number two. Ben had been conducting his own private investigation of Mitch Kruger, even after he'd handed in his report to Jack? "And number two, aren't you done with this case? Aren't we both done?"

She'd been reluctant to even think about the case for weeks now, ever since she'd spoken to James Kruger in the interrogation room at the police department. "*I'm* done," Sally continued without waiting for Ben's response. "I spoke with James, you know. The day they picked him up for smashing my windshield."

Ben was maddeningly nonplussed by her confession. "And?"

"And I asked him to tell me all about his aunt Mary. Mary and Ronnie were only fifteen months apart in age and grew up to be very close. So close that when Mary Ann developed cancer about five years ago and needed a bone marrow transplant, Ronnie was the donor."

"So they were closer than we realized," Ben mused. "That's interesting."

"It is," she agreed carefully, "and it also gives me pause. The sisters were close, or at least not as distant as we thought, although James mentioned something about an argument a few years ago. Still, it's possible Mary came to visit Ronnie before whatever happened to precipitate this entire case. That would make the hairs on the area rug less suspicious, wouldn't it?"

He eyed her, sizing up the situation. "Sure. The reason the hairs on the rug are suspicious is that we thought Mary wouldn't be seen anywhere near Ronnie."

"I've been wrong before, Ben. Horribly, publicly wrong, and I can't make that kind of mistake again." Sally swallowed. "Pride goes before a fall and whatnot, and I can't let my pride get in the way of my common sense. We're grasping at straws, tortured theories and gut feelings when we say that Mary was killed. Everything about this case tells me I should back quietly away and move on." She avoided eye contact, not wanting him to realize that she included Ben in that "everything." "I thought I was doing something good at one point, bringing a murderer to justice, but I can't fight something I don't understand."

"But you were right. Did you read my report?" The intensity of Ben's cobalt-blue eyes sent her heart racing into a traitorous overdrive. "You were correct. Whatever her relationship with her sister, Mary Ann Hennessy is gone. She's vanished, and no one has seen or heard from her in almost a year. She had tickets to go to Hawaii, but only boarded the plane to San Diego. After that, she was never heard from again. You know what that means, right?" He leaned still closer. "Ronnie took that plane ride. That's how she got to Vegas. Sally, Mitch Kruger got away with murder, but we got him on the wrong victim."

She felt her anxiety mount. "And so what? Without a body, there isn't a damn thing anyone is going to do about this." She brushed her hair back. "I'm frustrated, too, believe me. But investigations take time, and sometimes they take luck. We've been unlucky so far, and enough time hasn't passed to turn our fortune around." She sighed. "It's not the right time for this. And it's not a good idea to follow Mitch Kruger. If you really believed he had committed murder and gotten away with it… The man is dangerous."

Ben leaned back in his chair with the calm air of a man in full control. "Sally, if I didn't know any better I'd think you were concerned for my well-being."

Her throat tightened, her face flushed and her mind went racing with all kinds of inappropriate memories of the last time he'd leveled that maddening confidence in her direction. Dammit. "Of course I'm concerned," she said, recovering as best she could. "I care about my colleagues, and I wouldn't want to see any of them turn up missing."

She could tell that hadn't been the answer he'd expected.

"But this locket proves that we're getting somewhere, and that my hunch is right," he said.

"And what hunch is this?"

"He knows we're looking for Mary Ann, and he's got trinkets linking him to her that he has to dispose of." Ben shrugged. "Maybe he's even got her body stashed somewhere, waiting until the coast is clear and hoping we'd all be so relieved that Ronnie Kruger is alive that we'd call the whole thing a domestic dispute and move on."

That was Sally's feeling, as well, but she wasn't quite ready to verbalize it. "We don't even know that this locket belonged to Mary," she noted. "MAH could be lots of people's initials."

He shook his head. "It's not even dirty, so it hasn't been outside or exposed to the elements. My guess is Mitch intended to throw it into the woods and instead it bounced off a tree and landed back in the parking lot. That would be quite a coincidence if it belonged to someone else, wouldn't it?"

"Yes," she mumbled. "That would be a coincidence." She traced her finger against the plastic bag, outlining the locket. "You could've talked to me these past weeks, you know. I'm not the enemy."

Out of the corner of her eye, she saw him adjust his posture, shifting slightly. "We were both feeling... strongly."

If that wasn't the understatement of the year. This was the problem with Ben, and with *them,* that she swung between wanting to rip his clothes off and wanting to slam the door in his face and never see him again. Except that lately, she leaned toward wanting to rip his clothes off. It was like she had no self-control. She lost her head when he was close by, thought things she didn't intend to think. Maybe those were only the pregnancy hormones speaking. She felt out of control in more ways than one these days.

"This isn't a reunion," she said quietly. "What happened a few weeks ago—" a flush bloomed on her cheeks at the memory "—that can't happen again."

He nodded. "I completely agree. That was a big mistake."

A mistake? Now wait a minute. "You… I mean… just because we're colleagues, and if Jack found out anything… I mean, there's nothing to find out. There can't be. We need to get back to being somewhat normal. Normal for us, at least."

Even as she said the words, she knew that *normal* would never factor into what she felt for Ben. When she looked at him, all she could think of was the feel of him inside her, or the sight of him lying naked in her bed. Such memories were dangerous and problematic and needed to be smothered with things like cold stares and avoidance, except that cold stares and avoidance made something inside her ache. She couldn't quite explain it. Then her breathing halted as she remembered the violent nausea that had just started to subside. Their relationship was irreconcilable with normal.

"Normal for us?" He gave a short laugh. "Sally, what's normal for us anymore?" he asked in a resigned tone. "Is it ignoring each other? Living on opposite sides of the planet?" He came closer, his eyes fixed on hers, each step heavy with significance. "Is normal for us pretending that nothing happened? Imagining that we didn't experience the hottest night of our lives together? Don't do that," he said when she flinched. "Don't pretend you weren't thinking the same thing."

She brought her hands down against her desk. He was close enough that the spicy smell of his cologne gripped her senses and sent her stomach into a spiral. She recoiled, feeling a sudden flash of heat cross her skin. "Sorry." She pushed back clumsily in her chair, covering her nose and mouth with one hand. "I think I'm going to be sick."

His mouth pulled into a troubled frown just before she closed her eyes. She felt as if she was on a boat, swaying this way and that.

"Are you all right?" He came around the desk and crouched beside her. Oh, there was the smell of his cologne again. Her stomach revolted. "I'm fine," she managed to say through clenched teeth. "I could use some fresh air, though."

He was over to the window in an instant, pulling the panes down as far as they went to admit a thin stream of cold air. "Here," he said, rolling her chair to the window. "Does that help?"

The air was bracing, trickling across her skin like fingers of ice. The cold hit the back of her throat and then her lungs, but the effect was to soothe, not shock. After some time had passed, her stomach calmed and she nodded her head. "Yes, that helps. Thanks."

He plopped himself back into the visitor's chair across from her desk. "You had me nervous for a minute there, Sally. You looked white, like you were about to pass out."

"I may be coming down with something," she said, wiping her fingers across her forehead. She felt warm, but her skin was cool to the touch. "The flu, maybe."

He leaned forward in his seat, his elbows on his knees. "Maybe you want to take the rest of the day off and get some rest?"

"No, I'm fine." She smoothed her hair and cleared her throat. "Thank you for your concern. Let's just keep it strictly professional from here on out."

He leaned back in his chair. "I got it, Sally. No problem."

Why was that so easy for him? And why did his casual agreement make her feel as if he'd just slammed her heart against the floor? "Great," she managed to reply. "I suppose you should give the necklace to the police, though I'm not sure what use they'll have for it."

"I told you, it's a gift." He dropped his hands on the armrests, easing back and splaying his legs in a wide stance. "It's yours to give to the police. This is your case. I'm only second chair, and I don't even think I'm that anymore. I want you to nail this bastard, Sally. Show them all how tough and smart you are."

The sincerity in his gaze trapped something in her throat. She sure didn't feel tough and smart right now. She clutched the plastic bag protecting the necklace. "I don't think I can do it, Ben. Not without a body."

"I know you, Sally. I know you don't give up, and you don't take no for an answer. When there's something you want, you go for it." He leaned forward until his elbows rested on his knees again. "I also know you don't need my help. You never have. You don't need anyone's help. So I hope you understand that I'm only doing this because I want you to know how much I believe in you."

The space between them melted. He was so close to her, his gaze locked on hers, his eyes focused with a clarity she'd never seen from him. His words left her breathless and wishing she was as clever as he seemed to imagine.

"I wouldn't know where to b-begin," she stammered. "How about that? I have a necklace, so what do I do with it?"

The corner of his mouth twitched upward. "Are you asking for my help? Because I happen to have some ideas."

Of course he did. There it was, that maddening grin of his, except now it didn't seem so maddening. This time, she found it endearing. "Yes, fine. I'm asking for your help."

"You're an actress, whether you know it or not, but I think you know it. You have a flair for the dramatic."

She folded her arms across her chest, conceding nothing. "And?"

"Dan Maybury has been actively trying to find Mary Ann Hennessy. He's interviewed her relatives over the phone, checked flight manifestos and basically tracked down every lead he had. Now it's all come to dead ends." He held up a hand. "No pun intended."

She groaned. "I would hope not."

"I spoke to Dan just yesterday. He reiterated the official position of the department, which is that they aren't moving until they have a body. They've exhausted valuable resources on this case and come up empty. They won't go further without a break."

"And?"

"Have you ever read *Hamlet?*"

She blinked. "Yes. Of course. Junior year in high school, then again in college."

"Then you know the play's the thing with which to catch the conscience of the king." He spread his hands wide. "The police won't act, so we will. Mitch Kruger killed Mary Ann Hennessy and dumped her body somewhere. We'll get him to lead us right to her."

"You want to...what? Stage a murder?"

"No. I'm not thinking that literally. I'm thinking

we need to snoop around, ask him some questions. Make him sweat. Hope he slips up in a way that leads us right to some damning evidence."

She sat back in her seat, digesting the proposal. Everything about this was crazy. Nuts. Bizarre to the extreme. And yet she was intrigued. She'd tried not to think about the case for weeks, it was true, but it still haunted her nightmares. Mitch Kruger had to be held accountable for his actions.

She saw something in Ben's face that told her he understood. He felt it, too—the need to bring order to chaos, to bring some semblance of right upon the colossal wrongs they encountered regularly. "This is insane. You realize that, right?" Because she didn't want to work with him if he was going to try to convince her this was a perfectly sound, reasonable plan.

He shrugged noncommittally. "I realize it's an unorthodox approach, how's that?"

She drummed her fingertips on the desktop. She'd been living with unorthodox for pretty much her entire life. "Fine. I'm in." She tried to ignore the way her heart skipped at the broad smile that broke across his face. "But there's a better way to catch the conscience of the king." She leaned forward. "We have to talk to the queen."

Chapter 13

Ronnie shook two aspirin into her palm. Her head was about to split, and she wanted to be able to close her eyes for an hour without feeling as if the room was spinning. She choked down the bitter pills with a gulp of water, feeling them slide down her esophagus. Fifteen minutes, and she should be feeling better—wasn't that what she'd always told the kids who'd come to her with headaches at school? Go take an aspirin, and then come lie down for fifteen minutes. She couldn't give them aspirin or ibuprofen or anything. Just mints. Sometimes that made her feel useless.

She straightened and walked back into the living room. She hated this room now. Mitch should've painted it right after…but then, she supposed he couldn't. He'd been a suspect in her disappearance, and if he'd started painting the scene, that would've raised

suspicion. Still. He didn't even do a good job cleaning
it. She'd found blood between two of the floorboards
that morning—just a speck of dried blood that probably looked like a mark on the wood to anyone else, or
possibly a clump of dirt. But it was blood. There was
blood everywhere in that room. She could still see it
on the walls beneath the antiseptic coat of primer, even
after three passes. Ronnie could walk over the floorboards and hear the dried blood creaking beneath her
from where it had seeped below the planks. There was
so much blood, and it would always be there.

She scrubbed the entire room with bleach, don-
ning a painter's mask to keep from inhaling the fumes.
Safety first. With furious strokes of the stiff bristles
of an old cleaning brush, she worked at the spots on
the walls and the ridges of the floorboards until her
arms burned, then continued scrubbing through the
tears that blurred her vision. *It will never be clean.
The blood is still there.*

When her head was pounding and her arms leaden
from the effort, she sat back on her haunches and
dropped the brush unceremoniously into the bucket of
bleach and water. The windows were wide-open, and
Ronnie was wearing a winter coat to keep from freez-
ing, and the room stank like death tinged with bleach.

She emptied the bucket and returned it to the base-
ment. When she came back upstairs, she looked out
the window and saw the two prosecutors walking up
the driveway.

Ronnie's heart skipped, and she cursed under her
breath. She had nothing to say to these two, and she
still had ten minutes before her aspirin was supposed
to take effect, though in truth she'd already started to

feel the edge of her pain dull. A quick glimpse in the mirror showed that she looked presentable, if a bit disheveled. But then she'd been hard at work, cleaning.

She plastered a smile on her face and opened the door just as the man raised his fist. She had a doorbell, but perhaps he'd been raised in a barn. "I saw you coming up the drive," she said brightly. "Can I help you?"

Her friendliness was rewarded with two serious stares. The man spoke first. "Mrs. Kruger? I don't know if you remember us. I'm Ben McNamara, and this is Sally Dawson. We're with the state's attorney's office."

Ronnie felt her skin pulling with the effort of her smile. "Of course I remember you."

Mr. Tall, Dark and Broad. She'd remember a face like his anywhere, and that woman…she'd known women like her. Entitled, better-than-you types. Ronnie didn't forget them, either.

Sally pointed her freckled little nose at Ronnie's coat. "It looks like we caught you at a bad time, Mrs. Kruger. Are you on your way out?"

Like you care about my plans. "No." She smiled. "I was cleaning my living room, and I opened the windows for ventilation. I was just about to shut them." She stepped back graciously. "Would you like to come in?"

Yes, that's good. Show them how generous you are with your time. You have nothing to hide!

Ben and Sally uttered quick thanks before stepping into the foyer. Ronnie offered to hang their coats, but they declined. "We'll be brief, thanks," Ben said.

Ronnie shrugged off her own coat before leading them into the living room. She closed the windows and settled on the couch. Sally and Ben hadn't waited for an invitation before plunking themselves into two high-backed chairs across from her. Mitch had purchased those chairs to replace the cream-colored love seat Ronnie loved so much. It had been soaked through with blood.

"How can I help you?" She folded her hands on her lap and pulled her shoulders back. Always the lady, always gracious. She could be the old Ronnie when it suited her purposes.

She noticed Sally's gaze darting around the room. "Is Mitch—is your husband home?"

"He works," she replied. "He was lucky to be able to get his old job back after, you know, being falsely accused of murdering me."

Ronnie didn't bother faking a smile this time, although she could have managed a genuine smile based on the way Sally squirmed in her seat. Ben must have noticed it, too, because he cleared his throat and leaned forward.

"We're still investigating our internal procedures. Needless to say, we're trying to figure out how to stop that from happening again."

He gave her a smile that reached the corners of his eyes, and Ronnie's pulse reacted. My, he was attractive. She wished she wasn't wearing old clothes and stinking of bleach.

"But none of that matters for today's visit," he continued, reaching into his coat pocket. "I'm here to ask you about your sister."

Ronnie felt the blood drain from her head. Mary Ann. She brought her fingers to her temple and closed her eyes.

"Mrs. Kruger, are you all right?"

The voice was Sally's, and the concern that registered in the tone was alarming. Damn, she needed to pull herself together, stop thinking about the blood on the floor and the bleach burning her nostrils.

"I've had a bit of a headache all day," she explained with a feeble laugh. "Sorry for that." She looked up again and blinked a few times as if her vision was slightly askew. "You want to talk about Mary Ann? Whatever for?"

Sally and Ben exchanged a glance loaded with meaning, and then Sally spoke. "When was the last time you saw her, Mrs. Kruger?"

"It's just Ronnie. And, well. You know." She forced a chuckle. "I've been missing myself for almost a year. I'd say maybe eighteen months ago. Why?"

"She's missing," said Ben. "No one's seen her since around the time you disappeared. Strange, don't you think?"

Ronnie felt her face get colder, her pupils reacting even as she tried not to seem alarmed by this line of questioning. *They can't possibly know.*

But her assurances did little to calm her, and her fingertips began to twitch. "That does seem strange," she said slowly. "But I can't imagine anything bad has happened to Mary Ann. This may sound irrational, but we're very close, and I feel like I would know." She smiled. "We're sisters. We've always had a strong connection."

Sally's gaze was razor-sharp and focused on Ronnie. "You share more than a connection, don't you? You share blood. Bone marrow." She leaned closer. "DNA."

Ronnie's heart thundered in her chest, and her breathing became shallow. "Why, yes, we do. Mary

Ann had leukemia. She needed a bone marrow transplant. I was a match."

"It's an interesting fact about bone marrow transplants, how they can turn the recipient into a chimera—an organism with multiple sets of DNA. The bone marrow from the donor creates blood in the recipient that matches the donor's DNA, but the DNA in the rest of the recipient's body is unique to the recipient." Sally eyed her, watching for her response.

Ronnie's lips twisted into something she hoped resembled a small smile. "I remember studying something about that in nursing school. Fascinating subject."

Sally lifted one shoulder innocently and shot Ben a look. "The blood we found on the area rug matched Ronnie's DNA, and that's why we assumed she was dead. But if Ronnie donated bone marrow to her sister, that means the DNA in their blood was the same. It could have been Mary Ann's blood on that rug—spilled in a fatal amount."

Little bitch. Ronnie felt her muscles quivering with a desire to throttle her. She tried to shake her head with something like wonder at the statement, but found her muscles too stiff for such movement. "That's—incomprehensible to me. I would have to have some sense of that. A feeling, a foreboding. We were—*are*—very much connected."

That's why Ronnie's gut had twisted for years when she caught something in her husband's eye. Whether it had been the angle of his gaze or the way his pupils reacted to her, something in his eyes had told her that her husband didn't love her anymore. It was the sixth sense she had about her sister that told her that Mary

Ann was the reason. Even with hundreds of miles between them, Ronnie just knew.

"I know this must be shocking to hear," Sally continued. "But it's what the evidence suggests. You and Mary Ann have the same blood. If it wasn't your blood on that rug, then it must have been hers." She lowered her voice. "Of course, that means that Mary Ann is probably dead. No one could have survived such a blood loss."

Ronnie's hand flew to her cheek. She opened her mouth dumbly and shook her head, waiting several moments before speaking. "No, that can't be true. To think that Mary Ann…dead? Murdered in my own home? And by my husband? I can't imagine."

"We never said anything about Mitch murdering Mary Ann," Sally said quietly.

Ronnie's gut clenched. "No, of course you didn't. I only meant—"

"It was a reasonable conclusion to draw," Ben said, jumping to her defense. "I imagine it's upsetting to hear us say these things. You saved Mary Ann's life, donating your marrow. It's understandable that an experience like that would bring you two closer."

Closer? That was one way to put it. Turns out the bone marrow transplant had not only reunited Ronnie with her sister, but had reunited Mary Ann and Mitch, as well. Rekindled the love affair that Ronnie found out much too late had always been burning behind her back. That explained Mitch's odd "business trips" to allegedly research new machinery for the hardware store, and all the late-night sessions chatting with someone on his computer. They'd been making a fool out of her. She'd pledged to love Mitch till death did part them, and she'd saved her sister's life, and they'd both gone and betrayed her, threatened her family's stability.

Ronnie's fists tightened around the hem of her sweatshirt. She'd done what she'd had to do, and no more than that. No one was going to hurt her anymore.

"I haven't seen Mary Ann." She gave a little smile. "Is that all? We could have resolved this in the doorway."

"Actually, it's not all." Ben reached into his coat pocket. "Obviously, we were wrong when we charged your husband with your murder, but we think we were only wrong about the *who,* not the *what.*" He opened his fist to reveal a little silver locket. "We think your husband may have killed your sister and disposed of her body. If we're right, you may be in danger, Ronnie."

Her heart flipped at the sight of the necklace. Ronnie remembered it. She'd found it on Mitch's dresser that night, just sitting out in the open. It had her sister's initials engraved on the back, and he'd even written out a card for her that read simply, "Love prevails."

"What's that?" She squinted at the necklace as if she didn't know what to make of it. "And why does it mean I'm in danger?"

"Mitch disposed of this yesterday morning at the reservoir," Sally explained gently. "It has your sister's initials on it. MAH. We think he's gotten wind that the police have been looking for your sister, and that he got scared and started to dispose of some evidence."

Dummy. He should've disposed of that necklace a long time ago. All he had to do was flush it down the toilet! She couldn't trust him to do anything.

"You're a victim in this," Ben added. "We know he's

been violent toward you in the past, and he could become violent again if he thinks he's being threatened."

Violent? Ronnie had to bite her lip to keep from laughing. Mitch, violent? Sure, he looked dangerous and talked a big game, but on the scale of butterfly to serial killer, he fell somewhere around puppy dog. The first thing he did when he saw Mary Ann's body was to retch all over himself.

"Do you see what you did?" she'd snapped at him as he stood there looking stupid, staring at Mary Ann. *"This is all your fault."*

The responsibility was his, but she'd had to take charge as usual, spelling out every last detail. Where to dump the body. How to hide the car. Where to store the rug. She'd had to save both their asses. Was Mitch idiotic? Sure. Violent? Hardly.

"Yes, he can get quite angry at times." She looked down demurely at the carpet, as if too timid to admit such a thing about her own husband. "But I can't imagine he'd…"

She allowed her voice to trail off as if something had just occurred to her. In truth, it had. The prosecutors bought her story. She was a long-suffering, abused wife. Her son thought his father had killed her. Her plan had been so perfect, and what? Now she was supposed to go to prison because Mitch had screwed up and kept evidence? No. She was done being victimized. He'd done it all, and his fingerprints were all over the remaining evidence. His case was lost.

She shook her head. "I just can't imagine he'd actually kill someone, and not my sister, of all people."

Sally cleared her throat and crossed her legs. "Ronnie, this is a little awkward for me to say, but we think your husband was having an affair with Mary Ann. We think they were planning to run away together, but that something went terribly wrong. Maybe she got cold feet or a guilty conscience, and threatened to tell you. In any case, we think that Mitch killed her and concealed the body."

"That would explain why he was so violent with you that night," Ben added. "He was angry about something, maybe his breakup, or maybe he'd already killed Mary Ann."

"Maybe he tried to kill you, too," Sally whispered. "You may have gotten away just in time."

Ronnie sat mesmerized. She'd thought the plan was perfect: stage her own death and then return in time to save her husband from trial. Explain the whole thing as a minor domestic dispute. A misunderstanding. All the time the police spent looking for Ronnie meant they weren't looking for Mary Ann, and the trail would go cold. Witnesses would forget conversations, evidence would disappear. She'd thought it was a solid plan—as solid as it could be, given the heat of the circumstances in which Mary Ann had died. There hadn't been much forethought to any of it. But until this moment, Ronnie hadn't realized quite how clever she'd been. They bought it. They knew about Mary Ann and the DNA evidence, and they still bought it. They believed her.

It's not as if she especially cared what happened to Mitch right now. He'd been so stupid as to keep that necklace, and then he'd gone and thrown it away in front of witnesses. Mitch was the cheater. He was the one to blame for the tragedy. If he had only stayed faithful to her... She'd made him pay, all right. Nine months in prison, and he'd earned every single minute.

Mitch was responsible for Mary Ann's death, not her. Mitch had disposed of the evidence. He owned the gun that killed her, and he was responsible for any fingerprints left on her car. No one could trace Ronnie to that crime, because it wasn't her fault. If law enforcement was sniffing around again, looking for someone to blame, then that person was Mitch. Ronnie wasn't going to jail.

She scrunched up her face, willing the tears to come. She'd gotten good at this part. Then again, all she had to do was think about Mary Ann and the way things between them had been at one point. Those memories touched a sore, and from there, the tears usually fell freely. As they did right now.

Sally was at her side quickly, crouching with a few tissues she'd pulled from her pocket. Maybe she wasn't such a little tart, after all. "I see we've upset you," she said. "That wasn't our intent."

Ronnie accepted the tissues and blew her nose. "You said everything I've been thinking since my memory came back. What if Mitch intended to hurt me more than he did? He's been so…angry." She balled the tissue in her fist and wiped at her nose. "I don't know anything about Mary Ann. I haven't called her yet. It's just been too much of an adjustment. But if he did do something to her…" She stared at the wall and shook her head, creating a faraway look in her eyes.

"Ronnie?" Ben's voice sliced the momentary silence. "Finish your thought. If Mitch did something to your sister, then what?"

She swallowed and met his gaze. She'd become such a hell of an actress over the past year. "Mitch sometimes fixates on the morbid. Often, when we'd go hik-

ing around the reservoir, he'd tell me that if he ever had
to hide a body, that's where it would be."

Sally tilted her head up at her. "In the reservoir?"

"Yes." Ronnie lowered her voice to a whisper. "He
said there's a hill that leads right into the water. He'd
just roll a car right down and wait for it to sink."

Sally visibly swallowed. "Do you think… Would
you be willing to show the police that spot?"

Ronnie nodded gravely. "Yes. Yes, of course I would
do that. For my sister."

She saw the prosecutors exchange a loaded glance,
and smiled to herself. Finding the body would be easy,
and watching Mitch take the fall would be the best
part of all.

"So?" Ben started up the car and reached for his
seat belt. "Thoughts?"

"She knows exactly where her sister's body is."
Sally clicked her own seat belt into place, her eyes
still fixed on the Kruger house. "She's decided to pun-
ish Mitch for something. Let him do the time."

"You think she was involved in the murder?"

"Don't you? The evidence was all over her face,
right down to the fake tears and betrayal of her husband when we gave her a way out." Sally shook her
head. "The house reeked of bleach. She's come home,
and all she can think about is her crime, and she's trying to scrub it from her memory."

"Maybe's she's just a neat freak."

Sally gave him a look. "She was bleaching her hard-
wood floors, Ben. No one in their right mind does
that. And why do you always need to argue with me?"

"I'm not, I promise. Just playing devil's advocate.

And look, I happen to agree with you. If she didn't do it herself, she was at least involved." Ben inched the car through the neighborhood, speeding away once he reached the highway. "Let's get back to the office and call Dan. We now have Ronnie saying she's willing to show us where she thinks Mitch would have dumped Mary Ann's car. That could be enough to spark their interest."

Sally responded by pulling a tube of lip gloss from her handbag and swiping the tip slowly across her lips, leaving behind a trail of something wet, shiny and, from the smell of it, strawberry flavored. His collar tightened. "You can't do that to me."

She spun to face him. "What?" Her eyes were wide, her shiny lips open.

He shifted uncomfortably in his seat. "I said, you can't do that to me. Put on lip gloss in front of me, or before you see me." He shot her a glance from the corner of his eye. "I'm trying to be professional and to respect boundaries, but now all I can think of is your mouth, and you using it to do wicked things to me."

She sat perfectly still, watching him. He was acutely aware of his heart throbbing in his chest and the growing erection in his pants. The woman affected him like no other, tested every inch of his self-control. Then she said in a breathy whisper, "What kinds of things?"

A bead of perspiration started on his brow, even as he willed himself not to tell her. "You don't need to know the details. Let's just say that in my mind right now, you are being very, very naughty and enjoying every moment. You're doing something colleagues shouldn't do to each other when they're trying to be professional."

"You're enjoying it, though? In your mind."

That was it. He was fully aroused. He pulled his coat down to cover the evidence. "Yes. Very much."

She sat back in her seat, and he hoped she was feeling as conflicted as she looked. He hoped she'd reconsider—

"Ben, could you stop here?" She pointed to a bakery on the side of the road. "I need to run in for a minute."

His forehead tensed. She was clutching her stomach. "Hey, you all right?"

"If you could just stop the car."

He shot into the parking lot and had barely stopped when Sally opened the door and jumped out. Without a word, she ran inside.

Ben sat stunned, wondering if it was that flu Sally had been talking about. She'd seemed okay otherwise, but these things could come on suddenly. When she didn't come out right away, he turned off the car. Then when more time passed, he opened his door and paced the parking lot. Finally, he saw her emerge from the bakery, her face pale and streaked with tears. "Sally, what happened?"

She paused before him, her chin trembling as she fought to retain control. "I need you to take me to the hospital."

Chapter 14

She'd managed to stop crying, but as they waited in the hospital emergency room, every cell in Sally's body continued to vibrate. Ben held her hand sandwiched between his own, but otherwise he didn't speak or ask questions. She was grateful for that.

A doctor in light blue scrubs and a white coat pulled open the curtain to the little waiting area to which Ben and Sally had been directed. He had dark brown hair tinged with gray at the temples, but he didn't look much older than them. He introduced himself, but the name didn't register and Sally blurted out, "Is my baby all right?"

There had been so much blood, just like when she'd lost the first baby. She felt weak from the sight of it, as if she was barely holding up. Ben's grip slacked momentarily, but he didn't let go. Sally no longer worried about secrets. All that mattered was knowing that her child was safe.

"We're going to check right now, Ms. Dawson. You said you're about eight weeks along?"

"Yes," she murmured.

A nurse entered then and said with a gentle smile, "Lie down, honey."

Sally obliged, swinging her legs onto the gurney on which she was sitting, and leaning back until her head hit the thin pillow. The nurse inched Sally's pants lower and applied a layer of cold blue jelly to her abdomen. As the doctor lifted a wand from the machine, Sally turned her head to look at Ben.

His eyes, blank and unreadable, were fixed on the monitor of the ultrasound machine, but his grip on her hand was strong. He'd offered to wait somewhere else, but she'd asked him to stay. It seemed important that he be there. She squeezed his hand. He looked at her, gave a sad smile that touched something at the bottom of her heart, and squeezed back. Sally felt the wand on her belly. She held her breath.

"Here it is," the doctor finally announced, positioning the monitor so Sally could see better. "That little ball right there is the baby, and see the blinking? That's the heartbeat."

Her baby's heartbeat. Sally's eyes began to tear up. "Is it okay?"

"The heartbeat is strong," the doctor assured her, his focus on the monitor. "Everything looks great."

"Then why... What happened?"

"It's not always clear. We'll have to take a wait-and-see approach, but right now I don't see any reason to panic." He consulted the chart he'd rested on the counter beside him. "You're a negative blood type, right? O negative?"

"Yes."

"It may be that your baby has a positive blood type, and we want to prevent you from developing antibodies against the child." He removed the ultrasound wand, and the nurse stepped in and efficiently wiped Sally's abdomen dry. "We're going to give you a shot as a precaution. Otherwise the heartbeat is good and strong, and the baby is measuring correctly. All looks good."

Ben helped Sally to sit upright, placing one hand against her lower back. "My baby is going to be okay?" she asked.

The doctor smiled warmly. "Nothing is certain, but I'm cautiously optimistic. The nurse will be back in a few minutes with that shot." He placed a warm hand on Sally's knee. "Deep breaths, Ms. Dawson. Healthy babies need oxygen."

She bit her lower lip and nodded. As quickly as they'd come, the doctor and nurse disappeared behind the curtain, leaving her and Ben alone. Sally looked down at their hands. Then she began to sob.

His arms wrapped around her shoulders, strong and reassuringly warm. The sharp smell of his cologne had mellowed, and now, far from turning her stomach, he smelled clean and familiar. Sally clutched him, not caring about what he might think of her now that he knew the truth. At that moment, as he stroked her hair and held her while she cried, Ben felt like a long-lost friend, and her heart melted against his.

When she finally broke the contact, his shoulder was wet from her tears, but he didn't seem to notice. His gaze locked on her face, his brows pulled with concern, and he stroked one hand down the side of her cheek gently, as if he feared she might break.

"You're pregnant," he whispered.

"Yes." Her reply was choked. She removed her hands from his muscular arms and brought them to rest, self-consciously, on her lap. "It's not yours."

"I figured that much."

There was a twinge of injury in his voice. "It's not anyone's," she interjected hastily. "I used a donor." She saw the questions in his deep blue eyes. "I want a family, Ben. I'm thirty-five years old, and it's not like I have any prospects—"

"I'm not judging you," he said. "What right do I have to judge you?" But he eyed the floor, looking as if he had something more to say. He stepped away from her as the nurse returned to administer the shot. "I'll wait outside," he said.

Before she could reply, he'd ducked behind the curtain and vanished.

The night he'd wrapped his car around a tree, Ben had the sense that the obstacle had appeared out of nowhere and walked into the middle of the road. Fractions of a second later, his face had slammed against an air bag and his muscles had tightened reflexively as he gripped the steering wheel, and when it was all over, he couldn't breathe. His chest constricted as if squeezed by an unseen hand, and he sat for what seemed like forever, trying to understand what had just happened. The shock was preferable to the reality that settled in, bit by bit, as time dragged on. The reality was that his fiancée was unconscious and bleeding, and his muscles felt as if they'd been pummeled raw. That was kind of how he felt right now, as he pulled into Sally's driveway: emerging from shock, and feeling raw.

He knew he had no claim to her, no right to tell her what he thought, and still he wanted answers. Not that he wanted to control her, but because he wanted to understand how everything he'd thought was happening between them could have been so wrong.

Sally was pregnant. The night they'd shared together had seemed like so much to him, and all along she'd carried this secret. Here he thought they'd been standing beside each other, but only because she had been concealing a chasm between them.

She was quiet on the ride, still anxious about the baby. She hadn't wanted to stop for dinner, and neither had he. The antiseptic smell of the hospital lingered in his nostrils, and he had no appetite. He put the car in Park and cut the engine.

"Thank you," Sally said.

"I'll walk you to the door."

"You don't need to."

"I want to."

He got out of the car and walked to the passenger side, offering her his arm. She looked weakened and tired, as if she'd just been through hell. Any protectiveness he'd felt for her before was only magnified now that he knew she was expecting a child. She lived alone, she'd spent all afternoon in the emergency room and her car was still parked at the office. What if she had another emergency tonight?

"I'd like to stay with you," he said.

Her gaze flew to him in alarm. "That's not necessary."

"You aren't feeling well, and you don't have a car.

Who would you call if something happened? Do your parents even know you're pregnant?" He waited for her response, but it never came. He sighed. "I didn't think so. Let me sleep on your couch. It will make me feel better."

She swallowed. "I'm not helpless. I'd rather be alone tonight."

They reached the front step, and he released her arm and turned to face her head-on. "Are you pushing me away because you don't want me to be here? Or because you think I don't want to be here? Because I sure as hell want to stay with you."

"I'm not your obligation." Her tone was defiant, but he sensed that beneath that proud lift of her chin, she was feeling just as drained by the evening as he was.

"Dammit, Sally, I care about you. I sat in the emergency room with you for five hours. I held your hand, and now I'm offering to stay here and take care of you." He gritted his teeth and balled his fists against his thighs. She made everything so damn complicated. "If I left you alone right now, I'd be the biggest bastard who ever lived, and I'm not. No matter what you thought of me at one time, I'm different now."

How foolish to imagine he could have ever proved such a thing over dinner. Here he was, prostrate under the burden of his desire for her, and she'd forged her impression of him long ago. To Sally, he would never be anything more than the jerk who'd betrayed her, and that infuriated him.

She pressed her key into the lock, avoiding his eyes. "You can sleep on the couch," she mumbled. "But only because it's late."

He fought the urge to snap back a sarcastic comment

about how gracious she was, and instead followed her into her home. In the darkness, it was just like his own, reverberating with a tomblike silence. He couldn't say he'd ever considered having a child as the answer to loneliness, but in that instant he thought that maybe he could understand. Like him, Sally had resigned herself to being a relationship leper, but that didn't mean she wanted to spend the rest of her life alone. She wasn't punishing herself for past wrongs the way he was.

"I'll get you a blanket and some pillows," she said, her tone weary.

He waited until she returned from the bedroom, clutching two large pillows and a wool blanket. Ben met her halfway across the room. "Thanks." He lifted them from her arms. "Are you feeling any better?"

"I feel physically exhausted," she admitted. "Every part of me hurts."

He could see the pain written across her expressive face, the way she twisted her mouth into a grimace. "I know you don't need me to stay, but I'm here tonight to help you. If you need anything, you let me know."

She nodded. "Okay." Then she turned and walked toward her bedroom. She hadn't bothered to turn on many lights, but he could see her hesitate in the moonlight that streamed through the large windows overlooking the lake. "It's nothing personal, you know. We tried to make it work in law school, and we both ended up miserable."

Speak for yourself, he wanted to say. "I was never miserable with you, Sally. When we dated in law school, it was like being brought back to life. I can't take back what I did to you, but you should know that. You made me feel alive."

The words sounded painfully ineffective to him, but he didn't have any words that would undo her years of hurt, of believing herself to be unworthy of love. She'd told him she loved him, and he'd gone and scorched the earth. He deserved whatever he got.

"I saw my baby's heartbeat today," she said, turning to him. "I can't even explain how powerful that was."

"I can imagine."

"Can you? Then you'll understand when I say that I have other priorities right now and other people to think about. I don't want to complicate things by engaging in a relationship that has no future. I want to be happy, Ben." Her voice cracked with emotion. "Every time I look at you, I feel that hurt all over again. We can be colleagues, and partners, and maybe even friends, but I hope you understand if I have to protect myself from falling in love with you ever again."

"The thing is, I don't understand that." His voice bounced off the walls, and he felt like a fool, standing in the middle of her living room, clutching a blanket and two pillows. He no longer cared. "I don't understand how you can walk away from something that has been consuming me since the moment I saw you again. Every day I go to work with a smile on my face because I know you'll be there. I watch for your car, and I listen for your laugh in the hallway. I came back to civilian life expecting one thing, and instead I found you, and I'm damned if I know what to do about it if you can just turn your back on me."

Beyond the pounding of his blood in his ears, he heard her breathing in the darkness. Time stretched on forever as he waited for her response.

Finally, she cleared her throat. "It's been a long night, and I'm tired."

With that, she turned and walked into her bedroom, closing the door firmly behind her. He stood in the center of the room looking after her, feeling more naked than he'd ever felt, and entirely alone.

Chapter 15

The car was right where Ronnie had said it would be, and the body of Mary Ann Hennessy was locked in the trunk. She'd been shot twice, once in the left shoulder and once almost square in the heart. The medical examiner concluded that the manner of death had been shooting, and ballistics traced the gun in the trunk to one registered by Mitch Kruger.

A coincidence if I've ever seen one, Sally thought wryly as she sifted through the photographs of the evidence recovered from Mary Ann's car. Ronnie had practically shown them where the body was hidden, and yet investigators couldn't find a darn thing actually linking her to the murder. So much time had passed that detectives would have difficulty finding an eyewitness who would testify that Ronnie, and not Mary Ann, had taken the flight to San Diego the night in question—after all, they were sisters, and the resemblance was striking.

Airline records indicated that Mary Ann had boarded the flight—her license, her ticket and her credit card were used. Nothing conclusive placed Mary Ann and Ronnie in the same state, let alone the same house, at the alleged time of the murder. Not even James's testimony was conclusive. The kid had been high and drunk when he allegedly saw the body in his living room, and now he had criminal charges pending, to boot. Mitch wasn't talking yet, and even if he did, it was his word against Ronnie's.

After the humiliation the state's attorney's office had suffered the first time she'd tried to bring Mitch to trial, Sally needed her case to be airtight, and yet she could sift through the evidence recovered from Mary Ann Hennessy's car a hundred times and it still wouldn't make her feel settled. If Mary Ann had been planning to run away, she'd traveled light, packing only a suitcase and a carry-on filled with essentials: toothpaste and a toothbrush, a change of clothes, contact lens solution and a case, and what remained of a paperback novel—nothing that would give any clue as to how her last moments had been spent. Each item had been coldly photographed and catalogued as per the usual process, but as Sally flipped through the images, she felt the same sadness she always felt about the victims in a case. This one, like any other, was a matter of human tragedy being broken down into its elements, photographed on a tarp and placed in a plastic bag. The pretense of order did nothing to erase the underlying chaos of the event.

Her ears pricked at the sound of Ben's voice down

the hall, and almost immediately her stomach slumped. After he'd stayed the night at her house, they'd spent the next morning in awkward silence. He'd driven her to work and then issued her a terse goodbye. That was three days ago, and they'd barely spoken since. She'd wanted to thank him for all he'd done for her, and to tell him that she harbored no hard feelings, but she no longer knew what their relationship was now that everything between them was so horribly wrong.

Sally picked up the cable-knit cardigan on the back of her chair and pulled it over her shoulders. Her shoes were flat and sensible for a change, and the sweater felt like a hug as she buttoned it. She was entitled to wear cable-knit sweaters and practical heels, especially on days like this, when she needed some comfort.

She'd blown it, she was sure. She'd been preparing herself for so long for the moment that Ben would disappoint her, pick up and leave her as he had all those years ago, that she had neglected to notice what was right in front of her—he cared about her. He didn't want to leave. He wanted to be a part of her life… maybe permanently. Sally could allow herself to sink into the warm, happy thought of her and Ben raising a child together, of holding hands and taking cooking classes into their retirement.

She swallowed. She could dwell on that image, but that would require her to accept that Ben might have real feelings for her, real feelings that wouldn't change without notice. That, she wasn't ready to accept. No man had ever loved her for real and forever, and she doubted any ever would.

The sound of his laughter carried down the hall and gripped Sally's heart. Amazing, the way he could so easily move on. Ben was remarkably skilled at controlling his emotions, and here she was unable to focus on anything other than how much she ached to believe he could love her as much as she loved him. Because she did think that she might love him. She simply couldn't trust that he would love her unconditionally in return, and with a child on the way, she would not settle for anything less than unconditional love.

Sally shuffled the images again and stacked them on her desk. She'd been living by her emotions for too long, and look where that had gotten her. Feelings were overrated.

The play's the thing—that's what Ben had said, and when they had confronted Ronnie, they'd managed to get her to lead them right to the body. Maybe showing her some of the photographs of Mary Ann's belongings could prompt a similar response? Maybe if Sally continued to lead Ronnie to believe that she wasn't a suspect in the case, the woman would continue to open up.

Sally reached for her phone, her fingertips nearly prickling with excitement. After three rings, Ronnie picked up. "Mrs. Kruger," Sally began, "I was wondering if you'd like to meet me for lunch?"

Things were so much better now that Mitch was back behind bars. The house, which had erupted in a series of loud fights and accusations since the police had found Mary Ann, was once again quiet. Ronnie had the bed to herself. James had breakfast at the table for the first time since she'd arrived home. Mitch was gone. Everything was as it should be.

Still, Ronnie's nerves felt frayed, like little ropes that had knotted and snapped. She'd combed the house for any lingering souvenirs, any remnants of Mitch's affair, and had come up empty. She'd been wearing gloves when she fired the gun, so Mitch's fingerprints were the only ones on the bullets and the trigger. There was nothing to tie her to the crime. He could protest all he wanted, and in the end it was his word against hers. What jury in the world would believe the desperate accusations of an adulterer and, as the scar on her scalp indicated, a wife abuser? Who would believe she'd killed her own sister? Even if anyone did believe it, belief wouldn't get her convicted beyond a reasonable doubt. Without evidence, everything was speculation.

Part of Ronnie had even convinced herself that she hadn't committed murder. No need to dwell on the past, what's done is done, and a myriad other clichés. She had saved Mary Ann's life, and her sister had repaid her by planning to run away with Mitch. Ronnie tried not to replay those final minutes in her mind, but now they felt dragged to the surface and laid out to dry like so many things hidden underwater—that moment when Mary Ann had calmly informed her that she and Mitch were in love, and that he was going to run away with her.

"We've always been in love," she'd said, the confession not even puckering the corners of her eyes, not even making her mouth twitch with guilt.

Ronnie had stood then, her vision bursting with spots of rage, and calmly left the room to retrieve the gun. *I gave you my blood.* And then with a few well-aimed shots, she'd taken that blood back.

Still, appearances must be maintained, as Ronnie knew only too well. That's why she dressed in a new bright red dress and drove to the prison where Mitch was being held. She was all dolled up and ready to give her husband a sympathetic ear and the support he deserved, every bit the image of the doting wife.

Mitch looked terrible. That industrial shade of orange jumpsuit did nothing for his skin tone. He sat across from her, a thick plate of glass separating them, and lifted the phone beside him so they could speak. Ronnie wrinkled her nose at the sight of her own phone. What kinds of germs were crawling on that thing? She sighed inwardly and gingerly lifted the receiver from the cradle.

"Sweetheart," she crooned. "How are you holding up?"

"You have a hell of a lot of nerve coming here." His eyes had narrowed to hateful slits.."Don't think this is over," he spat.

"Of course it's not over, darling." She leaned forward, closer to the glass. "We're going to get you the best legal counsel money can buy. The thought that you had anything at all to do with Mary Ann's death, well…" She shook her head. "It's beyond imagination."

A sick smile teased at the corner of his mouth. "Don't think you're getting away with anything. I have the goods on you."

Ronnie sighed. "No you don't, my love. Don't you understand? *You* cleaned up the scene. Dumped the car, dumped the rug. Your fingerprints are all over it. All of it. I, meanwhile, have a cut on my head from being thrown into our glass table."

His jaw tightened. "I never touched you. You gave yourself that cut out in Vegas."

She slowed her voice as if she were talking to a child. "I know that and you know that, but no one else does. You see? But you don't need to worry, because I'm starting to get my memory back. I suddenly remember coming home that night and seeing you with Mary Ann. You were arguing. She wanted you to run away with her, but you were conflicted. See? You're not the worst person in the world, darling."

She leaned closer to the glass, her eyes focused like lasers on his. "But here's the interesting part. Mary Ann went out of her mind. She pushed me and I fell into the glass table, slicing my head. Blood all over. You panicked, believing she'd killed me. Then in a fit of rage, you shot her. I regained consciousness later, and that's when I panicked. I fled for my life in a daze of confusion, believing I was in danger. Of course, I came home when I realized you were about to be tried for my murder." She lifted one shoulder coyly. "Extenuating circumstances, Mitch. I'll make you look good in front of the jury. Just a man who made a mistake, and loves his wife. I'd never say that I saw you shoot my sister."

"That's exactly what I think you're going to say," he growled. His knuckles were white on the phone. "You're going to say that I killed her, maybe that I meant to kill you, when the truth is that I'm the one who came home from work that night to find you checking Mary Ann's pulse as she bled out on the rug."

Ronnie waved her hand impatiently. "Crazy talk, Mitch. I would shoot my only sister after I gave her my bone marrow to save her life? No one's going to believe it."

"There's something, Ronnie. There's something you overlooked, and I'm going to nail you for it."

She sat back in her chair, smiling sweetly. "You are

a doll, and so very brave. I mean it—we're going to get through this together," she whispered before brushing a kiss on her fingertips and pressing them to the glass. "Take care, darling."

He was still shouting, but Ronnie had heard enough from Mitch. As long as she continued to tell him she would testify that he'd acted in a fit of blind rage, he'd keep his mouth shut in the hopes her testimony would make the difference between being charged with manslaughter or murder. Of course, once she got to the stand, all bets were off, and she'd swear she saw him shoot Mary Ann in cold blood. She wasn't stupid.

She calmly hung up the phone and walked away, brushing past the guards and sweeping out into the cool autumn sunshine. When her cell phone rang, she plucked it from her handbag and squinted at the number. "Hello?"

It was the prosecutor, Sally Dawson. She wanted to have lunch. Ronnie chirped her agreement. What was the choice? She had to remain in law enforcement's good graces. But the hair on the back of her neck rose nevertheless. Mitch had told her he had something on her, something he planned to nail her with, and now the prosecutor wanted to meet?

Ronnie pulled her coat tighter. Something was not right.

Ben wasn't watching Sally. Not intentionally, at least. It wasn't his fault that he'd developed a hyper-awareness of her comings and goings, or that he'd been walking back from the library and noticed her slipping out of her office, wearing her coat. She froze momentarily when their eyes met, then tried to recover. He stepped into her path. "Going out?"

"That's not your business," she replied as she buttoned her cream-colored coat.

Her cheeks were flushed, but then the color of that garment tended to bring attention to the pink in her complexion. Something hit him square in the stomach. He missed her. The thought made him feel desperate. "I've done nothing wrong here," he said, his voice lowered to a hushed whisper. "Please don't shut me out this way."

She turned her face to his and sighed. "This is difficult for me." Her eyes darted furtively around the hall and she lowered her voice, even though no one was around. "I appreciate all you've done, but…"

He should have been offended, but instead he softened at the sight of the fear in her eyes. She was still scared he was going to run, just as he had so many years ago. "How are you feeling, Sally?"

She blinked. "Fine. Better. Everything is better, thank you."

"Good." He meant it. "Where are you headed? Can I walk with you?"

"I don't want to talk about it. I need some time—"

"We don't have to talk about anything. We can walk in absolute silence if you want. I just want to walk with you."

She swallowed and looked to the side as if considering how she could decline the request. Then she nodded. "Okay. Let's walk."

The air outside was crisp and dry, the remains of the leaves withered into small brown fists that clung haphazardly to the branches of trees along the street.

The sky was thick with gray clouds that would hover menacingly but never unleash rain. Sally had stuck her hands in her coat pockets, but as they walked, she allowed their shoulders to brush. The simple, brief contact, accidental as it might have been, cast light on something he'd been ignoring for too long. He loved her. He always had. Now if only he could make her believe it.

"This is where I'm going," she said, stopping in front of a little restaurant. *Fresco.* He'd never been here before, but he liked the dark wood paneled glass doors and the brush of warm air that escaped from inside when they opened. "I'm meeting someone for lunch." She cleared her throat. "Ronnie Kruger."

"You're—wait a minute." He took her gently by the elbow and led her to the edge of the sidewalk. "Why are you meeting Ronnie Kruger? And why didn't you tell me?"

"She's involved in this, Ben, and we haven't been able to get her...yet." Sally pulled her bag higher on her shoulder. "I'm going to talk to her, just like we did at the house. I want to see if she'll open up."

"Sally, you think she killed someone. Her own sister. You were going to meet her by yourself?"

"It's a public place and the middle of the day. Nothing is going to happen." She shifted. "But fine. You want to join us?"

Ben pulled his jacket tighter. He'd worn his gun today, and he was glad he had. Ever since James Kruger had stated that Sally's life was in danger, Ben had been on heightened alert. He didn't know what Ronnie Kruger's real story was, but he didn't like the idea of her being alone with Sally now. "Yes, I do."

She gave a little shrug. "Suit yourself." But he knew she was glad to have him there. After all, they were partners.

Ronnie had arrived first, but she rose when she saw Sally, and smiled as if they were old friends. "Ms. Dawson," she gushed, her figure awash with vibrant red hues. "How nice to see you."

Sally doubted that was true, but she returned the smile nevertheless. "Mrs. Kruger. It was nice of you to meet me on such short notice. You remember my colleague, Ben McNamara?"

The woman's eyes grazed his figure. "Of course I do."

Sally couldn't stop the stab of jealousy that coursed through her. She had no reason to be jealous when other women looked at Ben. He wasn't hers.

"It's a pleasure," Ben said with a friendly but efficient nod of his head.

The restaurant was warmly furnished with dark wainscoting and butternut-colored walls. Sconces cast subdued light over the interior, and on overcast days like this one, when little light came through the windows, the interior room felt cozy. They slid into a small booth in a corner of the restaurant, and Ben seated himself next to Sally. Their thighs touched, sending her heart into a skitter. She thought of the baby, and of him acting protective of them both at the hospital, and wondered whether a happy ending was possible.

Dangerous thinking.

"Mrs. Kruger, I appreciate that this has been a difficult time for you," Sally said.

The woman heaved a dramatic, self-sacrificing sigh.

"Deep down, I always knew this day would come," she admitted. "Call it intuition. I'm just struggling to come to terms with what transpired that terrible night."

"I can imagine. Thank you for being so willing to cooperate with the investigation."

"Nonsense," she said with a wave and a smile that sent a shiver darting down Sally's neck. "I want nothing more than to be helpful."

They were interrupted briefly as a waiter took their orders, and then Sally decided to get down to business. "Mrs. Kruger, I know you've said you don't remember anything from that evening, but I'd like to show you some pictures of the items police recovered from your sister's car, see if anything jogs your memory."

Ronnie inhaled. "Oh, I don't know if I'm up for this."

"We can stop anytime you'd like," Ben assured her. "You're in control, so if you get uncomfortable, just say so."

She nodded, closing her eyes tightly. *For dramatic effect,* Sally mused.

Finally, Ronnie said, "All right. I'm ready."

Sally had a series of photographs in her bag, and she set them on the table, one at a time. Mary Ann's hairbrush. The shoes from her suitcase. Her toothbrush. A tube of lipstick. Some of the items were waterlogged and filthy; other items showed no signs of having sat at the bottom of a lake for almost a year. Ronnie identified her sister's favorite brand and color of lipstick and relayed a story over lunch about lipstick on her prom date's shirt collar. Then she explained the hairbrush in great detail, telling Sally and Ben that Mary Ann's hair had been thick and curly, almost wiry in texture, and that after searching for years for the right brush, she'd found it and promptly purchased five of them. "Five," Ronnie repeated for emphasis. "In case she lost or wore out the first four."

Mitch's wife, Sally realized, was full of stories, and based on the level of detail she seemed to recall, Sally suspected most of those stories were lies. Ronnie barely stopped talking the entire meal. Each photograph brought with it a new tale, and none of them were relevant to the investigation. Sally caught Ben stifling a yawn at one point as he picked with disinterest at his sandwich, and her cheeks colored. If she had thought she was going to be able to get a hint of information from Ronnie today, she'd been sorely mistaken. The woman was good at this little game.

When Ben stood to pay the bill, Sally sighed and reached for her cell phone to check the time. Nearly two o'clock. What a colossal waste. She set the phone on the table and finished her glass of water.

"Nice phone," Ronnie said, dabbing the corners of her mouth with a napkin.

Sally hesitated, wondering at the sudden tightness in the woman's voice. "An oldie," she ventured.

"I can't believe you actually brought that. It's been sitting in water—shouldn't it be in a plastic bag?" Ronnie sat back, her lips pulled tight with visible agitation.

A plastic bag? What was she talking about? Sally considered the phone without responding. Then it clicked: Ronnie thought this was Mary Ann's cell phone. Perhaps they had the same model. She started to correct the mistake, but then remembered the overwhelming smell of bleach at Ronnie's house. Had she been scrubbing Mary Ann's blood from the floorboards? And was she now imagining that this was her cell phone? Intrigued, Sally decided to play along.

"The phone is dry," she said. "You...must recognize it."

"Yes." Ronnie's gaze was fixed on the phone. "It's my sister's."

Sally tried to keep her voice casual despite her mounting excitement. She decided to play a hunch. "It's interesting how much information you can get from a cell phone these days, isn't it? Pictures, messages. Practically a person's whole life."

"Hmm." Her response was pinched, and she didn't offer anything more.

Sally was dizzy with excitement. As soon as she returned to the office, she'd call Dan Maybury. They had never found her phone, but they had to check Mary Ann's cell phone records. There was something on that phone that Ronnie didn't want them to see.

Ben returned to the table. "All set?"

"If you'll excuse me for just a moment, I need to use the restroom," said Ronnie.

Sally watched as she walked to the back of the hall, and waited for her to disappear around the corner before turning to Ben and whispering, "It's the cell phone. Something's on Mary Ann's cell phone."

"What?" He sat next to her and leaned close enough that they touched again. "How do you know?"

"She practically told me." Sally lifted the cell from her bag. "I must have the same model Mary Ann had. Ronnie sat through lunch and nonchalantly told us nonsense stories about every item in that trunk, but the second she saw this phone, her face went white. Ben, she must be racked with guilt, desperate to clean up all traces of the crime, and she must have thought she'd destroyed the cell phone."

"She probably did. The police never recovered one."

"But *she* thinks they did! And it doesn't matter. We've already subpoenaed the cell phone records. We don't need the actual phone."

They stopped talking as Ronnie reappeared, tugging at the hem of her jacket and delivering a frosty glare at Sally. "Sorry about that," she said. "I'm ready to leave."

They rose and walked out of the restaurant. Ben attempted pleasant chitchat with Ronnie, but her responses were terse and distant. Sally didn't care. She fought to keep from breaking out into a large grin.

Halfway to the office, Ronnie pointed to a red Toyota. "My car," she said. "Do you mind waiting for just a moment?"

Sally and Ben stood on the sidewalk, and once again Sally noticed how close he was to her side. They'd already managed to convince Ronnie to lead them to Mary Ann's body, and to think they may have just cracked open this case *again*. She had to admit they made a hell of a team. She reached over and brushed her fingertips against his, and her heart surged at the way his eyes widened. Maybe it was about time to give Ben another chance. Maybe the risk of a broken heart wasn't as great as the risk of losing him.

Ronnie slammed the trunk of her car, jarring Sally from her thoughts. Her gaze flew to the object in the woman's hand. A handgun, pointed right at Sally's chest.

"Come on," Ronnie said. "Let's go for a ride."

Chapter 16

Ben couldn't see the gun from his position in the back of the vehicle, but he knew it was a .32, and that Ronnie had the barrel pressed against Sally's side. "Drive," she ordered.

Sally's movements were calm as she turned the key in the ignition, but Ben could see the tension in her shoulders. "Where are we going?" she asked.

"Just drive. You—" Ronnie looked into the backseat at Ben. "Put your hands on your head. If you move, I'll shoot her."

"Yes, ma'am," he said lightly, but inwardly groaned. He'd never be able to reach his gun like this.

"May I put on my seat belt?" Sally asked, lifting her hands in the air.

"Any sudden moves and I shoot."

Sally nodded and slowly pulled her seat belt across

her lap, clicking the buckle into place. Then she put the car into Drive and headed down the road. Traffic was light, but this time, Sally didn't drive quickly. Ben's heart thundered in his chest, the rush of blood in his ears blocking out all other sounds.

This wasn't how it was going to end. He just had to think.

"I'm not sure what went wrong here, Ronnie," Sally ventured after a few silent minutes. "I thought we had a nice lunch."

With one hand, the woman kept the gun pointed at Sally, and with the other, she opened Sally's handbag. "Where is it?" she asked.

"What?"

"The phone."

"In the front pocket."

Ronnie dug eagerly and emerged with the phone. "You shouldn't have brought this."

"It's not evidence," Ben said. "It's her phone. The police never recovered Mary Ann's cell phone."

Ronnie frowned at the device. "No," she said. "It's Mary Ann's. I remember it." She tucked it into her coat pocket. "What were you trying to do—trick me? Get me to confess something?" She sighed. "Take a left here."

Sally turned the vehicle as directed. "What's on that phone, Ronnie? What has you so scared?"

"That's not your concern anymore."

The hair on the back of Ben's neck prickled at the chill in her response. "You're going to kill us."

Ronnie glanced at him. "I'm a survivor. I've got to look after myself and my family."

"No offense, Ronnie, but shooting us doesn't help

you *or* your family." Sally winced in the rearview mirror. "You don't need to jam that thing in my ribs, for God's sake."

"Stop talking. Get on the highway."

"Where the hell are we going?" Sally was emboldened, and her voice rose in irritation.

"Somewhere private."

They drove for what seemed like forever down the empty stretch of highway. Once they arrived at their destination, Ben thought, he'd reach for his gun. But what if Ronnie saw him move, and shot Sally? What if she shot them both, right there in the car? Ice ran through his veins.

No, she would need the car to escape. She'd let them get out first, and then he'd make his move. He could reach forward quickly and grab Ronnie, easily overpower her. Except that gun was pointed right at Sally. Right at her baby. His gut clenched.

"You shot your sister." The voice that spoke wasn't his. It sounded much too calm. "You murdered your own sister and then engaged in this elaborate cover-up."

Ronnie rolled her eyes. "I guess you think I should have just confessed? Of course I had to cover it up." Her mouth tightened into a thin line. "But it's Mitch's fault. He's the one who needs to pay."

"He's going to pay," Sally said. "He's going to jail for a long, long time. Maybe the rest of his life."

"If you shoot us, you'll be going away, too," Ben said.

Ronnie snorted. "You think I'm sticking around here? I've hidden before, and I'll do it again." She gave Ben a smile. "You ever been to Vegas? They sell *ev-*

erything there. I have three different passports. I can disappear." Ronnie poked Sally with the gun. "Take this exit."

Ben's mind began to hum. She was going right back to the reservoir. It was almost too much to hope that investigators might still be at the scene, and even if they were, Ronnie would make Sally drive around to a different location. There were plenty of vacant areas around the reservoir that would be perfect for dumping two bodies.

His muscles coiled. He'd been in a war zone, in places where death and violence hovered on the periphery and sometimes intruded closer. Now he was on the front lines, with only minutes to formulate an escape for both of them.

If not for him, then for Sally. She had everything to live for.

Sally sighed. "You know, I have to apologize for my driving. I'm really a terrible driver."

Ronnie straightened her posture. "You've been fine."

"No," she insisted. "I'm really bad at driving. I have—what do you call it, Ben?" She glanced at him pointedly in the rearview mirror. "A lead foot?"

"That's right," he said.

The car accelerated slightly, pressing him back into the seat. "It's dangerous," Sally continued. "I should know better. I've prosecuted reckless driving cases, DUI's—you know, driving under the influence," she explained to Ronnie. "You can really do some damage with a car."

She kept watching him in the mirror, throwing

pointed glances at him. What was she looking for? The needle on the speedometer rose as the vehicle picked up still more speed. She was rushing them to their deaths, when what he needed was more time to think!

She met his gaze again in the mirror, this time making a gesture with her eyes at Ronnie. "You were in an accident once, weren't you, Ben? I think you hit a tree?"

Hands still firmly on his head, he realized for the first time that he and Ronnie weren't wearing seat belts. "Yes," he said cautiously. "That was a long time ago now."

"A tree," Sally mused. "That had to have hurt."

That's when the car shifted direction, and he realized Sally was speeding them toward a large oak tree at the side of the road. He had only seconds to brace himself against the impact, and he slid to the floor of the vehicle and tucked himself between the seats. There was the deafening sound of metal crunching, and glass showered into the car. Ronnie screamed and fired a single shot. Then there was silence.

Sally had struck the tree on the passenger's side, and Ronnie's crumpled body lay on top of her.

"Sally?" he asked. "Are you okay?"

She didn't respond.

Ben's hands were covered in blood, but he couldn't determine the source. There was no time—he had to get Sally to safety.

Wincing with pain, he clawed his way across the glass-splattered backseat. The passenger's side was smashed, and the doors wouldn't open. He fumbled at the handle. Locked. The damn door was locked, and he couldn't open it. He cursed. Childproof locks. He peeled the jacket from his back, wrapped it around his hand and smashed at the window once, then twice. The glass splintered and gave way, leaving a gaping hole that he was able to pull himself through. He reached inside to find the lock for the driver's side door, and pressed it. Then he opened the door, catching Sally's limp figure as she started to fall out. He held her with one hand and unfastened her seat belt with the other, then pulled her onto the grass.

"Hey, buddy, you need help?" A car on the road above them slowed.

"Call the police! Tell them it's an emergency!"

Ben dragged Sally farther from the car, his heart racing at the sight of the blood on her shirt. "Come on, honey," he whispered. "Wake up."

He checked her for wounds, finding nothing but some small cuts and an expanding purple bruise on her forehead. The air bag hadn't deployed. She'd probably hit the steering wheel. She was breathing; that was good. He pressed two fingers to her throat. Her heartbeat was strong. But bile rose in his throat nonetheless. Her eyes were still shut tight.

"Wake up, Sally." He pulled her limp hand to his lips and kissed it. "Honey, talk to me."

She groaned and stirred, pressing a palm to her forehead. "Ouch." Her eyes opened, and she blinked at him. Then her hand flew to her abdomen. "My baby," she whispered.

He couldn't stop the emotion that swelled in his throat. "Help is on the way." He ran his thumb across her forehead, brushing back her hair. "Try to stay calm."

He could see that was impossible. Her breath was

raspy, and she clutched at his bruised arms. "Are you okay?"

"Fine," he lied. "Quick thinking. You saved us both."

A tear streaked down her cheek. "I had to tell you that I love you."

He kissed her hand again, distrustful of the words. They were now joined in tragedy. It was only human for her to feel this way. "Sally…"

"No, I mean it." She propped herself up on her elbows. "It scares me half to death, but I love you. Can we have another chance? Maybe it's not forever, but…" Her voice trailed off.

"It's forever, Sally." He drew closer to her, cradling her head in his hand. "I love you, and I promise that this time, it's forever."

There was a rustle behind them, and Ben instinctively reached for his weapon. His heart jumped at the sight of Ronnie's pale face, streaming with blood. Then he saw the gun pointed right at Sally. "Drop it, Ronnie!" he shouted, aiming his weapon at her. "The police are on their way, and you need medical attention."

She didn't seem to register the words, and he realized that the blood on Sally's shirt was probably Ronnie's. She looked delirious.

The sound of distant sirens pierced the silence, and a bracing wind rushed through him. Sally shivered in his arms, though whether from cold or fear, he couldn't tell. "I said drop your weapon, Ronnie!"

But she didn't drop it. She turned her gun toward Sally with pure hate in her eyes. There was the sound of a shot and a scream, and Ben's world went black.

Epilogue

Sally had brought him flowers. She didn't know if that was appropriate, but it seemed to her that when someone took a bullet for you, the least you could do was bring flowers. She clutched the bouquet against her chest as she walked down the hall to his room, not knowing why she had butterflies in her stomach. This was Ben, after all.

Yes, that was the thing. This was Ben. Seeing him had always given her butterflies.

Every hospital smelled the same, she mused. She hated that smell. She looked forward to visiting him somewhere else, or better yet, bringing him home to her house so she could take care of him herself. The thought made her happy.

She paused at the entrance to his room and took a breath. Then she tapped on the door lightly.

"Come in."

His voice. Her heart somersaulted.

She stepped inside the room, suddenly shy. He was propped up, left shoulder covered in bandages. He had cuts on his arms and an ugly purple welt on his cheek, but he was alive. He smiled when he saw her. "Sally." He held out his good arm to her. "I was waiting for you."

She ran to him, burying her face in the side of his neck and inhaling his smell. His cheek was prickly with stubble, but she didn't care. She pressed her palms to his beautiful face and kissed him, delighted that he kissed her back and wrapped his arm tighter, pulling her close. "I missed you," she said. "And it's only been a day."

"I missed you, too."

"The surgery…was it awful?"

"They got the bullet. I won't be setting off metal detectors for the rest of my life. And congratulations—I hear the police arrested Ronnie."

"She's in custody. And guess who's turned state's witness? Mitch. Just as you thought, he's been saving evidence of Ronnie's involvement in the crime as insurance. You know what Mary Ann had on that cell phone?"

"I can't imagine."

"A picture of Ronnie's dog, Pookie. She took a picture of the shar-pei seconds before Ronnie shot her. In the background of the photo, you can see Ronnie coming toward her with a gun."

Ben whistled under his breath.

"I know. Mitch didn't know that Mary Ann was planning to confront her sister, and when he came home that night, it was already too late. Still, he had the presence of mind to send himself that photo. Ronnie didn't know that part."

"Why didn't Mitch just go to the police?"

"Because if he turned in Ronnie, he'd be implicated in the cover-up. He admits to disposing of the evidence. Best-case scenario was that Ronnie would turn up alive, all the charges would be dropped and both of them would walk away."

Ben rubbed her back. "They didn't count on you."

"They didn't count on *us*," she corrected. She gestured to a spot on the bed. "May I?"

"Of course."

She sat down beside him and wrapped her arms gingerly around him. He had stitches on one side and a gunshot wound on his shoulder, but she wanted nothing more than to touch him, to feel for herself that he was still with her.

"James is back to being an orphan again," she whispered into his chest. "I worry about him. I can't help it."

Ben brushed his hand down her back. "Any idea what he's going to do now?"

"I've already contacted one of his uncles in Pennsylvania. He's staying with that friend of his again, but he needs something more stable than that right now. He needs his family, and he mentioned at one point how much he admired this uncle."

She felt Ben shift, bringing his head down to kiss the top of her head. "Thanks for coming to see me," he said into her hair.

"Is this what it's like?" She sighed, pulling back to trace his lips with her thumb. "I've never minded being alone, and now I count down the seconds until I see you."

"I've ruined you."

"You've saved me. And you saved the baby." She gazed into his blue eyes. "I don't know if anyone told you this, but you dived in front of that bullet. Ronnie aimed it straight at my heart." Sally's voice choked. "You jumped in front of it without thinking."

He trailed his index finger along her jawline. "That's not true. I was thinking of you. Both of you."

That did it. Now she was crying. She took his good hand in both of hers and kissed it. "I was so scared. I don't want that to ever happen again." She pressed his hand against her heart. "I always thought I'd be alone, and then suddenly I found out I was expecting, and then you walked back into my life. I have everything I've always wanted, and I hardly feel like I deserve so much happiness. But I'm not going to question it."

Ben smiled. "Don't question it. You know, for two people who were destined to be alone, you have to admit we're perfect together."

"Perfect," she agreed, watching the way her hand fit with his. "And one day soon, when you're feeling better, I'd love to go on a real date with you, and maybe in time, I'd like you to think of this baby as yours, too."

"I don't know, Sally. Next thing you know we'll be shopping for furniture together and buying a new house. Then before you know it, I'll be picking out a canary diamond and asking you to marry me."

Her heart swelled at his smile. Maybe he was joking, but she didn't doubt the truth behind his words for a second. "I like canary diamonds. But, Ben, if we're going to be in love, we should get one thing straight from the start."

His eyebrows rose. "What's that?"

"I do the proposing around here." She leaned in and planted a kiss on his lips.

Ben laughed from deep in his stomach and pulled her closer. "I wouldn't expect anything different."

* * * * *

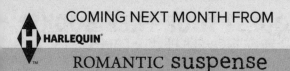

COMING NEXT MONTH FROM

ROMANTIC suspense

Available April 1, 2014

#1795 DEFENDING THE EYEWITNESS
Conard County: The Next Generation
by Rachel Lee

Terrified of men ever since witnessing her mother's murder as a child, Corey finds an unexpected ally when the killer returns for her years later. But more than protection, the mysterious government agent Austin Mendez proves to be the one man she can't resist.

#1796 HER SECRET, HIS DUTY
The Adair Legacy • by Carla Cassidy

Debra will sacrifice anything to see Trey achieve his political dreams, even letting him go after their one night of passion. But an unplanned pregnancy and unknown danger soon threaten to unravel both their worlds.

#1797 DEADLY LIAISONS • by Elle James

On vacation, secret agent Casanova Valdez helps his innkeeper Molly when the "just for fun" ghost-hunting event she'd planned for guests turns into real danger. But saving the day might mean losing his heart to the beautiful B and B owner.

#1798 LETHAL AFFAIR • by Jean Thomas

On assignment in St. Sebastian, FBI agent Casey McBride learns his ex-fiancée has been hired by his suspect. To keep Brenna safe, he brings her into the fold, falling for her all over again, only to have her become a target.

YOU CAN FIND MORE INFORMATION ON UPCOMING HARLEQUIN® TITLES, FREE EXCERPTS AND MORE AT WWW.HARLEQUIN.COM.

HRSCNM0314

REQUEST YOUR FREE BOOKS!
2 FREE NOVELS PLUS 2 FREE GIFTS!

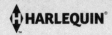

ROMANTIC suspense

Sparked by danger, fueled by passion

YES! Please send me 2 FREE Harlequin® Romantic Suspense novels and my 2 FREE gifts (gifts are worth about $10). After receiving them, if I don't wish to receive any more books, I can return the shipping statement marked "cancel." If I don't cancel, I will receive 4 brand-new novels every month and be billed just $4.74 per book in the U.S. or $5.24 per book in Canada. That's a savings of at least 14% off the cover price! It's quite a bargain! Shipping and handling is just 50¢ per book in the U.S. and 75¢ per book in Canada.* I understand that accepting the 2 free books and gifts places me under no obligation to buy anything. I can always return a shipment and cancel at any time. Even if I never buy another book, the two free books and gifts are mine to keep forever.

240/340 HDN F45N

Name _____ (PLEASE PRINT) _____

Address _____ Apt. # _____

City _____ State/Prov. _____ Zip/Postal Code _____

Signature (if under 18, a parent or guardian must sign)

Mail to the **Harlequin® Reader Service:**
IN U.S.A.: P.O. Box 1867, Buffalo, NY 14240-1867
IN CANADA: P.O. Box 609, Fort Erie, Ontario L2A 5X3

Want to try two free books from another line?
Call 1-800-873-8635 or visit www.ReaderService.com.

* Terms and prices subject to change without notice. Prices do not include applicable taxes. Sales tax applicable in N.Y. Canadian residents will be charged applicable taxes. Offer not valid in Quebec. This offer is limited to one order per household. Not valid for current subscribers to Harlequin Romantic Suspense books. All orders subject to credit approval. Credit or debit balances in a customer's account(s) may be offset by any other outstanding balance owed by or to the customer. Please allow 4 to 6 weeks for delivery. Offer available while quantities last.

Your Privacy—The Harlequin® Reader Service is committed to protecting your privacy. Our Privacy Policy is available online at www.ReaderService.com or upon request from the Harlequin Reader Service.

We make a portion of our mailing list available to reputable third parties that offer products we believe may interest you. If you prefer that we not exchange your name with third parties, or if you wish to clarify or modify your communication preferences, please visit us at www.ReaderService.com/consumerchoice or write to us at Harlequin Reader Service Preference Service, P.O. Box 9062, Buffalo, NY 14269. Include your complete name and address.

HRS13R

Debra will sacrifice anything to see Trey achieve his political dreams—she'll even let him go after their one night of passion. But an unknown danger soon threatens to unravel both their worlds.

Read on for a sneak peek of

HER SECRET, HIS DUTY

by *New York Times* bestselling author, Carla Cassidy, available April 2014 from Harlequin® Romantic Suspense.

Trey closed his eyes and allowed the vision to play out. There should be children in the pool, laughing and shouting as they splashed and swam from one end to the other…*his* children.

A sense of pride, of joy, buoyed up in his chest as he thought of the children he would have, children who would carry on the Adair Winston legacy.

And in his vision he turned his head to smile at the woman who'd given him those children, the woman who was his wife. His eyes jerked open and he realized the woman he'd seen standing beside him in the vision wasn't Cecily at all. Instead it was Debra.

Irritated with the capriciousness of his own mind, he poured himself a cup of coffee and went back into the great room, where he sank into the accommodating comfort of his favorite chair.

Lust. That was all it was, a lust he felt for Debra that refused to go away. But he certainly wasn't willing to throw away all his hard work, all his aspirations, by following through on that particular emotion. That would make him like his father, and that was completely unacceptable.

No matter what he felt toward Debra, she was the wrong woman for him. He had to follow his goals, his duty, to pick the best woman possible to see him to his dreams, the dreams his grandfather Walt had encouraged him to pursue.

Besides, it wasn't as if he was in love with Debra. He liked her, he admired her and he definitely desired her, but that wasn't love.

Debra inspired his lust, but Cecily inspired confidence and success and encouraged his ambition. If he used his brain, there was really no choice. The lust would die a natural death, but his relationship with Cecily would only strengthen as they worked together for his success. At least that was what he needed to believe.

It was almost eight when his cell phone rang and he saw that it was Thad.

"Hey, bro," he said.

"Trey, Debra was telling the truth," Thad said. His voice held such a serious tone that Trey's heartbeat reacted, racing just a little bit faster.

"A malfunction of the brakes?" he asked.

"I'd say more like a case of attempted murder. The brake line was sliced clean through."

**Don't miss
HER SECRET, HIS DUTY
by Carla Cassidy,
available April 2014 from
Harlequin® Romantic Suspense.**

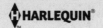

HARLEQUIN®

ROMANTIC suspense

DEFENDING THE EYEWITNESS
by Rachel Lee

Return to *New York Times* bestselling author Rachel Lee's *Conard County*, where a killer lies in wait

The note wasn't a threat, exactly. But for Corey Donahue, who'd witnessed her mother's murder as a child, it felt very menacing. Surprisingly, the one person she trusted to show the note to was a man merely renting a room from her— Austin Mendez. Traumatized since childhood, Corey had never trusted men...until Austin moved in.

Six years undercover had caused Austin to shut everyone out...until Corey. The vulnerability she hid from others made him yearn to break down the walls she'd erected around her heart. And with a killer closing in, two lost souls were discovering the trust they'd lost—and much more—in each other's arms.

Look for *DEFENDING THE EYEWITNESS* by Rachel Lee in April 2014.

Available wherever books and ebooks are sold.

Heart-racing romance, high-stakes suspense!

www.Harlequin.com

HRS27865

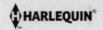

ROMANTIC suspense

DEADLY LIAISONS
by Elle James

People have been known to perish at McGregor Manor...

Opening her B and B to a group of ghost hunters, Molly McGregor hopes the spirits rumored to be there will appear. She needs the weekend to be a financial success. But when disembodied voices and hazy images nearly lure her to her death, Molly's driven straight into the arms of a sexy but mysterious guest—Casanova Valdez.

Nova knows what it's like to be haunted—by memories of a case gone bad. As a secret agent, he's confident he can protect Molly but is not exactly sure he believes in ghosts. But as the mysterious incidents targeting the gorgeous redhead become increasingly more dangerous, Nova must question if it's the handiwork of a ghost...or a killer.

Look for *DEADLY LIAISONS*
by Elle James in April 2014.

Available wherever books and ebooks are sold.

Heart-racing romance, high-stakes suspense!

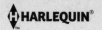

ROMANTIC suspense

LETHAL AFFAIR
by Jean Thomas

Falling back in love with his ex may be more dangerous than being trapped on an island...

Brenna Coleman's past has caught up to her on the island of St. Sebastian...and she's not happy to see him. FBI agent Casey McBride has a job to do, and he won't let feelings for his ex-fiancée foil his mission. While investigating the activities of Marcus Bradley—a powerful billionaire commissioning a series of Brenna's paintings—Casey discovers the island's darkest atrocity. With Brenna at his side, he can't ignore the love they once felt—and still feel— for one another. But as Casey keeps close watch on Brenna, one question remains uncertain: Who is keeping close watch on *them?*

Look for *LETHAL AFFAIR*
by Jean Thomas in April 2014.

Available wherever books and ebooks are sold.

Heart-racing romance, high-stakes suspense!

www.Harlequin.com

HRS27868

HARLEQUIN®

A *Romance* FOR EVERY MOOD™

Love the Harlequin book you just read?

Your opinion matters.

Review this book on your favorite book site, review site, blog or your own social media properties and share your opinion with other readers!

Be sure to connect with us at:
Harlequin.com/Newsletters
Facebook.com/HarlequinBooks
Twitter.com/HarlequinBooks